HELL IS OTHER PEOPLE

HELL IS OTHER PEOPLE

Michael Uhrin

Copyright ©2000 by Michael Uhrin.

Library of Congress Number:		00-190418
ISBN #:	Hardcover	0-7388-1669-8
	Softcover	0-7388-1670-1

All rights reserved. No part of this book may be reproduced or transmitted in any form or by any means, electronic or mechanical, including photocopying, recording, or by any information storage and retrieval system, without permission in writing from the copyright owner.

This is a work of fiction. Names, characters, places and incidents either are the product of the author's imagination or are used fictitiously, and any resemblance to any actual persons, living or dead, events, or locales is entirely coincidental.

This book was printed in the United States of America.

To order additional copies of this book, contact:
Xlibris Corporation
1-888-7-XLIBRIS
www.Xlibris.com
Orders@Xlibris.com

Contents

Hell is Other People 11
Boulevard of the Allies 22
The Outsider 28
A Fragile Dish 39
A Holy Family 46
A Road For Emily 53
Sitting Pretty 68
A Surreal Patient 76
The Coal Mine Machinery Company 80
A Good Woman Is Hard to Find 85
Whiskey and Walter 96
Uncle Art 108
Another Fixture at the Mill 120
A Provincial Poet 138
A Modern Scrivener 175

*This short story collection is dedicated to the
French philosopher who penned the proverb titling this book:*
Jean-Paul Sartre

We ought not to look so much for beauty and unity in a work as for character and diversity of subject.

-Gustave Flaubert

HELL IS OTHER PEOPLE

The most common and universal problem of life never changes—things are not always what they appear to be. This troubling thought shot through Mrs. Angelo's graying head as soon as she saw her son enter the house in his drab olive Army uniform. Her Little Tony's dreadful face was full of anguish; tragedy was eating him alive. He was coming home to Pittsburgh after WWII and now, as much as she hated to think about it, the whole routine of her happy homelife had suddenly stopped. Once her Tony entered the tiny house located in an alley behind St. Joseph's Church, his Army uniform gradually faded into nothingness.

As Tony walked clumsily into the brick row house in the Bloomfield section of the city's Italian neighborhood, his younger brothers and sisters gathered about him joyfully as though he was a god. They loved him dearly and all they wanted was to be held and patted and playful, and yet it could not happen; it seemed Tony didn't understand them anymore. They were strangers and even distractions to his gloomy solitude, and he desperately sought to avoid looking at their youth; he wanted nothing to do with them and their silly questions about the war and what it felt like to be home.

Tony's mother instantly realized her son had been brutally changed by the war; she quickly sent the children off into the back yard to play. She looked at her Little Tony and saw that all he wanted to do now was to withdraw into his own solitary silence. His face was deeply pained and sunken in grief; his wrinkled shirt softly announced his careless confusion. Tony had hardly greeted his own mother; all he mentioned to her was that he had seen many of his friends die in battle. The memory of their miserable and lifeless bodies on the battlefield now haunted all of his thoughts. What little Tony did share in the way of conversation was about gambling, death, booze and women. When his teen-age sisters came into the kitchen to speak to him it was as though they were invisible. Tony's thoughts were lost in solitary anguish, and this was concerning and even ominous to Mrs. Angelo. She saw something dreadful in her Tony; it was what had destroyed her own husband's spirit. This same menace now promised to rob her of her oldest son. The war had been tough on the Angelos. It was while her Tony went off to war that Big Tony had died in the Homestead steel mill when a cauldron of molten steel exploded.

The tiny and resolute Italian woman was now worried sick. As she worked cleaning the house, she knew what to expect; and it was not going to be good. Mrs. Angelo looked at her Tony as he sat at the kitchen table. She barely recognized him after three years of being in the Army; his commanders had sent him all over Europe. He had seen the Italian town where his maternal grandmother was born, and he even visited Rome. Tony's Army checks had kept the family alive every month after his father died. It felt as if Big Tony now had Little Tony return home to take his place. Tony hadn't learned of his father's death until that very afternoon; there was no way to put it into a letter since Mrs. Angelo had never learned how to write. Her young Tony now sensed he was all alone. If he was anything he was her insurance policy. He would have to support the family once he got a job at the steel mill; US Steel would find a place for him.

His mother saw him for what he was, and it was very worrisome. She knew that men enslaved themselves with what they should not want yet are too weak to resist. His bony hand on the whiskey glass was shaking, and the sight of him made her nervous. She fretted about what might happen to them if he couldn't work in the steel mill. It was from this same mill that his father had spent paycheck after paycheck on whiskey in the taverns along Homestead's Eighth Avenue. 'If my Tony makes a hell of his life, it is his own fault she thought to herself. I have six other children to raise and Tony's twenty-four years old. He's going to have to fend for himself now; that is the way life is. He's a man, and he's going to have to be responsible.'

As she peeled potatoes and shucked cornhusks, the bright yellow corncobs glistened unseen before him. All the dinner preparations were a mystery to Tony as he watched her work at the kitchen's old wooden counter. He sat at the metal kitchen table and stared out the window at the coal trains going by in the dingy valley under the Bloomfield Bridge. Tony shyly told his mother that the smoke from the steel mills along the river, which he had seen coming into Pittsburgh on the train, reminded him of the fires of hell. His mother didn't know what to say. Why would he mention such a thing as this? It was ridiculous! She was now worried about what might happen to him because all that day, he was joyless and unable to care about anyone or converse about anything other than death.

His mother didn't know what to do or what to say, but she knew she needed help. She sought to console her son, "Tomorrow I want you to go to Mass and talk to Father Dominic; he will help you. No matter what happens to us Father Dominic will always be here to help the Angelos. He buried your father, and he had the whole church there. They sang hymns during his funeral mass. It was like heaven the day we buried your father. All the Italians from the neighborhood were crowded into the Church, and they huddled about us in our grief as one big family. They were there with us in our wretched hour of torment for they loved your father like he was their own brother." Tony was distracted and barely heard a word of what his mother had said. The whistle of a coal train and the locomotive down in the valley below their house sent an eerie chill of the recent past through him. He thought over and over about the fact that his father was dead, "Why didn't anybody in the Army tell me about it?"

During the early evenings dinner Tony never talked to any of his siblings but just sat numb at the head of the table—his father's old place. The evening slid gradually away into the oblivion of childish chatter. The children were finally excused from the table and went back out into the brick alley to play. Later on, after helping his mother with the dishes, Tony joined her sitting on the couch. She smelled the whiskey on his breath, and a terrible pang stung her heart. She mused to Tony that he was now destined to go into the steel mill at Homestead, "America needs strong and healthy men like you to make steel for the new cars. Everyone returning home from the war wants to go out and buy one. Even your grandfather over in Altoona has bought a Ford." The newspapers advertised them, and they reported progress was now just around the corner.

Tony was impassive, frail-hearted and scared. When he put his arm around his mother's shoulder, he was overcome with a terrifying emotion. In a fit of deep sadness he cried for almost an hour. He said he was frightened, life seemed to be going too fast for him to understand. How was he going to get over his war memories? He didn't want to talk about the war, and yet he felt he had to. After a while he calmed down; his trembling voice sounded hurt and unsure, wounded. His mother knew he would never be the same Little Tony he was before he went off to the Army. He was now jittery and nervous; it was as if his heart was burning through him like the cigarettes he lit up non-stop, one after another.

"The war taught me one thing about life, Mama. Death is always the same, and it is forever surrounded by memories. They haunt me; I'll never forget them; I doubt anyone going off to fight a war has ever witnessed anything as brutal as what I've seen. I wish I would have never experienced this sickening hell in Europe. The Germans were killing the Jews in concentration camps. They used these big rooms to gas Jews, and then they cremated their bodies in huge ovens. I was in the platoon that got there with Eisenhower. Our Army film crew made a record of all the destruction that took place in the concentration camps. Even our commanding officers told us that they had never seen or heard of human hatred like this. Only a few people in these hellish camps survived. I had never seen such scrawny kids, men and women were but bony stick figures who could barely stand. They were weak and hopeless and disillusioned with humanity. They despaired at man's mean love of revenge. It was terrifying, it was all madness and insanity and it was cruel beyond belief. The Army chaplain told us there was no way to understand it. The whole scene was sheer madness, and then it refused to leave me alone. I never slept for days on end because there was no way for me to figure out what this horror meant. Its brutality was beyond belief.

"Now that I am home I don't ever want to leave Pittsburgh, I will never leave Liberty Avenue or the Church or the Homestead Mill or eating fish sandwiches on Friday at the bar. I tell you, Mama, I will never leave this place. This is where I am going to stay forever and ever. Bloomfield will be my life and the Homestead steel mill and the Union will be my future. I'll get a job and everything will work out. All the memories of dying Jews will go away and I will never have to think about them again. Never. They'll disappear forever."

There was silence, and then a soft sound of sorrowful desperation came over him. There was a flash of false vision and the sadness in his voice made him cry out as he spoke, "I never want to see or hear the word Europe ever again. Never. It was nothing but a living hell of human madness. I couldn't take it Mama. I couldn't take the death I saw there. The battles killed all my friends. I saw dead people every day; I saw a crushed baby, a man without legs, and a woman's intestine torn open. I saw her die clutching her bloody little girl. Then the girl stood up and cried out, 'Mama, Mama, Mama.' She had no one to go to. It was all horrible and frightening. I was going down an alley no bigger than the one outside our house-only this one was in the concentration camp. All these poor men's eyes were looking out at me. They were barely alive, and a few of them were exhausted by the misery of starvation they had lived through. I saw these sad men's eyes pleading for help, and all I could give them was my sympathy. My heart broke then, Mama. I found nothing but death all around me, and I became disgusted. The misery of these men moved me to love them and all men from that moment on. I was walking among corpses and then I knew one thing, I told myself this one thing over and over, 'We are all brothers.'

"I was stunned and sick to the stomach, staggering around in my own heartache for weeks. I read newspapers about the camps. I couldn't get away from them, and I couldn't understand them, Mama. What was it that I saw with these eyes in the concentration camps? Wasn't this hell's own damnation? I wandered about; I was lost for weeks and then one morning I saw a scrap of something in a corner of the burned out room where I was sleeping. It was a dried-out newspaper that said a Frenchmen over there reported that, 'Hell is other people.' Well, he was right, Mama. Those people over there made the war a living hell for one another. I never want to ever think about that place again, Mama . . . only . . . I can't get the men and women from the concentration camps out of my mind anymore   I am worried, Mama, I . . . I think I am going crazy . . . What should I do, Mama?"

Mrs. Angelo now cradled her lost soldier boy in her arms like a little baby; she comforted him and worried about him, as she thought back upon their first day together. He had been away from home too long during the war. They had kept him fighting the battles too long. Her angry heart was now mad at the world, "Why is it the Italians have to suffer the most? Why is it always us? Why us? Why do we have to suffer this way? Why did my boy have to go to their lousy war over there? Why is my Angelo so sick now? Why can't he even sit still anymore? He's a grown man and all he did was cry all afternoon upstairs in the bedroom. He chain-smoked away the whole day, and then in my kitchen he had to drink like a crazy man. He drank glass after glass of his father's whiskey. Big Tony bought it so they could celebrate when his son came home after the war. Why? Why did he have to drink it all up in one day? One glass after another and it went down like water, like water!"

As darkness settled into their Pittsburgh rowhouse, Tony's mother went to the back porch worrying about her poor dispirited son. He saw her quivering in the darkness, and he glimpsed her silhouette on the insulbrick wall as she held herself up against the wooden porch rail; it was rotted and falling down. Worms and maggots were at work on it and the rubbish strewn out in the back yard. Then she stood up straight, and Tony heard her strong voice bounce off the walls of the alley behind Cedarville Street. She would never give up loving her children for they were why she lived. It seemed to Tony that the only truth he knew could always be found in his mother's heart. He loved her so much as her voice echoed throughout the alleyway next to the house. She called to her kids with their dirty hands playing in the yards along the alleyways. The streetlight was on and they knew they now had to come home to get ready for bed.

An anxious and tired stream of noisy children ran into the house and then went reluctantly toward Tony. As their feet went to the wooden stairs between the living room and the kitchen, they abruptly paused before their brother. Clumsily they smiled and kissed him goodnight. He barely noticed them; they were lost in his anguished memories of the concentration camps. It was as though they were nothing more than shadowy reflections stranded in the deep, sad pools of his thought; his innocence and youth were perishable memories long gone the way of all flesh. His mother got the children washed and ready for bed. In the meantime Tony picked himself up off the tired couch, his sweaty shirt stuck to his damp skin. He was sick of this life of his as he went out into the backyard to smoke a cigarette. He kicked a tin can around the brick yard for a while and he used an Army penknife to cut a loose piece of clothesline swinging free in the autumn air.

As his mother got into bed she heard a dark creak on the cellar steps and figured Tony was going to have a beer from the refrigerator. She had told him to help himself. She had bought it especially for him, but she never imagined he would be drinking from her husband's whiskey bottle. He did it in the same way Big Tony used to when the Union was about to declare a strike against the steel mill. She had no idea of what her boy had been through or why she had lost a husband. Life was life and you simply had to live it as best you could; there was no explaining it.

Mrs. Angelo's own life belonged wholly to her children. They worried her, but there was nothing she could do about it because she knew she was doing all she could. All she was capable of now was worrying, and what good was it anyway? Her own son drank away an entire afternoon, and a whole bottle of whiskey was gone. If her mother found out, there would be bickering. If her father came over and asked for a shot of whiskey, what would she say happened to the bottle hidden in the kitchen cabinet? This was serious; it worried her more and more. What was she going to do when her mother and father came over from Altoona in a few weeks for Thanksgiving? What was she going to tell them about her little Tony? What if one of the children told them that Tony had drank a whole bottle of whiskey? They had watched him with their big eyes, and even they knew something was clearly wrong. Children always know, and they always jabber on. They were sure to tell grandma and grandpa. Why did it have to be this way? Mrs. Angelo trudged up the stairs with a thousand fears woven into her heavy heart. All these things went through her head as she reached the top step.

The warm wooden rowhouse closed in on her as she put the children to bed and fell off to sleep, exhausted from a full and busy autumn day. Thanksgiving was a few weeks away, and she would soon be busy with the holiday baking and cooking. Relatives would be coming over from Cleveland and Altoona, and they would help her with the Thanksgiving Day meal as they had during the war. How good her two sisters were to her! After her husband died she could never have made it without their help. A smile warmed her thoughts; at least she could be thankful for her eldest son this year. It was good that Tony was now home with them after being away for so long. He would go to Mass with her and the children in the morning, and she would encourage him then to go over and get a job at the Homestead steel mill like his dad had done. In a few years he would find a girl and get married, and then they'd have children. A number of the cute Italian high school girls in the neighborhood had pestered her in the last few weeks about when Tony was returning home from the war. Before long wedding bells would have him in front of Father Dominic with the love of his life, and all would be well. "I cannot wait to see my grandchildren, they will look just like him, I know they will have bright brown eyes just like Little Tony had when he was a baby. Now that he is a man all his happiness is gone; but maybe he will be better later on. The war will be a distant memory then; Father Dominic at St. Joe's will marry them." Dreams of the Church and Tony's wedding day put Mrs. Angelo happily to sleep.

Early Sunday morning found the sun warming the red brick wall of their bleak row house; the tattered venetian blind was pulled down to keep the neighbors out. Mrs. Angelo thought of the front stoop as she woke up to the hot brightness she had to face, "The stoop needs washing if I am going to have Father Dominic over to the house later on today," she thought to herself. The house was warm and silent for a moment and the springless bed where she had loved her husband and then birthed her children was her only haven from endless work; it was the whole story of her life and she never wondered about it. "I will have to wash the sheets tomorrow, then the children's clothes and the ironing; but that can all wait because after Church today I will talk to Father Dominic, he will probably deliver the only sermon he knows, 'The only true gold in this world is the golden rule.' The old Italians in the back of the church will fall asleep again as they do every week when they hear him telling it all over again. If he spoke to them in Italian, they'd listen to him."

"I know Father Dominic will help my Little Tony and I'll cook spaghetti today too, and maybe he will come to dinner. I'll beg him to come over to the house. He did that once in a while when we were so poor when we first got married. He used to give Little Tony a bath in the kitchen's stainless steel sink." This memory gave her endless pleasure and she told it to the children while Tony was away at war. They marveled at it and told Father Dominic all about it when they saw him on the street. He would bellow out a great big Italian laugh that echoed off their poor hearts like sunshine. How good and kind Father Dominic was to the poor. In every one of them he saw Christ; and in every good woman he saw only his mother, and she was everywhere on the streets of Bloomfield or in the department stores in downtown Pittsburgh.

Then the church bells on Liberty Avenue began to toll. They rang throughout Pittsburgh on Sundays. This moment was Mrs. Angelo's quiet hour, the only one all week that she had to herself. The Church bells refreshed her memory as she thought to herself about her life. Mrs. Angelo began wondering about how her husband loved this moment together with her every Sunday. The steel mill took him from her and now the war was eating away at her son. Why must the poor always be giving up the blood of their eldest sons to the wars? Too many Italian women in Bloomfield had lost sons. She was the lucky one, and she wondered about this to herself. She was thankful, she prayed that God would always be so good to her. Tears welled in her eyes as she thought about her husband and now her son's drinking all day.

Then her children crawled into her thoughts; she had to get breakfast together. What was she going to make extra special for her Tony now that he was home? Her heart leaped with joy thinking about her little Tony. He was so strong and so handsome, and the girls in the neighborhood knew it too. That is why they were always asking about him when he was away in Europe. Her heart loved these little Italian beauties who scoured the aisles and found her in the back of the Church on Sundays or on the streets of Bloomfield or shopping for vegetables at the A&P. Her Tony would be fine, he would be a good strong man who would soon be working over in Homestead making steel like his father had done for decades. When the Church's chiming bells ceased ringing she got up out of the dull warm bed and went into the other bedroom. It was a little odd that Tony had not slept in his bed among his siblings. "I'll bet he had to sleep on the couch because he was too drunk to climb the stairs," she worried. Then she was concerned about the children telling Father Dominic about Tony's drinking up all the whiskey in one afternoon. Mrs. Angelo's tired, aching limbs climbed down the wooden stairs to the cellar to get her morning shower.

Her sleepy eyes suddenly shot open in terror and disbelief, there before her was her oldest boy. Her poor Tony was gone; he had hung himself from the cellar's black, wooden rafters the night before. His whitened corpse was sad and limp as it hung down into the black coal cellar. She ran over to him, her thin arms reached desperately up for him. The feel of his cold body penetrated her broken heart. She quickly stepped on a nearby bucket and pulled him down from the dusty rafters. Her bony arms strained as she laid him gently on the brick cellar floor. His head rested limply on her lap as she glanced up at a picture of the Pieta as she cried out, "Oh my God, my Jesus Christ Almighty what is this hell? Why Tony? Why my Little Tony? Why me?" The raw mean voice of grief tore into the air to fight off the wickedness of death; it cut mercilessly into her lonely heart. Her frail arm reached up to pull his bleak boniness to her as she prayed, "What misery has this war brought home to me? What hell has my poor boy been forced to go through for them and their stinking war? My Tony, my Tony, my Tony . . . No, I don't understand this, not now not never. Why did they have to take my Little Tony away from me?"

Amid the tears, her heart reached out for words and her shrieks filled the coal cellar; the steel furnace nearby echoed with their wretchedness. The harsh cold words cut into the silence enveloping her misery. She clutched her Tony and pulled him closer to her heaving breast. Tears flew onto the floor as she cried, she pressed her poor boy in anguish as she called out to him, "Now it is over my son, now you can rest forever . . . it is over my Little Tony, you are home now with your Father . . ."

BOULEVARD OF THE ALLIES

On those long and warm and idle Sunday afternoons when memories of the busy hum of the industrial workweek has died down from the steel mills, silence becomes the keystone of thoughtful men and women. It arrives slowly and simply as the monotonous, droning of mill machinery gradually grinds to a stop. Far off in the distance, the side streets of Pittsburgh are soon saturated with the softly muffled laughter of innocent children. This thoughtful silence then grows calmly in the hearts of men, they come to know it as their own; they can feel it grow old within the darkness of their fading memories. Deep down, within the shaded and leafy boulevards of the city, the shy and softly made noise of childhood is intermingled with the silent memories like water and wine. It mixes with the sweet sound of women's heels on the sacred steps of churches. Their hollow and empty naves are enclosed by massive wooden doors calling out for parishioners who have left the city of faith for the eternal ennui of the suburbs. Synagogues reflect upon this holy, child-like noise in the empty caverns of their tomb-like halls that are peopled only by long wooden pews. Silence is woven in the clang of rusty church bells and waxen votives as they are gently lit by trembling and wrinkled hands as a way to warm the world with forgotten hopes and prayers. Outside these gothic mausoleums graced by the granite despair of moldy cemeteries, the heart of silence is light and joyous and twinkling with communal harmony.

Along the ancient city's industrial boulevards, the quiet mirth of children can be felt as it mixes with humanity's heartfelt failings amid the silent sounds of the city's consciousness of itself. It is only palpable in reminiscence; treasured memories are traded like rare coins in coffeehouses and dusty used bookstores. Words are so precious that they are never spoken here except in reverence. Poets listen to them and then peer deeply into themselves where they see nothing but their own sincerity; it is as sweet and as tired as their softly worn bibles of old poem-prayers. The poet's carefully written words are the epitaph of their experience of a certain world, it is small and clear and quickly forgotten. Like the glance of a pretty girl the words beckon them forward and then are gone as swiftly as they arrived.

Great cities destroy everything within them that is not as timeless as the sky. I pensively glimpse at the poets from a distance; their hearts pass before me like smoke drifting toward heaven from their cigarettes. These souvenirs hasten the memory along to a lost industrial riverbank of brick buildings, foundries, railroads and steel mills. They have now grown silent as a slowly moving river; it is curling magnificently around the bend amongst the weeds watered by the past. The truth seems to follow in silence in the wake of the past like a steamboat or a barge full of coal being pushed by a forlorn and lazy tugboat; the truth drifts in unity toward the city's three rivers that flow together to form a triangle.

Amid the softly tolling of church bells, the beery leftovers from the local tavern's night before now seep up in the shaded sunlight from an old limestone pavement. I see a child-like harmony surrounding the working man nearby who is out for a lazy Sunday stroll in the Point Breeze section of the city. Frick Park is there, its winding and gentle walks are paved with black coal, slag and burnt ashes from the old and forgotten steel mills of yesterday. They are now sleeping like the man on the park bench dreaming of when the steel mills will slip slowly away and then die without an epitaph. The man escapes from the drudgery of his family for a few hours by seeking out some rest on quiet sidestreets shaded by green and leafy trees. There, in the spring-like wonder of his contentment, he finds a niche; he is safely cocooned in its sanctuary of verdant quiet. Lulled into sleepy dreams gently warmed by the summer sun, the presence of the dull future is entwined by the sweet memories of the past deep within his solemn brow. Sprawling like a motionless and lazy corpse, he dozes in comfort amidst the scenes of fading tugboats and barges, train whistles and trestles from a distant and forgotten past. The smoky sky of industry itself is slipping away in forgotten rainy footsteps to evaporate like the poetry of childhood. A living memory of old Pittsburgh has calmly dissolved in the soft, sulfury air, it has swirled away and is now gone for good. All that remains of the industrial revolution are the silent rusty train tracks, noises of creaking old tugboats and other river-loving vessels on the water. The random groaning of wet wood is muffled by the wet, silent worship of the water beneath them.

The creaking is infinitely consoling to these weary men on the park benches who are longing for some sanity and rest. They are escapees from their hard work and all of the world-weary troubles born of women and children. These old men lament the passing of that glorious time; it is the thing they know as their own, old industrial memories. They miss the confusing mosaic of the mills and their poisonous smells, the boom of the rolling, fabricating and finishing of steel. The lies about seniority and how much the Union was looking out for their best interests are fast and fading dreams. The mills and the good money they brought home are gone now; what little that was saved is now spent. Nobody truly has an interest in these old men or what they did; their memories have rusted away into oblivion among the city's graveyards. The metal made by these men has a memory that has rusted away to nothing in McKeesport, Duquesne, Aliquippa and Homestead.

All of the immigrant and working class chaos that once was at the core of every Pittsburgher's life is drifting slowly down the river on the last barge of coal. It can be seen rounding a bend in the hearts of these innocent old men; each is a little stream of thought that flows into the rivers that refuse to leave the city. They will stay here till the industrial memories of the old city are gone, turned to ruins by the men and machines of tomorrow. For now these war-weary workmen have retired their ambition; they are as motionless and still as a fearful kitten abandoned in an old wooden house where they grew up long ago. Lost and forlorn, their memories are safely entombed in dusty and unread history books; the past is yellowy and forgotten as their cigarette stained fingers. Their noble actions are inscribed as History inside ancient libraries and museums carved in the minds of architects from Greek and Roman times.

The great men of the steam, iron and steel age of America were once divided into two camps—Capital and Labor. Their local battles made them weary of battling one another after a while; the old and perennial hatred in their hearts is now part of a lost and forgotten industrial estate. The deed encompasses a wasteland of abandoned coal mine shafts, rusting steel mills and ancient iron railroad tracks covered with lifeless dry rot and weeds. The old men and their lives, like their work and habits, have merged with the earth, which once gave birth to the coal mines. These fed the barges, the train cars, coke ovens and the steel mills along the rivers. The peasant men and women and the true substance of their lives is summarized by an epitaph that reads like the words on a crumbling industrial tombstone:

The city of my youth is dead.

At any moment these tired old men sleeping it off on park benches, who once labored in the great steel mills along the rivers could expire and be placed into a wooden box. Thus settled, they and their memory could be sent out to the graveyard where they could take their weariness with them and rest forever among the leaves of grass. Here on the park benches, in the midst of the busy city, they are happiest when awakened softly by the chattering of old women lumbering off buses from a day's shopping in the department stores downtown. Their memories of Union men is always fondly cherished and enshrined in a niche of soft and beautiful love songs sung in church every Sunday. The memory is like the men, completely relaxed and unassuming, sprawling like heroic soldiers from a war in Europe half a century ago. The faces of these men are always consoling and courageous for they possess a rare treasure—humility. Their courage dwells in their hearts silently and peacefully as a thing unto itself.

These old women know and love the truth, it sometimes seems as though they live only to admire it. The tired old men take all of life's goodness for granted only because they now understand for once the real meaning of their own simplicity. It calls out to them with a quiet voice and says over and over, repetition is the mother of study. Humility for them is worthy of pursuit only if it is the conscious discipline of the mind. They know that it is essential for survival amidst the thousands of diversions freedom forces upon their children and grandchildren whose harried vanity they can no longer fathom, it is unreal. Their own blood knows nothing of their heroic struggles, the battles and wars are a smoky mirage from the past, it lives on in the men and is never forgotten. These working men intuitively know humility to be a fulcrum upon which the iron bar they once moved, by all of their effort, was the impossible object of their own confusion—ignorance.

On certain occasions, when the old women are comfortably back at home from their shopping trips, they seek out solace in a house of worship. There they find these same old men silently napping on long wooden church pews in the cool autumn air; there is no lasting comfort on these hard religious beds of wood. The old men are oblivious to the world in the silent abyss of their sleep, their snoring saws carefully through a time that no clock will ever measure nor record. They no longer dream about the dreadful battles of their youth. Their dreams are only memories of their lost buddies; they linger on as souvenirs of Veterans or Armistice Days. They pray that both will never be forgotten. The Great War still rages on as a memory of their father's experience: the poisonous mustard gas and cannon shells can never kill the love they possess for their fallen boyhood friends. They were wounded or died; and sometimes they dream about them being mustered out of the military inside old Pittsburgh's own Hunt Armory.

Now, and at the hour of their death, these old men are the prayerful descendants from a Great War who seek out solace from the arched windows of churches. They gradually waken with coughs and phlegm-like memories swallowed like the truth of religious childhoods. The alcoholic pain from the battles of WWII echo in the nave-like emptiness of their minds. Faded ribbons of red, white and blue dissolve in their sightless eyes and become as soft and sacred as the candles lit near the altar of all sincerity. The sentiments of these men's hearts mimic the waxy tapers they dimly observe from the darkness of their tomblike thoughts; time is flaming valiantly and burning in silence out of respect for the dead.

THE OUTSIDER

No one preys upon the poor so religiously, so relentlessly and so regularly as the poor themselves do. It is for this very reason that no one hates the poor more than the poor, they seek to escape from one another for a reason. Their hard-won experience produces a kind of knowledge that is never forgotten, it is born of the eternal hatred of being despised by virtually everyone. Nothing is more unfortunate and truer than the injustices the poor must continually face in their everyday lives in a city like Pittsburgh. The poor people here know that their enemy is always near or among them, lying in wait and ready to pounce on them as soon as they let down their defenses. Their situation is often surrounded by a covert falsehood, they know it soon enough and through and through by names such as rape, robbery and murder. These are lurking everywhere. They are faced by the poor hourly, daily and weekly, year in and year out, and they never disappear. These enemies bring only chaos into the city. The true thieves in life continuously seek to destroy the existence of others. In so doing the real enemy of the downtrodden is always within their tight community—it establishes the hatred of others as life's only goal.

No one ever came to know these things more fully than the Pravda family of Pittsburgh's Homestead district. At the turn of the nineteenth century the Pravdas had struggled out of the poverty of czarist Russia and hoped to trade it for something better in the industrial heartland of America. Pittsburgh was their destination once they landed in the busy port of New York. The Pravdas then traveled by train to Pittsburgh and soon were living among relatives in Homestead. The neighborhood up the hill from the steel mill became their newly adopted homeland. The father and his muscular son quickly found jobs in front of the Bessemer furnaces of the great Homestead Steel Works where they worked like slaves.

After a decade of grueling manual labor before the open-hearth furnaces, the Pravdas had, thanks to the thrifty mother of the family, bought a brick rowhouse up on the hills overlooking Homestead. She never wondered about the fiery orange shadows dancing like lightning on the Monongahela River where molten steel was made. Her husband told her all about how steel was manufactured, poured and rolled into iron sheets, beams, plates and rods, but the paunchy Russian woman could not have cared less. Her sole occupation was the survival of her family. What little money she accumulated was spent buying clothes and food. If there was extra, it was sent back home to her poor mother in Russia. Money was precious, and it brought four of Mrs. Pravda's sisters to America. Mr. Pravda was against this, but the old woman always got her way; she fought ruthlessly for her family. Mr. Pravda always gave into her, and she loved arguing with him late into the night.

For them fighting was a continuous way of life that would go on for days. The neighbors said they lived by way of grudges, spiteful comments and threats. Poor old man Pravda usually lost most of the battles waged with his temperamental wife. Language to them was merely a weapon they used on one another mercilessly. To regularly escape her wrath, the old man took refuge in one of Homestead's taverns on Eight Avenue. When his wife learned he was keeping some of his pay from her, she demanded a good Catholic school for her two daughters in return. Mascha and Irina beamed when they learned that their parents were sending them off to Holy Cross School. The church school was run by Irish immigrants right down the hill next to the steel mill in Homestead. Mr. Pravda grumbled about this and then decided he had to get his way in the household. His Russian heart took up this matter silently, but it was secretly searching for vengeance.

The poor Pravda family was one of the good families in the neighborhood always willing to help others. The old man was a hard-boiled optimist who never doubted the good nature of anyone.

Everyman was a saint in his happy eyes. He had even decided on his own plan to get back at his wife; they would take in a Russian boarder because he felt sorry for him. The terrible and bitter man was from a farm town not far away from the town where Pravda had grown up. The recent Russian immigrant promised to pay Mr. Pravda the back rent as soon as he found a job. Little did old man Pravda suspect that his slow-witted tenant was not only lazy but also less than honest. He refused to work, but Pravda argued with his wife and simply refused to believe it

The boarder once appeared to be a friend and yet he was always down on his luck—laziness for him was a disease for which there was no cure. Lazy men are always poor and dreaming of riches, and this will never change. Mr. Pravda truly wanted to aid him since the wretched man was clearly in need of help, and he had to get it soon. Old man Pravda argued with his wife about taking the boarder in for the winter. Mrs. Pravda said his clothes were ragged and his winter coat and hat were nothing more than tatters worthy of the rag pile. She said to her husband that even the ragpicker who came around with his horse-drawn cart in the back alley behind their house would probably not give the boarder's clothes a second thought if given the choice of whether or not to collect them. The man's clothing like the man himself was marginal, suspicious, smelly.

When the winter wind blows along the rivers of Pittsburgh, it is almost as harsh and cold as old Russia. Mr. Pravda used to tell the men at the Homestead mill this; they loved to listen to his stories of growing up on a small farm on the outskirts of Moscow. Down at the steel mill, old man Pravda loved to stand with his back to the open-hearth furnaces when a furnace door swung open. He would confide in his son, "Nothing is so great as the Russian winter and yet nowhere is it so beautiful as in Pittsburgh along the river when you have a great furnace to warm your backside." The tall, burly son always looked upon his father as a hero. He accepted whatever his father said for he admired him with a great Russian love. Father and son celebrated their hard work at the

Homestead steel mill with weekly visits to the taverns along Eighth Avenue every Saturday afternoon. Old man Pravda was greatly loved in Homestead; the people of its steel mills and taverns never doubted his view of things.

Mr. Pravda, as he was known throughout Homestead, told his wife they must do something to help the strange fellow who now looked as though he might not make it through the winter unless he found a job. "If we do not do something for him, who will? And if not now when?" There was an argument, and then the old man was overcome with pity. He sought to make his wife feel guilty, harsh and cold hearted. He said to his wife with an imploring voice that the poor man would have to sleep on the street or in an alleyway next to the house, "He could freeze out in the February cold and all because you refused to put him up for a while." At Christmas time he told his wife that the man was like Jesus, Mary and Joseph looking for an inn, but nobody would have them. "Is this how wicked the world is that we live in? We must make it better, we must help this man and get him through the winter or else he will freeze to death on the street in front of our house where there is enough warmth to warm one more soul." With these words, Mrs. Pravda finally gave in. The boarder would be offered a place in the small attic that was converted into a tiny bedroom. Mrs. Pravda had one condition, and she delivered it to her husband as though it was a threat, "He can stay for three months but once spring arrives, he will have to leave and find another place to sleep."

These words had been spoken the night before Christmas, and the old man was overjoyed. His greathearted prayer had been answered. He finally got his way for once. The holiday found him drunk and sleeping on the small living room couch. The work at the steel mill furnaces had worn him down, but now that he had gotten a little accomplishment, a gift to humanity out of his wife, he dozed off drunkenly with his heart filled with contentment. It had been accomplished only by constant whining and arguments. "The poor man is an immigrant to Pittsburgh and he has yet to find a job in one of the steel mills. He is a Russian like us and he is a good man, I can tell by looking at him when we are in the tavern together drinking beer. Once he gets a job and settles into America he will be fine, you wait and see." Mrs. Pravda was silent, her whole mood was suspicious of her husband and his constant bullying. It was like his big beer belly that was always in need of food. She was solemnly reluctant to let the poor man stay in the attic, but she was finally overruled by her stern, overly generous husband, "Besides, what harm can come to you from being kind?" she thought to herself. Mr. Pravda must have repeated it a thousand times to her before she finally gave in. When she agreed her heart was full of uncertainty. Trembling misgivings plagued her from that day forward, as soon as she saw the man she thought she knew him. Then she suddenly told herself that her old eyes were growing bad for they now always fooled her. When her husband told her to go get some eyeglasses, she laughed at him contemptuously and called him a fool, "So now you're a doctor and you are going to tell me what to do?" The arguments went on and on and they were as regular as the dawn.

Mr. Pravda told his wife constantly about how cruel and unjust life was, "This man went out for two solid weeks was still unable to find a job. The company owners are greedy and unfair. Many of the machine shops, steel mills and foundries he's gone to have refused to hire him because he doesn't speak English. That's not right." Mr. Pravda did not have any idea that their poor boarder was his own worst enemy. The man had a mean streak, which was evident in his attitude toward others; he was skillful at making enemies, and this he accomplished wherever he went. Mrs. Pravda had seen it in Mr. Loezsch, but her husband refused to believe it. She was being argumentative for a reason; her cranky opinions were often too harsh, suspicious and doubtful.

Mr. Loezsch refused to work around the house when Mrs. Pravda asked him to shovel coal into the furnace on Saturdays. He hid his face from her and always sought to avoid her suspicious eyes. Chores were always left undone; this usually happened when her husband was down at the tavern on Eighth Avenue drinking up the quiet of the wintry afternoon among his Russian pals from the Homestead steel mill. She began to resent Mr. Loezsch once she noticed that he could not keep a job for any length of time. As soon as a job was offered to him, he worked for a week or so. Once he got his pay, all he cared about was money and how quickly he could spend it on booze and good times. As soon as coins or dollars reached his hand, they were gone for beer, vodka, whiskey and cards for he had picked up a real mania for poker in America. He often played poker till after midnight in the paddle-wheel boats or tugs down along the river.

Mr. Loeszch finally got a job on one of these paddleboats, but he fought with the captain. Working on another barge he again made everyone miserable. On land it was the same and sometimes worse. Another job he landed at a cork factory on the Allegheny River produced nothing but enemies of his fellow working men. Wherever he got a job, it never lasted but a few days. At best it went on for a while; but within a few weeks, he was told to leave the premises. The reasons appeared to vary and yet were always the same. Mr. Loeszch told old man Pravda of his troubles and complained about America—the country was no good. He would buy a beer for old man Pravda at the tavern, and he always had an excuse about losing his job. Mrs. Pravda got to calling him a man of a thousand excuses. She said he was forever lying, cheating and blaming others for all of his own problems.

To Mr. Pravda, Loeszch was someone else entirely as they sat there at the bar drinking after a day's work. Mr. Loeszch would confide in him that one job after the other could never be taken on because it was too dirty or too hard or too demanding in the physical effort it required. After a hard day's labor and several beers, old man Pravda agreed with anything that he was told. He was too tired to question or argue with anyone, least of all the poor boarder who bought him beer after beer; a man cannot be all that bad if he is always buying you a beer. The poor man needed sympathy and Pravda wearily showered it upon him month after month. As long as Mr. Loeszch provided him with beers at the tavern now and then, it seemed to Mr. Pravda that his Russian boarder was a fine man who could do no wrong. Once in a while, as they gazed out the tavern window at the snowflakes filtering down from the heavens, all their troubles evaporated in a haze of wintry mill smoke, steam and furnace gases as they drifted off into the dull, sooty sky. Inside the warmth of their whiskey-fired Russian brotherhood, the bar, where the mirror gleamed with shiny bits of hopeful noise from the laborers and steel workers gathered there, was like a great family of workingmen out for the evening having a good time away from the mill.

The one good job Mr. Loezsch did land after a solid month of searching lasted only two weeks. On payday he struck the foreman of a boiler shop. The fault was always someone else's. The man had told Mr. Loezsch about not scattering coal over the floor in front of the furnaces where he was told to shovel it. Mr. Loezsch got angry with the foreman, and then left the place in an uproar. Several men chased him from the boiler shop yelling at him never to return. At the end of the day, after drinking all afternoon, Mr. Loezsch came warily back to the house hoping that the Russian neighbors in the neighborhood had not heard about his latest failure. Word was now getting around, and he was aware that someone had been telling Mrs. Pravda certain things about him. He was suspicious and yet still furious about hitting the foreman. He felt scorned and was angry at his fellow workmen and perhaps at all men.

To ease his misery Loezsch had gone out and gotten drunk and then trudged up the stairs to his tiny attic bedroom looking for another fight, but no one was around. Loezsch slept away the rest of the cold afternoon and then awoke in a terrible fit of depression and seething. Nothing was right with the world. His wallet was almost empty and he had no idea of how he was going to support himself in his new homeland. The language was foreign; the work was difficult, and nobody seemed to be willing to help him get a foothold on the rotten ladder of life. How did he know when he left his Russian home that he would have to learn a new language just to get a job shoveling coal? Nothing seemed right, and it wasn't his fault. Life in America was out to get him; and he suddenly felt he had to do something out of revenge in order to even the score.

In the twisted mind of this sorely bitter man, the Pravda family who had offered him shelter now seemed to be nothing more than a living threat, taunting him at every turn. All they did was remind him of his failures, his poverty and his wretched inability to adapt to America. As he stared out the small window at the smoky sky above the steel mill, Mr. Loezsch thought about the Pravdas and their damned jolly faces; he had convinced himself that he now hated them. Like a slowly fired furnace, he was gradually growing angry and he would soon boil over in a rage. The smell of the cabbage, sauerkraut and kielbasa the Pravdas were cooking up in their kitchen down on the first floor irritated him. He was now sure they were unfair; he told himself that he despised the Pravda family because of their camaraderie. The merry air of kindness they exuded so cheerfully to one another was proof they hated him. That he was Russian and their spite was aimed at one of their own people stung his iron heart to the core. It hardened him to their hearty goodness that drifted through the house. Even their cooking penetrated everything in such a way that the mere smell of food being prepared in the kitchen was a malicious insult. Deep within his angry heart he felt the word "home" was foreign to him. He grudgingly mused about the injustice of the world: "The old man and his son come home from the mill everyday, and when they sit down to eat they gobble down more in one night than I do in a whole week. They are greedy when it comes to the bowls of food put on their table. I've watched them while I'm eating. They think they own everything; they hate to see me put even a piece of their crusty black bread in my mouth."

Mr. Loezsch climbed out of his cold hard bed and crept down the wooden stairway with the few coins he had left to his name. He would go out to a tavern and get some whiskey to drink. Tomorrow he would travel back to his homeland and see about starting over. America was not the place for him. It was all railroad smoke, steel mills and coal mines and he wanted nothing to do with them here in Pittsburgh. The raw filth of the sulphurous smoky skies disgusted him every time he looked at them from his tiny attic window. To distract himself from this miserable scene, Mr. Loezsch strode silently down the wooden steps holding onto the thin wooden banister. When he got to the landing on the stairway, he was seething at the smell of the sausages, galumpkies, pork and cabbages. Mrs. Pravda had invited their Polish neighbor, Mrs. Milarski over to the house. She was now teaching Mrs. Pravda and Irina how to cook Polish dishes. Loezsch's poor hungry heart quickly decided to get even with the Pravdas, but he didn't know how it could be done.

Then a winter shadow caught his eye. It was one of the Pravda daughter's coming home from school. Mascha was frail and alone. A fearless man now sought revenge. Mr. Loezsch quickly scanned the hall. All the doors along the first floor hallway were closed tight to keep the coal-fired heat from the furnace in the rooms during the winter. With everything to his liking he quickly hatched up a scheme as wicked as it was cruel. Mr. Loezsch crawled quietly down the steps. The jealous eyes of the outcast echoed deep within his wily and wretched heart. It was akin to that of the worms that never leave the ground. He was one of them and they had something in common: he, too, was forever tearing things down. For Loezsch every good thing could be ground beneath his feet with his own restless words of ridicule, resentment and rebuke. In so doing the entire world was thrust meanly below his own poor level of rabid selfishness. For a moment an illusion swam within him like a snake and he felt exalted. Thus redeemed he came to believe that nothing was really any good anymore. This was his whole attitude, and he had made it into all that it was. This mean thought now ruled his every action. Like a giant pair of steel pincers at the mill down the street a terrible and jealous hope for revenge suddenly got ahold of him. A passionate fury now forced him into action. He would show the Pravdas, he would prove he was equal to them by getting even with them once and for all.

The girl turned around and came through the frosted glass front door. Mascha was innocently turning to close the door when he resolutely strode forward for the attack.

There was a cold, dark shadow slipping down the staircase, and it now crept like a snake toward its unsuspecting prey. A moment later his big unruly hand was secure around the girl's mouth. Mascha's frantic eyes were fixed upon his maddened face, it etched in her trembling heart his raw will as he dragged her into the cellar. In a moment of terror and survival her sharp teeth sank deeply into the hand that held her. Mascha was crying out wildly for help at the bottom of the wooden cellar steps as she was dragged to the dirt floor, "Mama, Mama, Mama," she screamed. Pots, pans and steel kitchen utensils went flying as the old woman frantically yanked open the kitchen door. From within the kitchen old man Pravda darted out like a stray spark thrown from the burners of the black stove, the burly son was soon on his father's heels.

Mr. Pravda ran furiously down the wooden stairs in a fit of haste and was quickly upon the dark scene. A tentative, crouching shadow stood up, leaped sideways and then bolted out the back door of the musty old cellar. Sausages were hanging from the ceiling. The door's loud creak sent the shadowy evil's footsteps echoing out of the room as it flew off toward the alleyway between the brick rowhouses. Then it went out into the alleyway that led down to the steel mill. There its presence dissolved like mill smoke into the cold, dark winter of the night never to be seen again.

A second later a great fury ran out of the kitchen, Mrs. Pravda instantly marched down the cellar stairs with her eyes full of terror. Her heavy tread on the steps sounded like the Russian army marching in to confront an enemy. She found her daughter who was scared and upset but had gotten through her ordeal unharmed. The old woman dusted off the young girl's housedress and then turned to her husband with a mean, questioning look.

Her hawk-like eyes could have torn him apart and killed him; he would have to deal with her now, and there was no escape. "I told you we should never have let that man in the house.

He was evil and I told you so but you refused to believe me. And now you had to find out on your own. Don't you think I know how wicked my own half-brother was?" Mr. Pravda stood as still as a bundle of iron rods. He was shocked and barked hastily at his wife, "He was your half-brother? Why didn't you tell me? Don't you dare tell me he was the one who escaped from the Russian prison."

A cold hard shadow of contempt now crept over the old woman's face as her lips moved angrily to confront her husband head on, "I couldn't say anything because I promised my mother. She said I should never tell you because if I ever did you would never forgive me. She said if you knew her son was a murderer you would not have married me before we came here. He was the reason she wanted me to leave Moscow."

Mr. Pravda now felt the cellar and its lone electric bulb on the ceiling spinning apart. The dizzy world itself was turning around, and he felt sick to his stomach. His arms and hands reached out as he sought to steady himself, but it was no use; he staggered forward and then sideways and then his face suddenly went pale. As his knees crumpled he swayed backwards and fainted into a heap; his big burly son sprang to catch the poor old man in his arms just before he hit the ground.

A FRAGILE DISH

People are often nothing more than an extension of the things that possess them. This was proven to me by the McMammon family of Pittsburgh, one of the city's most private collectors of European art. It is reported that only the elite museums across the world appreciated their rare treasures in the secluded family's private museum. I know this because the McMammon's only daughter, Frances, and I were once engaged to be married a few years ago. It was a time when I was uncertain of what I should do with my life. Commitment terrified me to such a degree that I hid myself in a series of romantic affairs. They held me captive as their tireless and spirited lover during a decade of thoughtlessly dreamy and passionate weekends. My indecision and confusion kept Frances and me apart, and so our wedding was continuously delayed; later it was postponed on several occasions. I finally put it off a fourth time, and Frances acquiesced to the fact that life was short and that she would simply love whoever came her way. I was greatly relieved by this turn of events, for I just didn't feel as though I was ready to marry one of the richest women in America. Like any one of the dozens of Pittsburgh fine art and antique dealers, I can recount the sad story of Frances McMammon from Fox Chapel only now after a decade of dreaming about her. For it was Frances who, some dozen years ago, became renown in all the finest venues dedicated to antiquity, fine art and the rare works of western civilization.

Ms. Frances McMammon was the daughter of a rich Pennsylvania family whose real estate in Titusville provided the Rockefellers with one of their first footholds into the petroleum industry. Titusville was where oil was first discovered in the nineteenth century, and the family sold its farmland to Standard Oil of Ohio. The McMammon's then moved to Pittsburgh and have always lived in a large Victorian brownstone down the road from my parent's home. Ensconced within the McMammon mansion were collections of fine paintings, rare glass sculptures, porcelains and objects d'art. European dealers were yearning to view, ponder and perhaps purchase for important collectors who long regretted giving up a hundred years ago. Americans were raiding private collections throughout Europe and the McMammons were offered masterpieces by several bankrupt royal families in England, France and Russia. The British Museum, the Louvre and the Hermitage all knew about the McMammon collection and the fact that it possessed one precious treasure after another. Their private museum encompassed over thirty thousand square feet under one roof. Long marble hallways led to rooms that seemed to flow from nowhere and then lead inward to a vast labyrinth. Locked away in museum cases were Sevres and Limoges porcelains, Monets, early Picassos, a Vermeer, a Rembrandt and a Faberge egg from the Russian Empire of Nicholas II. Ms. McMammon had inherited these precious treasures from her mother and father at mid-century. During the last quarter of the twentieth century, she began offering items up for sale periodically from my fashionable Shadyside boutique in Pittsburgh or on the Upper East Side of New York.

When the Metropolitan Museum learned that the McMammon collection was going to be gradually sold piece by piece by a private dealer, it stationed a handsome young Italian, Frederic Vaughn Bivant, to travel now and then to my exclusive antiques shoppe periodically to determine whether any of the finest pieces in the collection might be acquired. Though I never had a chance to meet Mr. Bivant, I was told he was a charming man whose gray haired temples made him look distinguished and even noble. His egocentric and self-possessed presence exuded art, culture and sophistication. He was rumored to be a friend of many powerful New York dealers, artists and rare art collectors. It was said that Vaughn Bivant was part of a strategy known to only a few; he was secretly said to be an unknown force in the art world. In stationing him here in Pittsburgh, the Metropolitan would be assured of keeping up with the Getty Museum over the next twenty-five years.

*
*   *

Frances McMammon was a generous and passionate soul with whom I fell deeply in love during my last year of college at Princeton. In high school, I got into a fistfight over her when one of the fellows in a geometry class referred to her as "a cute dish." She rewarded me for this act by asking me to the Fox Chapel Prom when she came out as the number one debutante at the Duquesne Club in Pittsburgh. Later, she used to take me on tours of her parents' art collection where I was left utterly astounded by the great works right here in the industrial heartland less than a mile from my own home. Frances loved to see me enraptured by the art, her vast home and her charming manners. I was enamored of her fine beauty. I could watch her for hours as we went through the stone mansion gazing at treasures any scholarly art treatise could have pictured on its austere pages.

Frances then left Pittsburgh to be educated at the Boston Museum of Fine Arts. She wrote to me at Princeton, and her letters told me about her travels. She studied at the Louvre and then finished her graduate degree at the Art Institute of Chicago. For a while I thought she might move to the windy city and take with her the collection that her parents and grandparents had amassed over the course of a century. I lost touch with Frances for a while, and then I found out some good news. When it was learned that her Chicago lover was suddenly lost to his own self-induced and dreamy alcoholism, Frances McMammon was said to be moving back home to her parents' mansion. An immense sigh of relief echoed throughout the hearts of the antique collectors scattered about Pittsburgh. My heart leaped with joy, and Pittsburgh's fine art collectors were overtaken with the news of Frances' return to the city. The crown jewel in their midst was to remain here, her presence thus insured the quality and prestige of their combined holdings.

Unfortunately, their celebration was soon interrupted. Within a year it was then learned that Frances was now involved not with one lover but three, and that she was now living a life no sane woman could carry on for very long. I myself was involved with her off and on at this time, and I will never forget where and when I was when I found out she was giving up her Monets to a lover who worked for the Metropolitan Museum. I was out at the Pittsburgh Field Club grounds, stepping down from a polo pony when one of the young valets ran up to me all excited and blurted out hurriedly as though the world were coming to an abrupt end, "Did you hear about Ms. McMammon? They say the moving trucks are pulling up to her mansion down the road and loading up all her Monets. People at the club just said she is giving them to that lover of hers, Mr. Vaughn Bivant."

A shudder of dread shot through my heart as I suddenly realized the precious landscapes I had been longing to add to my collection and to that of the museum would soon be gone. This art was now destined to fall into the hands of some clever young man whose love of money was about to steal Frances' art treasures from the city. I ran off to the car and felt the steering wheel slip haphazardly in my sweaty palms as I drove recklessly to the McMammon mansion. I was hoping desperately that I might get there before it was too late. I had to stop this madness; I had to convince Frances to give me a week or two to raise enough capital to purchase the paintings for the Carnegie Museum of Art.

As I hurriedly approached the McMammon mansion's porte cochere, I realized all of my hopes and dreams were totally lost. The dark house looked spiritless and robbed of a future; my heart sank in dread of what I hoped had not happened. I stepped out of the car and saw the tire tracks from a large moving truck. It must have left only a moment ago for the contours of the tires were still glistening in the soft, pliable mud along the driveway. My heart was pounding wildly as I rushed into the house where I found my beautiful Frances lost in utter agony. Balled up on the dull red velvet couch where we had often made love, Frances was now wrapped in a bulky burgundy sweater. She resembled a bunch of mohair twine that might unravel at any moment.

The antique lover's motto of "buy low and sell high" seemed to have broken her heart during the recent transaction that had inevitably gone the other way. She was so limp with sadness that she could barely pick up her head to look at me as she spoke, "I had to give my Monets to him, Jerzy, and I don't . . . I don't know if I should have. But he said if I didn't he would leave me—I refuse to live my life without his love." Her voice trailed off as she sipped at a large glass of Merlot. I summoned a glass from a marble shelf nearby and tried to console myself that everything would be all right. She was alive, and that was all that really mattered to me. I tried to get a grip on myself but the moment enveloped me of its own accord. I was stunned, hurt and furious with her.

We had discussed the Monets as being a gift to the Carnegie for over two years, and now they were gone and off to the old country. Frances had found out that Vaughn had nothing to do with the Metropolitan Museum; he was an independent broker from Europe who made a living selling purloined impressionist paintings. The Monets were now on a panel truck headed to New York and then to Venice. There after a few years in the humid air of the ancient canals they would deteriorate and be lost forever. They would finally be sold to some greedy private collector, lost to the art-worshipping public who adored them. Speechless, I listened to her in anger with no real understanding of all that had happened over the last few hours. Her voice was a wretched catalog of self-pity and hot tears; she was miserable and spiritless, broken hearted. Some sense came to her after an hour or so, and she finally confessed all that had happened. Her trembling voice repeated over and over in a monotone that rambled back and forth wearily that, "Wretchedness is everywhere." Frances droned on helplessly for a while and then regained some of her old composure. But as she spoke I knew she would never be the same.

"Frederic found out about you and the other man I have been having an affair with on the week-ends. He threatened me. He said unless I could prove my love to him, he would leave me forever. He and I were lovers, Jerzy; but I could never tell you about him. I knew that if he left me I could never go on. The whole of my life was slipping hopelessly away." A great pain slowly sank into my chest; I was angry and jealous, stunned and deeply hurt. Her voice was full of dreary sadness. I could sense she felt the world was crashing down all around her. I glanced over at the case where she kept her rare jewels and the treasures from her porcelain collection. All the shelves were empty. "What happened to the Picasso, the Renoir, the Tiffany lamps and the Faberge egg?" I said excitedly, my voice evidently suffused with worry and disgust. I was now feeling that the worst words of my life were soon going to be echoed off the hollow hopes of all my fears. A great pause ensued as she lifted her sobbing head out of her weary hands and looked up at me pathetically. Her voice was full of tears and misgiving. "They are all gone, Jerzy. I had to give them to my dear Vaughn. He said that if I truly loved him I would have to demonstrate my love by sharing them with him."

The realization of this folly suddenly catapulted me into a painful reality that swallowed up the rare beauty of the woman sitting next to me. It seemed I barely knew all that had been going on; an old truth was unraveling like a rare canvas rolled up in a dark corner of the great mansion. Her soft, auburn hair was dull and lifeless and as forlorn as the tender features I had grown to love over the years. I leapt out of the red velvet wing chair and ran down the hall to an ornate walnut-paneled library. I didn't want to believe my eyes; all the rare texts were gone from the shelves on which they had been stored like priceless gems of history. My mind was racing—I was completely consumed by fear and trembling. A moment later I felt myself overtaken by disgust. I suddenly grabbed hold of myself and awoke to this dreadful catastrophe, I then scurried back down the long dark marble hall to where Frances was perched lifelessly on the couch like a young bird that had fallen out of a nest.

There on the soft velvet couch nursing her wine I saw a woman who was more like a small frightened little girl. She was holding a Sevres dish, which fell to the terrazzo as her pained voice trailed off in misery, "Love is a terrible thing, it tears us apart. All my own love of art is gone forever. My art was like the lovers who treasured me. I was once their idol and am now I am no more." A maddening moment ensued and Frances bolted from her seat—she flew out of the huge bronze doors of the mansion fastened forever upon a dream. I ran helplessly after her and watched her scarf stream down the driveway as she was cried out in agony, "I have to find that truck, I must . . . I must."

As she rounded the bend with her red hair flying wildly, I instinctively knew that she was now hopeless. My heart was being squeezed in a great vice of pain. I started to perspire and worry. I wanted to run after her, but my feet were frozen to the ground. My shirt was now soaked with sweat and frustration; my eyes sought out Frances. I saw her head bobbing along the distant road in the moonlight. It was a dark pearly scene of serenity stolen from one of Albert Pinkham Ryder's late seascapes. Within a moment she was gone for good. I realized the antique emotions from our love affair were now burning in my chest like an old and molten flame that would soon go out in the cold wind of my anger. Tears streamed down my face; a profound sadness crept into the silence of my struggling heart. As I turned away from the road and headed back to the mansion, I felt the object of my being was now lost forever. She vanished into nothingness. She was now nothing more than the sound of rustling leaves in the nearby oak trees while my heart had become a lonely souvenir—the mute memory of a crazy love affair with a rich and beautiful woman.

A HOLY FAMILY

An arc of blue-black pigeons turned casually in the autumn sky above the church tower on Forty-fourth Street in the heart of Pittsburgh's industrial district. Hanging like streaks and dabs of dark paint in the soft blueness, the pigeons circled about the tower in an instinctual routine as old as the ancient hills. Below them, perched on the church bell tower, elderly pigeons huddled together against the impending coolness of the evening air. Their bleary and beady pigeon eyes were suspiciously affixed on nothing in particular at day's end. Time itself promised to turn the late warm afternoon into an evening of idleness. Some of the old gray pigeons sitting along the church tower resembled the old retired men sitting on a nearby wooden bench. Clumped together on their own they sought out the shade alongside the church where they jabbered among themselves in Polish about the last baseball game of the season.

Not far away an unseen sweaty human figure climbed up the steep Pittsburgh street. Upon its face was a tortured and sorrowful look stolen from the fiery rim of hell from which it had just escaped. The head of this humble shadowy man looked over. Down the tree shaded alley along the church it saw Mrs. Pushnick tenderly looking after her little ones swarming about the hem of her faded housedress. Embedded in the hard church facade before him were the stony faces of a holy family. Apathetic church windows whose hollowness was made more severe by their distance, looked like they were frozen in place by the torpor and ennui of eternity.

The whole world was motionless save for this man who was nothing more than an impossible series of tired and worried motions. The sweaty shadow limped along in dreary misery, it was unaware of anything human save himself. He was no more than fifty feet from the tired old Polish pastor napping comfortably in the priest house. The pigeons were as motionless as the sky, like the clergy below them they were ignorant of the human pain and suffering struggling in the shadowy form before them on the street. The tired, stooped figure was slipping away toward a bloody oblivion as it reached out for help below on the sidewalk. Only the cast iron fence was there for him; the dry October sun had warmed it like a piece of hard dried up biscuit. The day now formed a mirage that drifted off behind him at the mill not far away on the river.

Two pigeons looked down upon him curiously; his hardship meant nothing. Mr. Dobreczech paused in pain, and his strenuous solitude strained against the massiveness of his plight. He was alone and struggling like a drunken man, but his problem was pain; he was injured and was now fearful that he would never make it home. He dreaded the fact that he might collapse and be as immobile and helpless as a raw piece of pig iron or an old rusted ingot down in the mill yard. He took a deep breath and tried to right himself, his back straightened for a moment as he leaned against one of the posts of the cast iron fence with his good hand. His determination was like that of a slow-moving steel mill locomotive that couldn't be halted or delayed. When he got his strength back, he slowly pulled himself along the black fence posts as though they were a train track.

Dobreczech was covered with sweat; he would stop to rest whenever necessary. A fear of falling down on the sidewalk gripped his heart; he fought it tirelessly amid his throbbing limb. It had been smashed and he needed help or he might bleed to death. He had **The Pittsburgh Press** wrapped around his hand, which had been hurt in the steel mill machine shop at the end of his shift. Mr. Dobreczech resolved to stand up; he strove to hold on until he got home near Bessemer Street. If he could get home he would be fine. Sweat that resembled tears trickled into the deeply tanned wrinkles of his craggy face. Nothing could hold him back as he pulled himself along, up the street with a look of silent terror upon his painful face. Each metal gate was a truth to which he clung in an effort to return home.

The autumn sun was drifting across the maples, through their foliage slid the chill of time. Hardened rowhouse windows looked imperious and unforgiving on Mr. Dobreczech for the first time. He felt worried and sore as his sweaty pant legs stuck to his wet aching calves. His heavy black work shoes with their iron toes were covered in grime; they looked as though they could not hold him up or take another step. Then he bit down hard on the toothpick stuck between his teeth. His good hand now reached along the spiked iron fence and pulled him along the sidewalk where he took a rest. The ancient weariness in his Sisyphean-like step rose up into a shadow on the ground at his feet, the steep hill loomed immense and impossible before him. He paused and there formed about him a cool shadow, a shaded alleyway between the rowhouses sent a breeze that soothed his sweaty and painful arm. The tarry black fence posts stood straight and stiff as soldiers; they supported him as his whole body drooped weak and helplessly alone on the sidewalk.

Mr. Dobreczech lumbered up the hill now more steadily and isolated in his final attempt to return home. He was dogged relentlessly by pain. His eyes could barely make out the wall of his own house since his heart and head were now swimming in delirium. As he got to the narrow shaded alleyway between the rowhouses, Dobreczech knew his legs would give out on him before long. He fought hard, and the staggering limbs pushed him onward in vain. He crawled along the brick wall and its coolness hit his cheek, home and hearth were almost his, and they were not far away. A few more steps and he would be there, only now did he suddenly realize that he was sure to collapse beyond the reach of help.

A moment later Mr. Dobreczech fell into the backyard cellarway where his daughter Pearl was ironing her dress for school. She turned to see her father slump down as a tired and bloody mass onto the cellar floor. Her heart jumped in fear at seeing his torn and bloody hand. "Mother," she screamed frantically.

HELL IS OTHER PEOPLE

"Come quick, come quick. Poppa's been hurt . . ." The heavyset old woman ran out from the other room of the cellar where she had been peeling potatoes for dinner. Her generally calm face suddenly took on a terribly worried look of concern; she was overcome with fear as she hastily wiped her hands clean on her apron. She rushed over to her Stush and bent down to help him; her eyes sought to size up what was what. She instantly stole a glance at the man's blood, a trail of it was on the slate sidewalk outside and her eyes followed it to his right arm. The old woman braced herself and sternly ordered her young daughter upstairs, her face a fiery blaze of haste. "Pearl, go quickly. Get me some clean sheets and towels to use as a bandage. I have to fix up this mangled hand." The thin young woman ran to the wooden steps and bolted to the second floor where the linens were stored in her mother's linen closet. Mr. Dobreczech was wilting and slipping toward unconsciousness; every attempt to get up from the concrete floor failed him. He gasped in pain as his wife approached. She raised him up, and he crumpled into a small padded chair. His arm moved slowly up into the air, he held out his injured hand as though he wanted her to cut it off.

Mrs. Dobreczech's eyes went right to the problem. As he flinched she carefully probed the deep and bony, bloody gash on his hand. "You'll lose your thumb; there's no way to save it." Without wincing she reached for a putty knife and did what needed to be done. The thumb and a piece of bone came free and went off into the bloody newspaper; they were set nearby, close to her feet. Pearl arrived and began cutting the cloth and handing it to her mother who now wiped the bloody mass carefully with water from a steel pan. Once the hand was cleaned up Mrs. Dobreczech took a deep breath and tried to fight back her tears. The throbbing wound was carefully placed on Mr. Dobreczech's lap and his wife reached for a bottle of whiskey. The hot and frantic temper of the time seemed to slow down; it took on the cadence of an amber fluid flowing gently from a bottle. He was handed a shot glass and he drank it down at his wife's hasty urging. When he was finished she had one too. Pearl felt the warmth of the whiskey flow from their breath and into her hot face. The old woman's hands were now trembling like the autumn leaves outside in the brick yard. Mr. Dobreczech was going to have another whiskey but his lips could barely open wide enough to drink it. A little while passed and then a sense of calm descended upon him.

Mrs. Dobreczech's face was now riddled with fear and anger over her husband's injury. The work at the mill was always hard, grueling and dangerous. After 26 years at the steel mill it had cost her Stush a badly damaged hand. She didn't know what to tell him as he slumped before her in misery. He had mumbled something earlier about a metal bar slipping and how it had caught his thumb. He couldn't get his hand free before a gear came down on it. Then he was running out of the mill delirious with pain. His mouth was a gash of pain cut across his face, "It was Jimmy Stentkowski who had got hold of the bar before it took off my hand, my whole arm could have been taken right out of its socket."

Mrs. Dobreczech went to the doorway where two of her neighbors appeared in their babushkas. They had seen blood outside on the sidewalk and had heard Pearl crying upstairs about not wanting her daddy to die. The women's faces were now pleading to help Mrs. Dobreczech in her hour of hardship. Mrs. Dobreczech had them come into the cellar and the three of them began to prepare a cot for Mr. Dobreczech to lie down. Suddenly a small, sweaty boy of five barreled into the crowd of adults. His face was torn into fearful shrieks as he desperately grabbed onto his father's sweaty pants leg. "Don't die daddy, don't die." The women's hearts almost broke. They rushed to pick up the boy whose small hands refused to let go of his father's leg. One of the women, a tall chestnut-haired Slav reached down and brought the anxious boy up into her arms. The women grieved at seeing Mr. Dobreczech in pain. He could have been any of their husbands. The women's helpless mouths were full of a silent truth pulled from the fiery heart of Pittsburgh's furnaces. The misery before them hammered away at the cruel injustice that Mr. Dobreczech now had to bear. They were drenched in sadness and anger, and there was nothing they could do. Then movement in the room broke the spell of their emotions. Mrs. Dobreczech and the other woman, Mrs. Mihalik, gently picked up the broken man and moved him carefully toward the tattered cot. He was in shock and despair and looked as though he might expire before the night was out. The neighborhood women gathered in reserved silence, tense and saturated with worry. The hot dingy cellar air where the family's clothes were soaking in a steamy tub seeped into their pores.

Pearl now appeared in the doorway of the cellar crying at seeing her father prostrated by pain. Little Stush took this as reason to despair further and began to sob. "Momma, momma," he cried out, "I don't want poppa to die." Mrs. Dobreczech and the two other women went to work. They settled the exhausted man onto the tattered couch; they pulled him up so his head was resting on a pillow. His hand dripped blood onto his shirt and pants so they removed these sweaty rags covered with oily mill grime. Pearl brought over a wash basin and for the first time saw her father's wounded arm was cut. She handed a sheet to her mother who then swabbed the other wound and bandaged it with a clean white towel. Then Pearl ran upstairs to get him some food and water as her mother cried out, "Go next door and get your uncle, tell him my Stush has been hurt." Pearl returned with a plate of holupkies and sausages and then ran out the cellar door.

The boy gazed tearfully at his father as he lay helplessly on the couch. The older woman from next door whose sweaty brow looked like a bundle of worries sought to console little Stush, Mrs. Dobreczech also leaned over to him and said slowly, "You are going to be the next man in the house and you are going to have to learn how to do things because your father needs you now more than ever." The boy's eyes were full of promises and hope. The sweaty women soon started a vigil that lasted all night in the cellar. They fed Mr. Dobreczech and gave him water to drink. Before long he passed out exhausted from his ordeal. Everyone was quiet.

Little Stush and Pearl's fear put terrible dreams into their heads as they crawled silently into bed in the upstairs bedroom of the brick rowhouse. The street light came on. The few cars moving about out on the side street subsided and then disappeared as silence ruled over the end of the day.

Outside on the dull, shoddy rooftops the evening sun was glinting sideways and turning the mill and rowhouse windows to deep orange and red. Further down the block, crimson sparks from the steel mill reflected magnificently in the water of the gray oily river. On Forty-Fourth Street the church and its tower loomed immense into the sky. Lazy pigeons twittered about, roosting in the last of autumn evening's warmth. In the distance, down along the Allegheny River, mill whistles from Blawnox Rolls and Heppenstall's sounded as men filed through a wooden door and headed off to their tool bins. The first snow was supposed to arrive soon. The leaves from the maples and sumacs scattered like dry thoughts across the pavement. The Church's housekeeper had not swept them up nor the pigeon shit from in front of the rectory again. Alas, the pastor mused silently to himself about this as though lost in prayer; this was the way of the world. The memory of eternity slid in his mind like a piece of raw steel or a shiny slice of starlight in a monk's narrow cell.

A ROAD FOR EMILY

The busy occupants of the stream of cars passing by see nothing more than a faint gray farmhouse in the distance for a brief second before it is eclipsed by a rolling hill nestled along the Pennsylvania turnpike. Wheels carry them in hasty anticipation as they travel along, and then they are gone, oblivious to the reality that swiftly slipped by. An abandoned and dusty road leading up to the farmhouse and barn has a long dirt driveway choked with lifeless weeds that stand waist high. The drooping presence of the dried out weeds discourages all visitors except the mailman to visit the old homestead built before the Civil War. The rough dried out weathered wood of the gray farmhouse has a barn off to the side, the wooden slats of both buildings have been baked and bleached dry by the hot sun for over a hundred summers. Time is measured here by the rate at which gravity pulls down the abandoned silos, chicken coops and the forlorn doghouse as they collapse in random, dry wood bundles.

 The shade trees behind the house, which once served to protect it from the elements, were sold off to a lumber mill for money during the Great Depression. What still remains of the oaks and maples in front of the house was the profile of neglect; broken tree branches were splayed and helpless beneath the forbidding winter sky. The tattered screen door of the house rusted through years ago was never replaced. The wooden front door behind this screen was warped shut and it can't be opened, no one went through it in over twenty-five years. Out back behind the farmhouse a milkweed drooped over the edge of the gutter, its autumnal seeds raining down along the perimeter of the back porch. Not far away inside the gutter a muddy-brown leafed sumac sprouted in the air like a withered flag of surrender; the farm and its owner had given up long ago. Both were gradually falling into the seedy depths of decay. Not far behind the barn was a fallen down wooden structure. It had been a long corncrib that stored corn for cows; now it was but a splintery mass of old gray wood that had fallen onto hard times and would never be the same again. Sagging wooden window frames on every side of the farmhouse were a history of what lonely desperation had befallen the place. The only sturdy building still in use was the solitary outhouse. A flock of squawking crows perched on it daily and soiled it season after season.

The rusty and crumbling tin of the chicken house roof sloped down into the earth like a shipwreck that had reluctantly been dragged inland against its will; its battle for life was over long ago. The coop itself had collapsed many years earlier; before the chickens were gone. The big snow of 1950 had essentially done away with the patriarch and then the chicken house; there never came a time to fix it. Emily Kreig's husband died that year shoveling the big snow. It was soon thereafter that the farm was neglected. Emily could no longer look after the place, and the one hired man who helped out now and then had just left once Samuel Kreig was put into the ground. People in Butler and on the adjoining farms began to talk about Emily's fading beauty. Before a score of years had gone by people in her parish said Emily's pretty face simply dissolved like clouds in the sky. The bright young beauty turned into a gray and stifling weariness. Her wrinkled old age soon clung to her like a house dress that had long ago lost its shape.

Soon thereafter, Emily's frail mind drifted like a cloud forever into the past. She went out onto the back porch to look at her fruit trees and to reminisce daily about how beautiful her life once was. Nowadays, Emily lived in the lost promises of the past. If she was out and about, it was only to refresh her memory for nothing in the future seemed to matter anymore. There were days, weeks and months that went by where the only things she thought about were the apple and the pecan trees down by the old barn.

She sometimes wondered how the barn was able to stand up for over a hundred years while other things around the farm had fallen into disarray. The buildings, fences and silos behind the barn were sloping, tilting and falling down, but she didn't know why. All she knew was that her prized pecan and apple trees stood out strong and brave and were at the heart of what was truly important. As long as they flourished and provided her with food she would be all right. In those trees was all that was beautiful about her life; the rest was gone and soon to be forgotten. A few things on the farm troubled her but there was little she could do about them. The chimney swifts in the fireplace kept her from sleeping now and then in winter, and a squirrel and some chipmunks had taken up residence in the rafters of the attic. Over the kitchen window was a spider web, saturated with dust and sunlight. It was stretched like a cloudy film that made every object seen through it as dull and as lifeless as the gray wooden farmhouse in which Emily lived.

The rusted old mailbox was a remnant of a finer time that had fallen into complete chaos; the flimsy mailbox had aged and was now a decrepit brown cylinder on a stick whose hinge was about to give way. It swayed in the wind and its fate was assured, time was biding its time. The mailbox was destined for the invisible junkyard of all man made objects where the temporary and the eternal seemed to be locked in a timeless embrace. Age and decay conquer all. A frail voice of reality drifted about the farm like wasps lodged in a hive being built under the dormer on the farm house roof. The sandstone foundation of the house was seeping into the soil like grains slipping through the infinity of time's sullen hourglass. The timelessness of the scene announced one fact—gone, the past is gone but never forgotten by our hearts. Here is where all of our life is lived out in a kind of truth no one can ever deny. The past is everywhere, and yet it cannot be comprehended; it is hidden in every tired and overgrown garden of weeds, decay and crumbling hope.

Spider webs covered the windows of the kitchen and made it impossible to see outside; a permanent fog of confusion slipped over the farm quietly years ago and it never departed. Spiders, chipmunks, squirrels and the skunks had inherited the place. The only greenery was by the barn along the row of apple and pecan trees, the rest of the place had fallen helplessly on hard times by a neglect that never goes away and yet can never be banned from human things. Emily Kreig seemed to be waiting for a certain end; her great and failing heart was as green and as patient as an abandoned country cemetery.

Emily had survived by living off the farm's meager produce for years, she did what she had to do and that was more than enough to get by. She had surrendered so much that now, toward the end of her life, she stubbornly decided she didn't need people bothering her about her farm anymore. A nebby real estate woman came around a few months ago. She asked about buying the farm and Emily had to chase her away. The woman's youth haunted her for weeks and then for months and months thereafter. "Well that woman won't get my farm, she won't ever get her pretty hands on my homestead cause it's the last thing I have. From here I can see my husband and my boys who are buried in the country cemetery across the way, I could never leave them. You'd swear these people don't have any sense of family anymore . . ." Emily thought resentfully to herself about this silky, young and prying realtor who pestered her for a whole week. This woman was the reason Emily stopped paying her telephone bill; old people have the craziest ideas sometimes. "If I kept the thing connected that real estate woman would just annoy me all day and night." Emily was independent, and she knew how to show people she meant business when it came to her farm. She had gotten rid of that real estate woman in such a way that she never again came snooping around as long as Emily lived. Besides, there were too many things that needed to be done, and Emily couldn't find the time to do any of them.

It was when Emily found the bottom step on the wooden cellar stairway all rotted out that she knew things in the house were getting pretty bad. The stairs had gotten progressively worse, but she didn't know why that was. For a while she was convinced that the squirrels and the chipmunks had eaten away the bottom step. It just seemed there was so much to do that it wasn't worth doing anything anymore. Mostly it was because everything cost so much money. Along with the bad wooden step there was a skunk nest under the back porch that bothered her to no end. When she stood on the sagging wooden porch to feed her two farm cats, she smelled the skunks more and more nowadays. It seemed as if even their presence was telling her, "Get out, get out of this place. You do not belong on the farm anymore. You should be among your people in the church graveyard across the way." This thought settled into Emily but it did not frighten her. She was exactly *what* she had wanted to be, she had in the end become *who* she wanted to be. Being a farm widow was a hard life to live, and soon it would be over. The only thing she ever really wished for was to be a good mother to her two boys but the government took them away from her. Now Emily was alone. She had her two cats and their little kitties, and they made the thought about the graveyard go away for a while. A worry took its place. If she did die who would take care of her new kitties? They needed her. "Who would look after Ginger and Chloe if I should pass on?" she thought to herself. There was nobody else around after her Samuel died during the big snow. People still talked about how it killed her Samuel and how the big snow blocked the Freedom Road for almost a week. People used horses to get around just like they did in the old days; Samuel loved going out into the snow on horseback. It just doesn't snow like that anymore either. "Everything has changed," Emily mused silently to herself, "Nature conquers all," I suppose.

    Emily looked out over at the tin doghouse roof from which her dog Ishmael used to roam among her big hydrangeas, "He was the best farm dog a woman ever had," she thought to herself. She looked at the rusted roof of the doghouse again and again and she felt a thought grow deep down into herself, "That is such a sad monument to such a good and loyal dog. He deserved better, but what could I do? I could never replace a dog that was that good and there was no use in taking the doghouse down so I just let it go. Sometimes you just got to let things go and hope for the best. That is the only way to survive sometimes."

Then Emily heard the skunk rattling around under the back porch and her thin finger and bony thumb pinched her nose as she went into the house. She had to get away from the spray. 'If only my two boys had lived through the war, they would have looked after me and the farm.' Samuel always used to say that to me all the time, 'If our boys would have come home from Germany, we would have had a happier life but it just was not meant to be. We never would have had to worry about keeping up the farm if Jim and Bud had come back from Germany in 44. They would have come home and helped us keep up the farm and we'd have made some real money then. Once I started hiring men to help out with the work on the farm we started losing money.'" Samuel was always worrying about money and running off to the bank during the Great Depression. He had us saving every nickel we could get our hands on. We lived off the vegetables, produce, chickens and cow's milk the farm provided. He even took the horse up to the bank in Butler so he wouldn't have to pay for the gas the truck would use. Saving money had become a kind of old time religion to him.

Emily thought about Samuel's words over and over as though they had been spoken yesterday, yet she had not heard them for almost twenty years. 'Remember the time when Jim planted those apple trees along the road leading up to the barn and I gave him hell because they were going to overshadow my pecan trees? You stood up for him. You took sides with him Emily, and you both argued with me. That was our first fight. He was 13 years old and I will never forget him watching me as I yelled at you and he was hurt by my argument. I will never forget him saying to me then, *I will run away from home.* And I just glared at him, and you packed him a lunch and he took it from the kitchen table and started down the road with his angry hand clutching the paper bag, biting his lip in revenge. The two of you were so fed up with me that day.

"Jim walked on and on in a huff. He went on for about three miles and he was almost to the Butler Plank Road, and by that time he was hungry. He sat down under a tree and ate the sandwiches and the peaches you gave him; it was as though the two of you just wanted to spite me that day. And by the time the sun was setting he was already walking back up the dusty farm road toward home. He seemed a man then. You said those apple trees were from the Garden of Eden and that they had been his Bar Mitzvah and had made a man of him in a certain way. He had stood up to someone for a principle he believed in, and maybe that is all it takes to be a man. Yet some men never learn it."

"And then when he came into the house at dusk, the sound of the wooden screen door hitting against the jamb and its echo following his footsteps woke me up from my evening nap after dinner. His pensive mouth opening up before me was saying, '*Walt Whitman once said that the best part of a man is his mother.*' He looked me right in the eye as I sat there with the newspaper setting on my lap and he went on, '*My strength is like my mother's strength, it is a happy strength borne of an honest toiling. It is filled with a simple magnanimity that you can never thwart yet alone destroy.*' And I looked at him wondering where he learned that word. Yet I knew that you had taught it to him because all the truth a man can ever know for sure is in his mother's heart. You had taught him that it lives on there patiently like the widows across America who struggled with broken hearts and dreams once their sons were sacrificed on the fields of Europe. You taught him about WWI when your mother lost her only son. You taught him what he knew, for every good mother is the same, and teaches her children in the same way. It was the way you had taught him everything else too, I was happy for him and for all of us. Bud looked up to him like a god at that moment as he sat there on the floor where the words were echoing in our hearts, wondering what had gotten into his brother. Bud had seen his brother's self-determination for the first time and he admired it in the same way you and I respected it.

Jim truly was the best man this family ever had. That was clear to you and me, even the boys understood it to some extent at that very moment. When the government drafted Jim into the Army he went because it was the right thing to do. You had taught him that too. A year later when Bud followed him it was only because he wanted to be like Jim. Our Jim was the ideal man and Bud was not going to be outdone, not our Bud.

"Once they went off to war we wrote to them every other day. We were so proud to tell them in the autumn about the apples that were coming off the trees in such great numbers; we had bushel baskets of them in the kitchen. Even the picky neighbors next door said they were the best apples they had ever eaten. I can still see Jim walking back home after running away in an angry huff that day, his jeans and shoes all dusty. He was utterly disgusted with me too. The next day when I finally let him use the soldering iron to solder the edge of that tin roof on the doghouse, he forgave me cause I never let him solder before. I figured I had to do something to make up to him. That was it, and once the doghouse was done he was so proud of it, Jim just about had Ishmael thanking him for the right to admire the fine work he put into it too."

"And I will never forget Jim and Bud going down to Pittsburgh. It was their first time in a car, and I was telling them about how you and I met. I drove them over to look at your father's old house and they grew more and more curious about you. I told them all about you and me. How when I met you your name was Rebecca Goldstein who the society papers said was the most charming and elegant woman in all of Pittsburgh. I remember how you wanted to leave your cocktail dresses and evening gowns behind. You wanted a new life. You said you even wanted to change your name to Emily too all because you didn't want to carry any of your past or any of its hypocrisy into the future of your new life here on the farm. I told them about how you and I eloped because we knew it was the right thing to do at the time, and that we never regretted it. Back then you said running away from home was like the Quakers leaving England to settle down in Pennsylvania. I said you will never know how prophetic what you said really was and you looked at me curiously."

"And then I told you, 'That's right, you are marrying a man from Butler County who can trace his family's lineage all the way back to the Quakers coming to America in 1620. I am descended from a Quaker family who came over from England with William Penn.' Your wondrous eyes lit up full of knowledge; you were thrilled by this little bit of Pennsylvania history that surrounded the man you were marrying. It was as though you knew you were right to run away with me."

"You were so joyous then. We got the farm going and just as things were looking up, the Great Depression came and turned us into great savers. Then dad left the farm to me cause I was his oldest son. When I showed it to you and you got tired of walking the 1200 acres you just said, 'I will see the rest later on.'" Only later on never got here cause you were carrying Jim and then a year later you had Bud and we were just trying to get through the Depression like most folks. It seemed that a certain truth came home to us then. It must be a tradition with the poor in America, no matter how much money there is they are always running out of it. That is how we became such great savers."

"Nothing is heavier than the heart that feels failure is ahead and is inevitable as the future," Samuel used to say. "There's no use of hurrying cause what you are rushing off to get to ain't going to be too much different than where you are already. People nowadays are nothing more than perpetual motion machines, and they are forever chasing after a past happiness that they can never catch up. Their memory holds them back because they have already forgotten it; it is hidden inside their haste only they don't understand that. Besides, good things last a good long time only they refuse to see it that way since their motion has their eyes perpetually focusing on where they are going. I suspect people are so busy they don't have time to understand the simple things anymore. Perhaps if they would stop to save themselves for the present they wouldn't have to be in such a rush about the future cause it will get here soon enough. If they had a little common sense they could be ready for it."

Emily thought to herself about him and his always saving their money. Then she fell to thinking about how poor she felt nowadays, "I don't know where Samuel put all the money his dad left to him because I cannot even put my old bony fingers on a hundred dollars. Not for the life of me do I know where all our savings went. During the Depression we had it a lot better than other folks whose older kids ran away so that the younger ones could survive. Samuel and I sold our extra eggs and made money selling milk from our cows. We saved most of the money, but I don't know where it went. The poor must have got their hands on it and spent it while I wasn't looking. What was left probably went to pay taxes on the farm and maybe some of it's in the Butler National Bank strong box where he said he was always putting it away. Only I never saw any of it. Samuel said he was putting it aside for a rainy day and I never saw it rain when I was outside, hanging clothes on the clothesline. I guess that is just the way it goes sometimes.

"Then Samuel and I were sitting on the front porch the day the Western Union man drove up. His rusty car made a cloud of dust behind it. That was the end of our happiness and we sensed it would never return. We knew when we saw his Western Union uniform and the telegram in his shaky hand that it was trouble. Only we didn't know how bad the trouble was. It was not until we learned we had lost not one son but both of our boys in Germany. Their platoons had met up and fought the great fight, but we lost them within a week of one another. Our whole life ended at that moment on that porch as we sat there in disbelief. Hopelessness descended upon our hearts, and we would not emerge from gloom for years and years. The thought of those two boys never coming home alive was too much to take. It slowly killed Samuel, I still don't know how we ever got through it."

After we buried the boys in the church graveyard across the road, he and I were over there all the time praying and sobbing over them. Their youth was lost so others could live. The dusty farm road leading up to the house grew long and darkened by our dull grief; our two boys were gone forever. Then after a while the farm just seemed to fall to ruin of its own accord and there was no stopping it. Samuel worked the farm but the whole feel of the place was not right. About the only things he felt good about were the apple trees and the apple pies I used to make every autumn. Samuel's favorite month was October when the apples would ripen red and delicious. It was as though we were eating Jim's apples. We thought of him all the time and how Bud used to look up to him; thoughts of them just hovered over us for years and years. We loved them all the more now that they were gone. It was those apples that opened up our eyes to all that we had done together as a family. Bud had dug the holes and Jim had planted the trees at my urging. Samuel's argument had somehow brought all of us together in a way we never thought possible. After Samuel died in 1950 shoveling the farm road during the big snow, my grieving over him and the boys descended over the farm, and it was never the same again. Then I got Ginger and Chloe from a neighbor, the farm seemed to gradually get away from me and after a while I gave up looking after it. The next thing I knew a bleached blonde real estate woman was coming around asking me if I wanted to sell the farm. I told her I could never sell the farm because it was home. She looked at me like I was an old grouch when she smugly walked away saying under her breath, "You can't stand in the way of progress forever."

*
*   *

Before long Emily Kreig passed away. She was barely a memory to anyone. The utilities were turned off and the mailman·who had been her only human contact and who had delivered her mail and packages for over thirty years retired a week before she died. Emily had given him a bushel of apples as a retirement gift. Nobody noticed her absence on the back porch as the overgrown weeds just sprouted and then perished and then were absorbed by nature as the years went by. The smell of death came and went inside the house, and then it just drifted away with the seasons. Six summers and six winters slipped silently by like swallows or chimney swifts without notice by anyone.

The ambitious bleached blonde finally came back to the farmhouse with a secret hope. That things had finally gone her way. She was driving her new station wagon, a big gaudy diamond was on her hand. It caught the sun when she walked among the dusty drifts of skunk dirt. Atop the broken steps she found the back door of the farmhouse open on this cool autumn morning. The windows throughout the farmhouse were covered with gray and black deathlike shadows. The skunks had left their nest under the back porch, which had finally collapsed sideways under the weight of snow several winters earlier. The blonde carefully picked her way across the remnants of the porch and went into the house swiftly as a hungry animal. The quiet enveloped her like the silence of an abandoned country church. She looked at herself in the fading mirror covered with ancient farm dust. A dried out piece of cracked plaster hung down from the ceiling lath where it had peeled away from its splintery wooden ribbing. Time had pulled it lower and lower. Cobwebs were knitted across the remainder of the ceiling like a flimsy net.

A shudder shot through her fearful heart but it was not enough to deter her. She didn't feel she belonged here; and she wanted to run out to her car and drive away but she smelled something, money. From that her courage took on a certain villainy. Blood flushed through her veins and gave her wickedness new strength. She boldly walked over to the banister and sized up what could be sold at auction and what had to be put onto a bonfire after the dirty deal was done. This took all of a minute; she had a figure in her head by then so she went upstairs. Dust from the walnut banister touched her slim hand. She felt death penetrate her thoughts as she reached the upper landing. Her eye never missed a thing. There on the floor of the bedroom was a bit of bleak sun glinting from a bleached skull setting on its side. The end had come for Emily Kreig. She was prostrate with her skeleton askew in a moth eaten housedress; her straw hat sat idly nearby.

The scene looked like a black and white photograph of a lost farm taken not long after the war. The spartan bedroom had never changed after her boys died.

Emily had fallen over into the kitty litter; a dozen cats had died there with her from starvation. That at least was what the authorities claimed in their official report. They were thorough with their investigation and brought in a Professor of Pathology from Penn State's medical school. Emily had sent them two dollars once after she got a request in the mail. The pathologist who looked at her bony remnants was a baby back then. He was there for a few hours, and his conclusion was that Emily Kreig had been living on apples and pecans. A basket of dried out six-year old apples along with a half-empty bushel basket of ancient rotten pecans were found in the kitchen. Another bunch of papery apples cores were found next to her bed. It seems that she must have died sometime in 1970 shortly after the real estate lady had dropped by to inquire about purchasing the farm for a land development company that Butler County wanted to call Cranberry.

A month or so later a lawyer and some officials from the Commonwealth of Pennsylvania got to poking around the house and found some documents, savings accounts and a key to a lock box at the Butler National Bank. When they got into the strong box they found 1.3 million shares of common stock issued beginning in 1902. All of the stock certificates were tied up in yellowy bundles with bits of farm rope. They were from a steel company down in Pittsburgh. Without any heirs to the estate it was soon evident that the Commonwealth of Pennsylvania had stumbled into a windfall. Within the next year all 1.3 million shares of preferred and common stock for the **United States Steel Corporation** were redeemed for cash that was then deposited into the bank account for the Commonwealth of Pennsylvania.

After much political fighting among the legislators, the Democratic governor was told that his own name on a nearby road would not be a fitting memorial for his limited contribution to this enterprise. However, as a sign of the commonwealth's gratitude the Governor and the state legislature finally negotiated a settlement. Together they decreed that a state road running through the suburban sprawl north of Pittsburgh would have its name changed to the Emily Kreig Road. One of the Butler alderman who had more than his share of chins thought it was a nice gesture for the Commonwealth to name a road for Emily. It would intersect one of the longest strip malls in the state running from Freedom to Cranberry, Pennsylvania. Arguments rose again and then ensued for over a year and a half in the state legislature, the Governor threatened to veto the road project until he figured out a way for one of his political supporters to become the sole road contractor. Things settled down very quickly after his old political crony from Philadelphia was appointed to his cabinet. Even though the project's final budget doubled from its original estimate, the Governor's share of the road construction costs secretly found their way to his New York bank account.

Some of the other greedy people who profited from Emily Kreig's estate were the land developers and the real estate folks. The bleached blonde got her percentage of the loot; her share permitted her to retire to Las Vegas, Nevada where she built her own condominium. She was a real prisoner of impulse who gave up the husband back home to become an expert on black jack and gin and tonic and never looked back. Her days were like the playing cards she loved, numbered.

The last time anyone bothered to check, Emily Kreig's dilapidated farmhouse was still there rotting gracefully away in the dusty nothingness of the Pennsylvania hills. It gradually fell into further ruin as the squirrels and chipmunks thrived. They had taken up living under the wooden remnants of what was once her back porch. Their offspring are now rubbing their little paws together and snickering with glee because the animal rights people from California have just had some legislation approved in the Pennsylvania State Senate. It declares that the animals living on Emily Kreig's farm are protected by a decree making the land a wildlife preserve. Over the weekend the Governor signed legislation that will ensure that the offspring of these animals will be forever fed from the coffers of the Commonwealth. Their food will be supplied in perpetuity by a company owned by the Governor's wife; the animal food will be paid for with money left over from Emily Kreig's largess.

The splintery and warped grayness that touched everything could be felt everywhere. It could be felt most securely in Emily Kreig's estate where it penetrated each and every object, known and unknown to her when she lived out her last bleak days. Now that she was in the earth alongside her husband and her two loyal sons, her silent shining beauty and goodness were gone and yet could never be forgotten as long as the trees she loved continued to bear fruit. Along the weedy road to the farmhouse, the only abiding things that stand tall and self-sufficient are the apple and pecan trees planted over five decades ago, seven years before WWII. Back behind the slanting tin roof of the chicken coop and the rundown doghouse, the Pennsylvania highway maintenance men now store their graders, tractors, construction machinery and road salt. Once a week they take their mowers out to the highway across the pasture to keep the interstate's green meridian neat and trim. On their return at day's end, the smell of freshly cut leaves of grass lingers in the late afternoon air of the abandoned country graveyard across the way. Its dull and mossy gunmetal gray tombstones honor the fallen. They are a lasting and shining monument to the sullen and worn out old farm whose memory will live on forever and ever.

| James Kreig | Samuel Kreig | Emily Kreig | Robert Kreig |
| 1924-1944 | 1897-1950 | 1899-1970 | 1925-1944 |

SITTING PRETTY

Joe and I grew up in Duquesne, Pennsylvania back in the 1970's when this bustling mill town located on the Monongahela River outside of Pittsburgh was still in its industrial heyday. "Billy Toricht," Joe would say, "once you and I get into business together we will be sitting pretty as the Mon Valley's best painting contractor." I used to just go along with him back then. We worked as house painters in the summertime and did odd jobs like cutting grass, digging graves and working for this wily beer distributor, who never wanted to pay us at the end of the week. If it wasn't for tips old ladies and other drunks gave us when we delivered their beer to their houses, we would have never made it. One year a minister in East Pittsburgh helped us out by hiring us to move his wife's furniture after they got divorced. That divorce saved our lousy necks that summer for sure. Lots of times we just paid ourselves with cases of beer owed to us by the beer distributor from the week before. Joe was always on the lookout for how we could make a buck, and he finally turned up to be the lucky one. He got a job working in production for the Pittsburgh Plate Glass Company over in Creighton, wherever that was. He said it was on the Allegheny River up the road from the Harmarville exit of the turnpike, but I didn't have any idea of where either of those places was, so it didn't make any difference to me. The first thing Joe did was go out the next week and buy a Chrysler convertible. He and I decided to celebrate with a party that night.

I don't even remember half of it anymore cause the booze fried my brain. All I recall is that we went down to the McKeesport bank to cash his paycheck from PPG. The bank teller was my cousin. She and I used to go to St. Mary's High

School a couple of years ago. She invited us to a party in Monroeville so we decided right then and there what was on tap for that night. Joe had this thin bunch of twenty-dollar bills on him that amounted to something just over a hundred dollars. After going home to pay his mom and dad the rent money that he'd promised them, Joe and I went over to the distributor to buy a couple cases of beer and head off to our disco party. We stopped in the State Store and got a couple bottles of Imperial whiskey. Joe said, "I feel like royalty, sitting pretty and on top of the world in my new car." I envied him too because he always seemed to be a guy who was lucky. Lady Luck was always good to my old pal Joey. He was now on the road to riches, and I envied him. We drove up to my cousin Linda's house where the party was going on. We met a bunch of our old friends we hadn't seen since high school. Joe started handing out beers and shots of whiskey and we were really whooping it up. The only problem was that within an hour we were running out of booze. Joe went to the car and headed down the road to get some more Imperial at the State Store. I wanted to go with him but this woman who was a friend of my cousin Linda wouldn't let me go. She said she wanted me to start selling dope for her. She promised me that I'd have more money than Joe would ever see in his whole life. The next thing I knew she had me in bed with her, and I told her I'd do whatever she wanted.

 The party went on late into the night—I passed out about midnight. I never thought about how I would get home to Pitcairn where I was soon to be living with this woman off and on. It turned out I ended up in a sleeping bag on the back porch of my cousin's house. During the party somebody said they had heard fire engines going off to a fire. Since we didn't smell any smoke everyone realized it must have been a false alarm down at the McKeesport mill. I felt delirious and fell sound asleep in the arms of my new girlfriend out on the back porch of my uncle's house. I was wasted the next morning when Linda's old man came out and woke me up.

He was all excited and nervous. "Billy, wake up. Did you hear?" he said to me like it was a kind of mystery about what had happened. "Did I hear what?" I asked. "Joey Toricht was in an accident with that new car of his. They say he almost bled to death down at the bottom of the hill by the State Store." I jumped out of the sleeping bag and looked for my fancy tennis shoes. I finally found them under the couch that was splashed with vomit from the night before.

Then I heard a noise. The woman I was with the night before had her head in a toilet and was throwing up her guts. I got scared and ran out of the house and then down the street without any shoes on my feet, I was off to McKeesport Hospital full of frightful visions of Joe being dragged out of a big pool of blood. The nurses at the hospital wouldn't let me into his room to see him. They said I wasn't a relative, so I went down to the steel mill to find his father to tell him what was going on; but he wasn't there. The men said he was at home, and one of them gave me some old work shoes to wear. So I ran over to Joe's house. His mother and father were all worked up. She was crying and blaming me for what happened—they were mad at me for buying all the booze. My head was pounding, and I got into an argument with them. They blamed Joe's accident on me. I just gave up by yelling at them, "I didn't even have any money to buy whiskey." They wouldn't listen to me and their angry looks only made me feel worse than I already felt. Joe's accident had me worried. All they cared about was finding someone to blame for it other than themselves. I trudged off in a huff and went home to get rid of my hangover. My head felt like a huge metal press down at the Duquesne Metal and Machine Shop that was stamping out pain like it punched out parts for new cars.

One endless month after another went by and the news was never any good. Joe was not going to get better and he blamed me for what happened to him. His parents had convinced him I was the one who ruined his life; they told him I was a bad example. After he went home from the hospital he started drinking. After a while I became his runner to the State Store. I cashed his disability checks and then picked up six packs and bottles of Imperial for him when his mom was out of the house. She gave me a dirty look if she saw me on the street, and I tried to avoid her now whenever I could. When his old man wasn't home we smoked dope together. It became obvious soon after that that Joe was never going to get out of the wheel chair. By now he was always depressed and moody. He got angry and threw things at me if I was late bringing in the stuff. I once got arrested getting him cocaine and heroin, and he didn't even care about my having a police record. "Hell," he said, "You got me into this rotten mess with that damn party at your cousin's house and look at me now." I was hurt and I never knew what to say to him anymore. His mother went to church constantly and his dad wouldn't let me in the house. If it wasn't for me their little Joey would have stayed working in the glass plant and had his car paid off by now.

After about six months, I got a job at the McKeesport steel mill but I went around for a long while in a daze, stoned out of my skull in the mill yard where I worked as a laborer. My girlfriend then got me selling stuff for her, and I was peddling it wherever I could. Young guys bought it up like candy. One of the black guys I was working with hated the idea of me selling the stuff. He told me I better be careful about who I tried selling it to down at the mill, the Union had spies everywhere. He said, "If Capitalism made sense then the McKeesport steel mill will never die, but I got a bad feeling inside me. The mills got a system, that's what I think and here's how they do it. As soon as the Union starts letting black guys like me into the steel mill, they'll start shutting the steel mills down. You just wait and see cause that's the way the white people do it nowadays. Whatever is done is rigged up to hold us down. I tell you the black people around here like me don't have a chance in hell of getting ahead." Then a few years later somebody said the steel mills were closing down and all around me I saw nothing that was any good—the radio reported that destruction of the rust belt was now coming down on the little guy faster and faster. They said the industrial northeast and parts of the Midwest just weren't going to make it. Shiny-faced TV reporters said we were History.

I began to hate the steel mill more than anyone could ever imagine. As far as I was concerned the mill was evil and it was now out to destroy me and all the Monongahela Valley towns where the steel business was born. Then two guys I know committed suicide when the newspaper reported that the Duquesne's National steel works was finally going to be closed down. I swear to God that I thought it was doomsday. I couldn't stand it anymore; I hated to see our lives torn down and carted off like scrap metal. Our whole world seemed to be collapsing all around us and nobody seemed to be able to help. I read somewhere in a newspaper that even the President had been observed sleeping on the job inside the White House while his wife tried to interest him in an astrologer who could show him how to improve the country.

Sometime later I went on welfare. Joe and I would see one another at the Social Security Office. Now and then he would speak to me, but sometimes he wouldn't. His old man had told everyone in Duquesne that I was driving the car that crippled his poor handicapped son. Then his mother died and the Union gave them money for Joe's mother's funeral cause she worked for them. I was a pallbearer. Joe and I cried the whole way to the cemetery like two babies who felt like they were doomed forever. This was even echoed by an old man with a scraggly beard who came up to Joe as they were putting his mother down into the ground. His mean voice cut into Joe, "The nut never falls far from the tree. You'll end up like your no good drunken father who never cared about my poor sister while she was alive. Everybody in Duquesne knows it too." Joe and I were quivering in fear of this man; his words hit us hard. The old man's eyes had tore into Joe and he couldn't forget them, he tried but these words were powerful and their truth haunted us and then hunted us down. Their hold on us forced us to run away from something and toward something else. Only we didn't know what was what anymore. It was as though we had to run in order to find a place to sit only we could never sit down for long.

I was doing most of the running, and Joe did his in his wheel chair. I would go over to Joe's place and he would have me working as his runner. My girlfriend sold the stuff to me, and I sold it to Joe.

Nowadays I get packets of the stuff for him and he shoots it up into his arm. His old man got so fed up with us partying all time that he just gave up and retired from Westinghouse in East Pittsburgh—packing up and going off to Florida to get the hell away from us. Joe started to live in the house alone like it was his since the old man just up and left. Joe said, "At least I don't have to pay rent anymore." We both laughed out loud about how he was just an old tightwad. He was a guy who loved to do nothing but complain. That damn guy was always harping on the two of us about something. If we wanted to get away from him we would go outside and drink the Imperial I stashed away in this Corvette I borrowed.

*
* *

All Joe and I do anymore is watch TV, get loaded and call out for pizza whenever we're too bombed out of our skulls to go down the road to the Eat 'n Park. Joe said to me the other day that he was waiting for one thing more. "What's that?" I said, "An overdose," he said. "And then it will all be over and I will be sittin' pretty." I didn't know what to say, so I turned on the transistor radio and we listened to a Pittsburgh jazz station. It felt like we heard the same song for weeks and weeks.

The other day I wheeled Joe to the car since he likes to go out for a Sunday drive now and then to get some fresh air. The house smells like a damn steel soaking pit where I used to work in the steel mill and Joe just had to get out. I was telling him about some guys who used to work at the mill and how they just got busted for ripping off an appliance store. They were running down Lysle Boulevard with a hot TV and the cops saw them. Joe was laughing, and I never figured it would be the last time he would ever go down that road with me in the car. A little while later we were going along Route 22 to Pittsburgh to see a Rolling Stones concert. I put an eight-track tape in the Corvette's stereo system. The metallic crack taste was in my mouth and my heart began to race, brimming with the jazz of my heart's lonely confusion.

    The jazz was nice and soothing. The blare of horns sounded like cymbals crashing against the mirror of my soul as sirens roared down the littered streets of the city. I wanted to chase after the men and their cries for help. It was where the poor and lonely illiterate men live by dying to get out of the poverty of their own understanding. In the spiritless neighborhoods of the city they are doomed by their own thievery of the golden rule that never made its way into the stolen radios and TV sets of their hearts because the jazzy light of knowledge was not turned on or set to the right radio station. Their reception is bad because it is always looking for the electric cord they are dragging behind them as they jump into the stolen cars they drive with music blaring out amid the silence of our lives that echoes and blends in with the cop car sirens as we roll along lost in the crack-lit smoke of the radio as it drones on and on now as a GE commercial "Brings Good Things to Life" ends with pure Jazz. Jazz. Jazz. Jazz. Jazz. We are off to a concert and the thrill of being around people is amazing as we stagger into the Civic Arena.

    Everything everywhere is Jazz as I hand the hash pipe to Joe. The Jazz is floating around in our heads like music at the Stones concert where sirens are screaming into our ears as the streets of the city float by in silvery darkness of another day gone down the drain. I wheel Joe out to the shiny new Corvette and he seems to be falling asleep as I get him into the car seat. I mean Joe is REALLY GONE, but I am tired. I am just about falling asleep on the front seat of the car. I am too druggy to drive anywhere but the steering wheel is moving groggily from side to side. I am pulling the car over to the curb down in front of Mercy Hospital on Forbes Avenue. I am telling God Almighty

I need some real mercy now. Then I am thinking that maybe I can just sleep it off here, and we can go home in the morning when I am not so wasted out of my mind.

When I wake up the Jazz is still playing softly on the radio after the Stones concert, and the sun is now in my eyes. The Corvette's battery is petering out, and before long it is dead. The jazz is still alive, and it is now a liquid music flowing like the hard, salty tears formed in my eyes as I realize I am more crippled than Joe is. I look at Joe leaning over like a saxophone player. He is locked in life's last battle; it is against his hardheaded stubbornness that he has landed. Joe's hand is clutching a pill bottle that he had emptied into his mouth during the Stone's concert. He said he was stoned with the Stones and his legs are now stiff and cold with rigor mortis. I am trying to figure out what the hell is going on when I say to myself, "He is dead." My thought is frozen in a single fear of what's going on; what will happen to me? "It was just like his old man to abandon me. Just when he knows something is going to go all wrong he decides he's out of here. He's no dummy; he packs up and goes to Florida and leaves me all alone. Now I have to figure it all out. Like this is the way families are supposed to exist anymore. Shit, where am I going to bury him? Wait, I know, I'll drive him over near Homestead and leave him at the gate of Calvary Cemetery; they will take care of burying him for me. I mean why did he have to go and die on me like this for? I got a police record all because of him. Joe told me that it was his old man who turned me in to the police. Like I need him dying on me inside a stolen Corvette. They'll add that onto my police record now too . . ." I pull myself out of the car and walk down Forbes Avenue toward town to catch a bus. "I better just get the hell out of this town before it's too late."

A SURREAL PATIENT

On the day the steel mill where I worked was closed down in Pittsburgh, a single dreadful sound reverberated through me. I felt as though a great tarry black metal door had been pulled down on me. From that moment the future forever vanished. Then the door closed, and finally it was gone. I tried to walk home, but my legs refused to believe the mill would never open again. I might have felt myself falling, and it was then that I reached out for something, I'm not sure what it was. I must have fallen down the steps of the Polish Eagle Club and lost consciousness for a while. It happened after work the day one of the foremen at the mill told us we were being let go. Most of the men expected it to happen, but some of us didn't see it coming. All of us felt bad about it, and it was all we talked about as a few of us walked home that day. Our mood of dejection permeated Fisk Street as we sluggishly climbed the hill wondering about what our wives and girlfriends would say when they learned we were out of work. I tried to tell myself that the mill's closing wasn't true. I went over to the Union hall to find out what could be done to help us out of this mess. A couple of men there said that the mill was bankrupt and had to be completely closed down because the bankers in downtown Pittsburgh were demanding their money be paid back on a series of old loans. They were taking over the steel mill and were going to sell off the machinery at the end of the month; Christianak Steel would soon be gone for good.

This Union news hit me hard; my chest was pounding, and I didn't want to believe the mill was gone. My whole life had been spent there since the 1950's when I graduated from high school. I had to get my bearings. I walked back over to the

Polish Eagles in a daze. Once I began drinking away the night, guys from the mill sent over shots of whiskey and bottles of beer. We were all worried and trying to forget that come Monday there wasn't a job for us at the bottom of the street. Somebody at the club called me a boilermaker. I said I would drink to that and the next thing I remember a couple of Pittsburgh policeman were hoisting me up from the whiskey-colored sidewalk where I fell. They were loading me into a van and told me I was a rowdy troublemaker. I bounced around on a cot inside the police van for a while; I must have dozed off. When I woke up hours and hours later the back of the police van had turned into these long white-tiled corridors. I heard this overweight nurse complaining about pushing another alkie down the hallway to surgery. I wanted to tell her I didn't ask her to do it, and that I wasn't an alkie either; but the whole scene seemed to be out of whack. We quickly went around a corner, and I couldn't figure out why they had me strapped down. I hadn't even done anything to them, and they were handling me like I was a wild animal about to tear them apart.

I saw this guy looking down on me with a mask, and I got worried. I must have looked odd to him because he looked at me curiously. His eyes made me feel like I was sick in a way that wasn't going to go away. He and another guy in a green gown were putting tubes into me, and I started to feel lightheaded, then nauseous. Then the nausea went away, and a surgeon was telling me he had to cut something out. I was nodding my head and screaming, "No" at him, but he said he had to or I would bleed to death. I just said to hell with it all, do what you want cause I don't care anymore. I must have passed out because I was terrified of the sight of blood on the surgeon's white apron. I knew right away, it was my blood. I felt them putting a broken bone from my arm back behind the muscles where it belonged.

I could see a mirage of veins and arteries slipping by. Slowly there were these small black dots that showed up in front of my eyes. I was absolutely sure of the size of them. They were ants gradually moving up and consuming my arm; there was a tiny army of drones and workers. Then somebody pulled a microscope in front of me. All of the time this is going on I got the impression this was taking months and months, so I said, "Hey, ants don't take months to crawl up over you." Then the black dots had lots of filaments coming out of them, and I said, "These aren't ants at all cause they are too fuzzy like," and then the dots grew slowly and more gradually like colonies of fungus on a petri dish. I suddenly realized these things moving up my arm like urban decay were the tracks from the medicine needles. I had to yell out to the nurse who was unconcerned. She was too damn busy scrubbing my belly down with this betadine—I figured I had to get her attention, "Hey get that damn brush over here on my arm where the fungus is growing before it's too late, these black fungi are going to eat me alive." Then I felt something like a hair inside me, and I grew terrified; this was serious. I pulled this long black hair from inside my mouth, it was caught on my tongue and I said, "Wait a minute. This isn't a hair at all it's part of that fungus, and it's already beginning to spread to my brain." I was absolutely lucid now and things were starting to make sense. I knew I had to do something before it was too late so I yelled out to the nurses, "Hurry up. Damn it and get over here! Get a hold of this fungus thing before it spreads and grows right up into my head!"

    The stern, dark-haired nurse and the black guy were now laughing at me as the surgeon smiled down at my stomach. I could see he shared their attitude toward me. He had a cigarette in his mouth and I heard them talking about me in the hallway where they had pushed me outside on a cold metal gurney with icy, chromed rails. "That is the craziest case of DTs I've seen in a while," the bossy nurse said. The orderly was shaking his head in agreement and talking, "This is one bad patient. I mean this guy was hallucinating and thought he had a black fungus growing up inside him. And then he yelled at us about how it was spreading to his brain. After that the surgeon said we had to give him something. I mean, this guy was a real pain in the ass for a while with all his screaming and crying out loud."

Then I said, "Hey you. You got to help me because this damn fungus is in my arm, and it's still growing." The next thing I know I passed out. When I woke up my girlfriend was standing over me inside the hospital room where a crucifix was nailed to the wall. She was dropping cigarette ashes down on my hospital bed, and I said, "See, that fungus is coming outta that damn brown butt in your mouth." Her face grew dark and mad. She started getting angry at me, and I said to her, "Go ahead and get mad, I'm telling you that fungus came right outta that cigarette in your mouth." She just stomped out of the room like I was crazy or something. And I never saw her again either, and I am damn glad of it too . . . cause she was the one who got me into trouble in the first place with that damn fungus of hers . . . I mean, hell, the doctors didn't even know how she got it there inside my arm and that just shows you how much they know . . . and if she didn't put it there in the first place then I wouldn't have had to come to the hospital . . . The police even told me that, they said she had called them to come get me once I fell down the steps onto the sidewalk. She was standing there complaining about how she couldn't pick me up. That's when the fungus must have made me black out. I'll bet she pushed me down the steps with that fungus helping her, I'll bet any money that's what happened.

Then the nurses reappeared and were looking at me suspiciously. I overheard them talking about me again too, "I swear to God I wish I knew where they picked this guy up. He is really something." And the other nurse with the hard-hearted old voice was tying me down again before they wheeled me up to the psychiatric wing. I guess they thought I was going to take flight. The last thing I saw was the nurse's dark profile against a shadowy wall. She was standing there smoking a cigarette and saying, "They found him down in front of the Polish Eagles, whatever the heck that is." Then their dark arms were reaching out toward me then they stopped. The black door was shut, and I could feel its oily hinges moving in unison and echoing inside me like a reverb.

THE COAL MINE MACHINERY COMPANY

Mr. Joseph Karchak was a mechanical engineer who once worked for the Coal Mine Machinery Company in downtown Pittsburgh. His tiny cluttered office was no bigger than a poor house, and yet it was good enough for him and his engineers who gathered there for Friday afternoon problem solving sessions. If some men are loved for their knowledge, others for their experience and still others for their ability to make money, Mr. Karchak was admired by virtually everyone in Pittsburgh's engineering community for all of these reasons. His engineers were the best around, and he knew it for he expected the best from them, and he demanded even more than that from himself. Everyone agreed he was one of the city's finest engineers as well as being a bit of an oddball for an eccentric habit he had perfected. Mr. Karchak was a leader in the field of do-it-yourself eyeglass repair, using bits of wire and leftover pieces of sticky black electrical tape.

Mr. Karchak's eyeglasses looked astonishingly like the square headlights of the old car he drove from the little town of Monongahela, located on the southern outskirts of Pittsburgh—known for its industry. Someone said Mr. Karchak's eyeglasses and the headlights must have once been interchangeable parts. Both were held together by similar bits of flimsy wire that Mr. Karchak was forever bending and manipulating in his fine, precision-loving fingers. The spectacles on his face were always being put back together again. When they fell to the floor of his engineering workshop, these spectacles appeared headed to oblivion on the concrete floor, but they usually struck the surface so that the electrical tape cushioned their fall. The eyeglasses themselves were arranged on his face as if they might fall off Mr. Karchak's nose at any minute. In a similar way the headlights of his car casually hung out of their sockets tethered by a flimsy hodge podge of a sculpture made of wire wrapped around itself like a coiling silver snake. The headlights dangled in front of the car as though they were bifocals that could plummet to the road at any time. When Mr. Karchak drove home to Monongahela, he was never sure the headlights like his eyeglasses would make the trip home on the bumpy, cobblestone roads without forcing him to stop by the roadside for a quick repair.

Mr. Karchak would always chuckle to himself when people at the Coal Mine Machinery Company commented about his old eyeglasses. He would usually smile and take his glasses off so that he could work on them. He twisted wire and bits of black electrical tape that held them together and then attempted to reassure the group assembled around the long coffee table that the glasses would be fine for another ten minutes or so. Occasionally at lunch, Mr. Karchak could be seen across the way in the engineering department getting a new supply of black electrical tape to hold the glasses together long enough to get him through the afternoon.

A favorite story was told by one of the accountants who marveled at the engineer's continuous tinkering. "If Karchak spent as much time doing the engineering of our mining machines as he did repairing his own eyeglasses, we would never turn out a final product. It would forever be under development." Another story that went around for a long while in the executive offices of the company was that if Mr. Karchak ever made it out of Pittsburgh and found his way to Detroit to work at General Motors' headlight department, night time driving would be doomed. Headlights in his hands would become a permanent work in progress that he would refuse to finish until it met his impossibly high and exacting standards. Mr. Karchak knew the head engineer at most of General Motors' divisions because most of them had tried to lure him away from Pittsburgh; he turned them down time and again because he loved the city. Besides, he couldn't move away from Monongahela where he had been born; his parents were there. His optometrist lived there, and that was where he got his first pair of eyeglasses. From everyone's experience, Mr. Karchak's eyeglasses were said to be more than two lenses he wore on his face. They were a part-time job, a hobby and an avocation. Someone in manufacturing once mused that Mr. Karchak's eyeglasses spent as much time in his hands being repaired as they did on his nose.

Mrs. Karchak came downtown once a month to pick him up at work. Together they strolled over to Kaufmanns's Department Store arm in arm for lunch whereupon she would go shopping for her children's clothes or one of her relative's birthday, wedding or anniversary presents. She was seen at the lunch table gently scolding her husband while he fiddled with his eyeglasses that had become unhinged or tangled up with the wire he used to hold them together. "Why don't you just go out and get yourself some new glasses?" she urged him testily. He sat there silently absorbed in his effort of reworking some of the wire or a piece of the electrical tape, fiddling for minutes at a time. Soon he was lost in wondering about how to perfect what seemed to be destined for failure later on that afternoon.

Mr. Karchak's eyeglasses were a diversion from worry. They gave him something to work on as he contemplated the design of a new mining machine or a better coal moving assembly. His eyeglasses were a way to divert his attention from an important project while the wheels of his mind worked tirelessly at something trivial so that he might think that much better about what really meant the most to him. It was clear that Mr. Karchak's engineering mind was always at work on something. Nobody could guess what it was engaged in from one minute to the next. He held over eighty patents. No professional engineer in all of Pittsburgh ever really doubted him or his engineering expertise. The engine of his calculating mind roared with ingenuity. He was the tutor of over a hundred engineers who loved him for his meek simplicity. His kindly manner had gotten most of them their first job or their first major projects at Bechtel, American Bridge or Westinghouse. Pittsburgh was an engineering town, and he was one of its princes. His reputation won him innumerable friends and associates throughout the city. The universities and most of the best engineers in the country knew him because his engineering work was faultless. This made him known everywhere he went. He was famous among a small army of Pittsburgh engineers. Dozens of them and their fathers had worked for him, and they all always felt a certain affinity for his brilliant and eccentric ability in mathematics.

When Mr. Karchak finally retired from the Coal Mine Machinery Company someone inquired about what he would like as a going away gift. The president of the company felt Mr. Karchak should not receive the gold watch everyone usually was given, he should be presented with something special. His secretary was recruited to make an inquiry of the friendly old engineer. She tiptoed over to his drafting desk one day and said, "Mr. Karchak, what would you like to have as a retirement present from the company when the time comes?" Without even looking up from the drawings on his desk, Mr. Karchak said as casually and sincerely as if he was guiding one of his engineers on another patent application. "It would be nice if the company would give me some of that good electrical tape they have over in the electrical department and a roll of that stainless steel wire they have in the engineering supply bin upstairs. I will need them to keep my glasses together and I don't want to be running all the way downtown from Monongahela every fifteen minutes when I feel my eyeglasses slipping off my head."

Two weeks later the tape and wire were packaged in a box and gift-wrapped in special paper which his fellow engineers, had covered with various drawings of Mr. Karchak's eyeglasses. This was presented to Mr. Karchak. He chuckled at the thumbnail sketches of him and his glasses, and he gratefully acknowledged a certain fact. It was no use giving a man a watch who hadn't used one yet in over forty years. Then the president of the Coal Mine Machinery Company saw Mr. Karchak in the parking lot with the new engineer, a recent MIT graduate. Mr. Karchak had hired him only a few months before and was teaching him how to wire together the wobbly headlights of his old car. When he finished he pulled open the car door, and his eyeglasses slid off his face and fell to the ground. Mr. Karchak reached down and picked them up; he pulled out a piece of his new wire and a roll of tape and just started working on them all over again as though nothing would ever really change. "See, this black electrical tape is just the thing for both eyeglasses and headlights," he said to the new engineer who looked on attentively. "I don't know what we would do without them. I tell you these have been some of the best materials ever invented since my old buddy Ben Franklin discovered electricity over in Philadelphia a while back."

A GOOD WOMAN IS HARD TO FIND

I had taken refuge on a barstool in one of Pittsburgh's rundown neighborhood taverns. It was situated in the center of the industrial district where I owned one of the city's small steel mills. An hour or so into my nightly drinking routine, I took out my wallet and glanced at a worn out photograph from my past life. A woman with stringy yellow hair, who had just left work, then drifted into the bar. She sat down next to me and said her name was Alice. Her fancy clothes hid a slew of secrets. She bought me a drink, and we talked for a while about this and that. Mostly it was about how rotten her dad treated her and how she was going to run away from home. She mentioned that her mother used to beat her and that she had to find a way out of Pittsburgh—she had to go somewhere nobody could find her.

    I didn't really know what to think, so I told her that she was beautiful, and that everything would work out for the best. It felt like the right thing to say at the time. She seemed friendly, moved closer and then told me, "I need a friend I can rely on." I said, "I could be your friend for a while. Your smile makes me feel like the virile young man I once was when I was in high school." She laughed. I was nothing but an old drunk to her, and yet she and I hit it off as the hours slipped away. We drank all night long to hide our rotten, rundown feelings about the world. Nothing was good about it anymore—we both knew it through and through. Nobody could tell us differently because our experiences could prove people wrong time and time again. On that point we were in complete agreement. We shook hands on the deal—the world was a rotten place for sure. There was no denying it. Our sad eyes told no lies. People treated one another like crap and that was just the way it was.

At closing time we stumbled out of the place and found some concrete steps behind an old rowhouse in a shady alley. The canopy of a sumac loomed over us, and the smell of its leaves filtered down with the beam of a street light. We started our miserable lovemaking on the hard pavement in the dark. The last thing I saw was some old woman shaking out a mop from her wooden porch in the moonlight; then my head went down in the dark. The partially nude, whiskey-eyed woman from the bar was pulling me toward her; my anxious face slid across the rough pavement. *I felt its rough darkness creeping over me; the night was fresh with sumacs and its blazing passion rose up like a flame to then throw the rest of my life into darkness forever. I didn't know it would be our last night together, I didn't know.* I was passing out, and there was red paint running down my cheek into my mouth. When I stumbled awake in the dull gray sky of dawn I found Alice unconscious and sour-faced. It felt as though she had eaten this big hole in my life, and it was so deep that I couldn't even get out of it. And everytime I looked around, her memory was everywhere. I could even smell it; her hair was splashed with vomit. My own face stung with a brush burn inflicted during the frantic madness of our drunken and sweaty love.

My head tried to regain its bearings upon the cold hard scene. A few moments later I stumbled down the cobblestone street to my father's steel mill. I barely thought it was my steel mill even though dad had been dead for over fourteen years. When I got into the mill yard a bunch of millworkers looked at me as though I was a menace, a maniac, a raving lunatic who was about to pounce upon them lounging about the time clock. "Get to work you sons of bitches, get the machinery up and running and make me some steel."

Once I had fallen into my office chair, I felt sure that I could not go much lower. This was my throne of misery off and away from the nightly bar stool. Shortly after that I heard the office telephone ring.

It always upset me, and now it was no different. It was my wife. She wanted to know where I had been all night, I told her we had a brawl at the mill and I had to stick around to calm things down. "I slept on the couch in my office, and I am in a bad mood. I'll see you later. . . ." I slammed down the damn telephone and wished that she were dead; the bang of the receiver in the telephone cradle made me mad again.

    A tall guy with a clipboard marched in with two men from the steel mill's grievance committee. They wanted to hold a meeting with me. The men had a complaint about the foreman who was my right hand man. I knew that nobody could accuse Mack of any wrongdoing, and I let them know it, too. Old Mack had held the whole damn place together for decades since the war. He and my dad were pals, and the company couldn't have survived without him. Who did these guys think they were—Almighty God or something? They made me sick with their whining. I wasn't going to put up with their damn grievance crap anymore. "Get the hell out of my sight before I close this damn mill down right now. If our order of steel to Ford doesn't go out today, the mill is kaput, a goner. I'll close it down, and nobody will have anything to complain about because the mill will be history." My rock-hard fist pounded on my wooden desk as their feet ran toward the doorway. I recalled the sound of their work shoes rushing out amid a flurry of shirts that headed after them. They now knew I meant business.

    I had given up on these damn committees. All that they ever did was complain, and then they ruined everything. Now the Union was sapping me dry. Their demands on me never stopped and they thought they could run this outfit without me. I marched out onto the shop floor and told the craneman to hurry up into his perch. "If these billets aren't loaded by nine o'clock, you can go home." Suddenly everyone was working, a tow motor flew by and picked up a pallet of shovels and took them down to the maintenance crew where a bunch of guys were on a smoke break. Other men with shovels were now moving coal, and I felt a deep pang in my gut. The whole damn place began humming and I ran into the office to get the ringing phone. It was my secretary calling. Her sharp voice was angry as she told me she would rather quit than be treated like a piece of crap. I hung up on her, and then a whirl of trucks and train cars were flying by, past the mill door. I ran out to see what was going on, and my head began pounding as if squeezed in a metal press. It was then that I felt that damn gnawing pain in my gut again. I ran back to the office and jerked open the bottom desk drawer and pulled out a bottle. I drank down half a fifth of Imperial whiskey in two big swallows and then I felt steadier on my feet.

A man in a blue shirt ran in and said they were about to get the next run of steel onto the rolling mill. "Do you want to inspect it or should I do it?". . . "I don't care what you sons of bitches do. Just get it right this time, Mack. Cause if it doesn't come out right I am closing down this damn place and the whole mill can go to hell. That's how much I hate this place." His old face was scared and worried. He looked like he hated me, but I couldn't do anything about that. Then he ran out, and the phone rang; it was our coke supplier jabbering away in my ear. "When are we going to see payment from you bastards? You are already past due by 90 days." I said, "Don't worry, you'll be getting your damn money soon enough. Once Ford pays me you will get your filthy money. Now quit calling me and get another load of coke down here by the end of the day or you'll lose one of your best customers . . ." I hung up the phone in disgust and sifted through some papers on my desk. The whole place was a hot cauldron of confusion now that the steel was being poured. Heat flowed from the furnace and into the office. I started to sweat as chaos ruled over another day. Nothing seemed to make sense anymore.

The pain in my stomach now fought back and tore a hole into the growing monotony of lies deep down within me. It rose up like a great fear I had to fight off. I reached down for the bottle and took another long swallow. Then I smashed the bottle to bits in the trash can and ran my hands through the file drawer on the other side of my desk. Whiskey bottles rolled around like heavy, brown bowling pins. I picked one up and put it down on my desk, I poured its liquid into a clear new glass. I held it to my mouth and took a long and soothing drink and then a dull mirage appeared; it was walking. A man came into the office and said the rolling mill run from last night was almost over, so where should they stack the plates? "Put the damn things on a train car because they gotta get shipped up to Detroit by the end of the day God damn it! Didn't Mack tell you we gotta get them out TODAY? Don't you understand what TODAY means anymore? Now is forever and it ain't never going to be here again. You gotta get your work done TODAY. Everything depends upon TODAY. How many times do I have to tell you damn people how to run a mill? Get out in the mill yard and put that damn steel up on those flatcars so we can all get paid by week's end and go home for Christ's sake."

The man ran out, and then Mack was there again with the clipboard. Someone was with him. The little, wiry guy was his son; he said it was lunchtime. I reached over and pulled some crackers out of a drawer and swiped some peanut butter across them with a piece of scrap steel and put the stale crackers into my mouth. I washed them down with Imperial, and I put my feet up on the desk. I scribbled some numbers down on some sheets of paper to determine how long the mill's money was going to last. This went on for a few hours until I was exhausted with worry; then I fell asleep. I woke up groggily when a sad shadowy guy came shuffling in saying he needed a job. He told me something about having three kids to feed, and he wanted to know if could I help him out. "I can't help every lousy son of a bitch who just walks in here off the street with some hard luck story." He was about to leave; he looked at me with these big sad eyes that were about to burst out crying so I yelled at him, "Go outside and talk to Mack. He should be somewhere out in the plant. Ask around and you'll find him. He'll take care of you. And you better work your God damn ass off here cause this place is losing money and I can't afford to lose any more God damn money."

Late in the afternoon the whistle blew at Heppenstalls over on 44th Street. The men stopped working and another shift of men came on. I heard the day shift punching out at the time clock and hid behind the door. The men going out told the men coming into work that I was in a foul mood. I went back to my desk to sulk. I finished off what was left of the bottle of Imperial. The telephone rang; it was my wife. I yelled at her again, "No, I won't be home tonight, I'm going out with the guys. We just got the Ford order done and we're gonna celebrate, damn it. Is that OK with you or do I have to get permission for every damn thing I do in this world anymore?" I slammed the telephone down, and the whole place was suddenly quiet. Silence was raging in my ears like a runaway locomotive. The stillness in the joint was making me upset. I was jittery as hell, so I grabbed my coat and went angrily outside into the warm night.

 I felt the darkness envelop me like a fluid as I walked along the same cracked pavement I knew like the rest of my life. Imperfection was everywhere, and I seemed to be drowning in it. The broken concrete fence surrounding the mill gave way to the crumbling brick wall, which turned into the rusted corrugated iron railing outside the mill yard. I turned right and went along a street paved with crooked Belgian Block. The glaring light atop a telephone pole looked down on me. I walked faster and faster to get to the bar. I was in a hurry because I had to have a drink. Things began to look better inside the tavern; and I felt calm as I pulled myself up on a barstool. I was finally in control and nothing could touch me.

 The skinny woman from the night before appeared as I was going through my wallet. It was one of the regulars who reminded me of Alice. She gave me a sickening look. Soon we were drinking all over again only this time I had to pay—and now she wasn't beautiful anymore. Her bleached blonde hair was cut ragged around the edges; her teeth were all rotten and made me feel sick. I wanted to get out of this place. Then she put her arm around me and started slobbering on and on about money, her problems and all sorts of crap about how she had been cheated all her life. I was tired of her and her kind. Some people are nothing more than parasites feeding off the living. They thrive on excuses and self-pity and are always looking for somebody like me to bail them out with sympathy. I pulled a couple of bills from my pocket and told her, "The night's young. Drink it away and life will be merry." She waved the bartender over and ordered a couple more beers for us along with some shots of whiskey.

As soon as it arrived, I threw a shot of grain alcohol down my throat—it burned hot as a furnace. A surge of alcohol swelled up in my nose that now felt on fire. I spotted myself in the mirror behind the bar. My face was a horrible, unshaven wreck. My cheek was scabbing up, and it made me feel like my bleeding heart had been torn open. I felt my sad head was looking for a place to go but all I could find was pain. It was sitting there inside me on top of this bar stool, and it had nowhere to go but down. I was pulled along with it the way a locomotive pulls a bunch of train cars down the track.

The door of the tavern swung open, and I could see cars, lights and people moving about out on the summer street. A breeze that washed in cooled my sweaty ankles, and I reflected upon the lights twinkling outside on the darkening, starry street. It was then that I understood the facts. I couldn't get Alice's nude form out of my mind; she was a desire I couldn't shake off. Her arm was around my shoulder and it seemed hard and inert. Her lips were sinking toward mine, and I felt myself falling into oblivion of passionate bad luck. A nude picture of her swam in my head as a living image of mad desire. An hour later we were swaying back out into the alley again. I fell against a wrought iron fence and looked up. A street light was wobbling back and forth like a bright white moon in the summer's chilly darkness.

*

* *

That and only that is all I remember because—that was what my whole life was about for the longest while. Then I discovered Alcoholics Anonymous, and now I am sober . . . well, at least for a while . . . I mean I've been sober on and off for a couple of days now, and I am probably not gonna make it . . . Once my dad's steel mill closed down, I had nowhere to go. This damn blonde and I both knew it. The time is better now because I don't have the steel mill and my dad's nagging memory to worry about. He always looked at me like I was a failure. Well, he could have been right because the profits from the mill are all gone and I really think I will make it for once, only not today but some day. But if I don't make it now then . . . when and if not me then who? And if not this time then maybe the next time. I don't know . . . All my workers hate me now that the mill is bankrupt. Even my wife despises me. She says I ruined over a hundred people's lives. She has taken her revenge on me by turning the kids against me, too. She says they're just like me—spoiled brats and lousy weaklings. She can go to hell. I usually just hang up the telephone on her when she calls me at the office that's all closed down and abandoned. All her rotten attempts to tear me down won't work anymore. If she ever found out about Alice, she would strangle me with her own two hands.

The tavern is often a hideout for me nowadays. It's where I can always find Alice and where we can be alone for a while. I often console myself by saying the same thing over and over, 'Why not drink with her? That way I can at least have a life of my own that nobody will destroy. There's a jukebox to listen to music. I can keep the bartender employed and help him feed his family . . . Hell, there's no crime in that is there? I remember the last time I saw Alice. She was dangling my Cadillac car keys in front of me and telling me how she was going to drive out of Pittsburgh toward Florida or California. Then it turned out she was only going to Johnstown. She gave me a nude souvenir of herself. It all fades as I reach into my sport coat and pull out my wallet. I look longingly at the tattered photograph of my old girlfriend who died in an automobile wreck years ago. The wrinkled photo of my Alice often makes me think that she is still alive and beautiful and that one day we will be together. I hope that she will eventually show up at our old rendezvous to rescue me from the hell of all hells, from the wretched hell of all that I am.

A mirror above the bar reflects the cigarette burning before me like the old and forgotten shell of my only legacy on this earth. The steel mill down the street rusts away as a squandered inheritance that can never be retrieved from the desperation that destroyed it. The smoky and rundown futility of all my work sinks into me in the form of memories of a barge out on the rusty water next to my steel mill; its dilapidated carcass rusts into the abandoned earth.

Amid the women in the booths and along the mahogany bar whose smoke scarred faces now know that I am broken-hearted and out of money, I am not even a passing thought. They used to like me when my wallet was full and my new Cadillac was outside, waiting to take them for a ride out to their Shadyside apartments where we holed up over the week-ends. Now they have no use for my gray hair or my whining heartache. At one time they would listen to it, but now that my wallet is empty they have taken up with another man, he owns a car dealership in Squirrel Hill.

My Alice was never like one of these bar flies; she was decent. She grew up in McKees Rocks and she was in love with me the year I went off to Princeton. When I flunked out it made no difference to her; she loved me for what I was and not for my money. We met in this very tavern in Etna not far from Tippins. We were carrying on when her old man beat her up and told her she had to get out or else he'd kill her. I gave her the keys to my Cadillac, and she gave me her photo the night she left. She promised she would come back, and we would run away together in a week or two. She just needed to get somewhere where nobody would see her black eye. She said over and over that I had saved her life with those car keys. She went out the screen door of the bar and I looked at her nude photo. She would be coming back for me. That night the police showed up at the house and said, "Your car must have been stolen by a woman," and I said, "What?" And they said something about this woman who had stolen my car. They said, "She died going around a snowy corner in Etna." They told me it was because she had probably never driven a car with power steering before. I was shaking, I said to the police, "No, it was not stolen, I gave her the keys to the car. She was going to bring it back over the weekend . . ."

The long, dreary mirror over the bar was our rendezvous every night; it was where our eyes always met. I would see her walking in the door behind me and her bright smile would light up the whole bar. The steelworkers from my mill knew her. The salesmen and real estate brokers, who hung around the bar all day, marveled at her. She made their day when she strolled in every evening. All the men at the bar would swivel around on their barstools, they loved to look at her and she knew it too. She was the Miss McKees Rocks, 1958. She was the finest lady I had ever met. She was all kindness and laughter, lightheartedness and charm. She was forever running away from the executives in the office downtown. They were always pestering her for dates. She was hired as a secretary for Westinghouse Air Brake, and then she moved over to Gulf Oil. Everywhere she went the people loved her. She used to say, "Men are always looking at me with their hungry eyes but my heart belongs to you, Mr. Christianak. I'm your gal."

That is what I called her from the beginning, My gal Al. And she knew I absolutely adored her. We were making plans to get married but once her old man found out he beat her up. I was going to kill him, but she talked me out of it. We knew we had to get her out of Pittsburgh and that is what we did. It was the only way for her to survive because he would have tracked her down. She was supposed to be driving to Johnstown to stay with one of her high school girl friends. That was twenty four years ago, and I was broken-hearted. Her death never left me. I could never get rid of her memory, and I see her in every woman who walks into the bar.

The women do not even bother with me now when they see the paunch on me. Something deep down inside them tells them not to have anything to do with the sagging bags under my eyes. Their feminine youth shining in the smoky mirror makes me look old and hopeless and completely worn out. Someone tells them that I used to own the mill down the street, but once they find out I am broke, they look the other way. They have to have someone with some real money.

All of these things pass before me, my memories wash up and then fade away. Alice is always in my thoughts. I knew she was the only one for me, but now she is gone but cannot be forgotten. She will live on as long as there are bars and bottles of whiskey, beers and wobbly bar stools. As long as I am alive I can always find her here for a moment, smoking her cigarette and leaning up against the bar all beautiful and happy and hoping to start a new life for herself once we get married. I feel her presence in the bar only it is really absent and my memory lies to me over and over. It hovers in that nude photo of her beauty that never faded for love is perfect only once. That is what she used to say to me. And now I am forever clutching her memory, ever wanting her; but I got someone else instead. She is not even good enough to stand in Alice's shadow; she is always pestering me at the bar.

I can't even have a drink on my own anymore because my wife tracks me down wherever I go. The bar owner knows it too; a few of the tired old patrons talk about it in the tavern now and then. They are on their way out; they've started shuffling out at closing time when the telephone rings. The skinny bartender hustles down to the end of the bar to answer its loud nagging ring. It has become routine at closing, and we both know what to expect. He holds up the black receiver and motions that the call is for me again. His thin smoke-scarred voice roars out over the juke box music. It is the same old thing that he's yelled out for years and which I've heard a million times, "It's your wife. She says she forgives you and she wants to know when you're coming home."

WHISKEY AND WALTER

American business creates almost as many alcoholics as it does millionaires. My Aunt Cecilia once confided this secret to me at one of her cocktail parties while I was struggling through college. Aunt Cecilia always understood me perfectly; she said that growing up in Pittsburgh in 1960 was not easy for a young man like me who loved to dance the polka. My uncle was an executive for United States Steel's research. He and my dad often held or attended parties for clients, executives and managers. I was just getting out of high school, and I dreaded these stuffy parties; but I always enjoyed dancing the polka with Aunt Cecilia and her friends. I was inevitably hired to be a waiter and wore a tuxedo for those affairs where I became something of an amateur dance instructor. My primary job was to shuttle huge trays of champagne, white wine and high balls back and forth from Aunt Cecilia's kitchen to the living room that was so large that it felt like a warehouse. I can honestly say I never saw Aunt Cecilia without a glass of whiskey in her hand. It was an essential part of her, and it was not so much an accessory as an extension of her shaky hand.

Aunt Cecilia had people congregate in the living room or out on the patio where lost and boozy corporate widows were in their minks. They performed their own personal parade before their wobbly, apathetic friends. On the other side of the room, cold and sober men fell into spontaneous groups of serious engineers and executives, narrow corporate lawyers or flamboyant, woman-chasing managers. Their chatty wives swirled about them extolling the genius of their spoiled children who roamed about New York or Rome or Paris. The women were a a collage of colorful dresses fresh from overseas. Their rumors, back biting, jealous stares and whispers filled the stone patio of the steel city's finest Presbyterian family. This is how Uncle Walter described himself, and Aunt Cecilia hated him for it. She despised his hypocrisy, and yet she could never give it up; her patio parties were too compelling. Horrible secrets flowed there like old fashioneds, gin and tonics, whiskeys and water, white wines and Manhattans. Aunt Cecilia, on her anemic, wobbly alcoholic legs that seemed as though they were made of whiskey and water, went to and fro among the people gabbing away about stock prices, Broadway shows and the latest Hollywood movie. Mother said these parties were monstrous, gaudy affairs that catered to corporate extravagance and were paid for by US Steel; the company picked up the tab for everything Uncle Walter ever did.

As I dressed for these monthly events, my mother told me I was handsome. She said that was why Aunt Cecilia wanted me to be there; her tiresome reason was always the same. Aunt Cecilia told mother, "Some women become so excited when they see Jimmy Stahl; he could pass as a twin for James Dean." I was not only a rebel without a cause, but one with even less money; so I worked these parties to pay for art courses I was taking at the University of Pittsburgh. Mother smiled politely when she heard these comments from Aunt Cecilia about why I had to be at a party that I absolutely detested. I just about bit off my tongue, but I had to go since I had to pay my own way through college. It was a deal Dad and I had made years ago, and neither of us was going to back down. Subsequently, I was making my own way in life while dad was hoping I would quit the university and head off to engineering school. If I did that he said he would pay all my expenses; but I said engineering was not for me, and so I had to pay for my own college tuition.

The popular story I had to listen to before the guests arrived concerned how Aunt Cecilia was a University of Pittsburgh cheerleader back in the days when Jock Sutherland was the football team's coach. Aunt Cecilia loved to talk about football, her college days and how she met Uncle Walter in her freshman year of college. After all, finding a husband was the reason she went to college in the first place; there was no denying it. Aunt Cecilia was proud of this fact, which she repeated during every party. Along with it came inquiries about whether I had found a woman to marry in any of my art history classes. Aunt Cecilia's jabbering always ended in a tired promise, "Wait until you meet a nice young brunette like your Aunt Cecilia. You'll get married and the next thing you know Uncle Walter will have you working for him at US Steel." Deep down in the honeycombed coke ovens of my determined heart I promised myself that this would never happen. Yet it was evident that Aunt Cecilia was making a concerted attempt to plan out my whole life. All I had to do was show up, and she would program it all in the same way she set up her parties. According to Aunt Cecilia, I was supposed to become a metallurgical engineer like my dad and then move to Fox Chapel outside of Pittsburgh. There I would have kids and spend the rest of my life slaving like a dog in one of her husband's research laboratories. My work would then guarantee his next new product, patent, annual bonus, Buick and the inevitable promotion.

The Buick was something Aunt Cecilia had to have every so often. As much as he might try to dissuade her, Uncle Walter always gave in once Aunt Cecilia found out about one of his girlfriends. Aunt Cecilia always got her way with the new Buick. I swear to God she lived for that Buick. It was her reason for being, her revenge for the girlfriends. Everyone at US Steel said the shiny new Buick was just a way of life for her and Uncle Walter; so he got her a Buick to appease her. It was parked in the circular driveway in front of their home like a suburban centerpiece. The new car announced to the world, "Uncle Walter just finished up with his last girlfriend." She would now be given Aunt Cecilia's old Buick as a going-away present. Once Uncle Walter and his roving eye just got a look at his cute new secretary a routine series of events always followed on schedule; in a few years, after he was done with her she would be provided with a bonus, a Buick, and sent to one of the steel mills out in McKeesport or Duquesne or Braddock. To those who didn't know the details of Uncle Walter's love life, the car in the driveway simply announced, "Look at us now, we drive a brand new Buick."

It was after one of these weekend parties of Aunt Cecilia's that I told mother, "I have decided to choose my own way in life." I told her I had a calling, and I will never forget how calm, patient and understanding she was with me when I mentioned to her that I was joining a Franciscan monastery north of Pittsburgh. I told her I wanted to join the order, and I didn't want to have anything to do with the hollow lives that many people around us sadly accepted. Mother was the only one who listened to me; she was my only ally. Father wanted me to go off to MIT and then graduate school at Carnegie Tech, but I decided that I wouldn't be an engineer. Mother came through for me by saying, "I know your father is going to argue with you because he thinks you are planning to lead a useless life in the priesthood." I prepared myself, knowing what I had to face. "I am going to study art, philosophy and theology. Father can't stop me. I'll pay my own way if I have to. He can forget about his alma mater. I am going to the common man's college at the University of Pittsburgh's College of Arts and Sciences. After that I'll join the monastery up in Herman." Mother told me that my eyes were burning with an earnest desire that said this fire in my heart would never fade. On graduation from high school I got a dirty look from Aunt Cecilia when I told her, "I am not going to work in the mill at US Steel all summer. I won't ever work for Uncle Walter." Aunt Cecilia gave in but slyly fought back when she told me, "Eventually I know you will be working for Uncle Walter—you just wait and see."

The next day I sat down with my father, whose quiet and reserved demeanor always seemed to conceal his true beliefs. He loved research on steel alloys. The steel mill was a kind of cathedral to him; it brought spiritual unity to the products of his work for the world at large. His childhood had revolved around the mills of Homestead, McKeesport and Duquesne. Growing up in Braddock, Pennsylvania, just up the Monongahela River from Pittsburgh where the Edgar Thompson works was founded, was the most imposing feature of his childhood. His life revolved around steel mills as a piece of steel stock revolves about a lathe. His eyes grew excited when he talked to me about his work. "I want you working with me in the specialty steel research center. You don't know how wonderful life can be when you're an engineer or a metallurgist. You'll be doing experiments, learning lessons through trial and error and making new alloys. Research on steel is a kind of laboratory; a beautiful philosophy of life in itself and engineering is a way of understanding it all. Opinions based upon facts create reality and once you acquire an understanding of the scientific side of steel alloys, welding and metallurgical engineering, you're sure to fall in love with it the same way I did."

I sat in stony silence before him; his worldview was completely foreign to me. I had no interest in industry, steel or steel making. I wanted to go to Pitt and make my own life. My thoughts fell together all of a sudden under the force of their own power. It was as if spontaneous generation had taken place deep within me and was evolving into a thought all by itself. My resistance gave symmetry to my beliefs that soon formed the cast iron mold for my independent character. "Dad, your whole life is steel research, new alloys and how to manufacture them. You have your engineering degrees, and Uncle Walter and you are partners at US Steel; you're inseparable. Uncle Walter and his immense ego dominate everyone in this family. Our life is only an extension of the steel company. Whatever you do is always done for US Steel and Uncle Walter. It's like we live in a company house and everything we do is owned, managed and done for the company. You've sold your soul to the company and Uncle Walter is never going to sell it back to you. . . But I am different, Dad, your life is not mine. When you were growing up, you just rolled out of bed and went down the street in McKeesport and headed into the Sheet and Tube mill. You and your brother's lives have been turned and shaped and molded a certain way, but mine is made of a completely different material.

Look at Uncle Walter, he's an egotistical bastard. Mother does everything to appease Aunt Cecilia because she feels sorry for her.

Uncle Walter treats her like crap, but nobody is willing to say anything for fear of losing their job at US Steel. Even mother says Uncle Walter is a tyrant and I agree with her. She says Aunt Cecilia is trying to wash away the thought of Uncle Walter with every glass of whiskey. Only it won't work, it never does and you know it too. I don't ever want to have anything to do with him. He is a part of your life, Dad, but I want my own life to be more than just another one of Uncle Walter's pawns, another of his metallurgists stuck inside his research laboratories. The labs are an empire, and they are taking over the world; but my life is not going to be colonized like everyone else's. I know you want me to be an engineer because the greatest men you've ever met were engineers. But I am not going to try to become another Thomas Edison, George Westinghouse or Charles Kettering. I want to do something else. I have to do something else that's totally new and different."

My father's cold hard features seemed to solidify and become as inflexible and rigid as the steel alloys he worked with. His wiry gray eyebrows twitched nervously before me. All his dreams for me and my life were wiped away, and he suddenly didn't know what to think about me anymore. How could I do this to him? I looked him in the eye and the words sprang from my mouth, "Once I finish my art classes at the university, I'll be leaving Pittsburgh and going to the monastery or maybe heading out to California in a Volkswagen bus." My decisiveness was something new to him. He had never seen it before, and he sensed that there was no use in arguing with me; my mind was made up. He was always too busy to talk to me. Now a look appeared on his face that said he had done something wrong, but he didn't really know what it was. Life itself seemed to be a formula that his keen mind just couldn't figure out, and his own son was now a curious thing to him. I was a complete mystery—an alloy of new thoughts about which he knew nothing.

This was probably the first time in our life that he had time to sit down together without any distractions. When Dad got out of his favorite wing chair by the bay window of his paneled office, he looked down the hill at the great steel mill, his mind wondering. He had talked to mother about my working there this summer. I went over and stood by him. His words echoed a deeply felt truth. "It sounds as though you are a man of steel and determination. I am sure you will be fine if you do what you choose to do." Amid the sad silence there was a gentleness that conveyed to me all that he felt as he spoke. "I want you to be good and happy; that is the essence of life." His presence sent a resounding spirit of confidence into me; it carried me joyously out of the room and through the next decade of my life.

As I was finishing my last year of college, mother had me working more and more for Uncle Walter and Aunt Cecilia. The parties and social events at their home became more frequent once Uncle Walter was made Vice President of US Steel. Aunt Cecilia liked to joke that the real reason they had moved outside of Pittsburgh was because most of Uncle Walter's work was now conducted on the golf course of the Pittsburgh Field Club. There, all of their friends and relatives from Jones and Laughlin Steel, Alcoa, Gulf Oil, Westinghouse and Pittsburgh Plate Glass seemed to be part of one big happy family. They all loved Uncle Walter and Aunt Cecilia, and my dad was simply brimming with joy when he was surrounded by all of his engineering pals. He was enveloped by powerful people whose discussions of science and steel kept him current on new advances. He was a leader in Republican fund raising at these cocktail parties where everyone sought out his advice. Senators and governors would stop by; the house became a Who's Who of Pittsburgh industry, engineering and power. The debates and deal making that went on during these grand parties kept the mills and the city of Pittsburgh alive.

During that happy period, Aunt Cecilia always dragged me out onto the dance floor of her patio where she told her girlfriends I was going to be a priest. A moment later she and I were dancing to the Pennsylvania Polka and drinking whiskeys and water to quench our thirst. Little old Presbyterian ladies from Pittsburgh's finer families were there clapping, yelling and telling me, "You dance too nicely to be a priest, I want you to meet my daughter."

By the time the night was over, my tuxedo was wet with sweat and I had danced with every woman at the party. Aunt Cecilia would corner me in the kitchen, stuff a $50 or a $100 bill in the pocket of my tux and tell me, "Now Jim, you have to be here a week from next Saturday night. Uncle Walter and I are hosting the American Iron and Steel Institute members and their wives. I want you here to meet and greet them and show some of the women how to dance the Polka. Your Uncle Walter and I are depending on you being on the dance floor because the women just love being with you. We're bringing a Polka band in from Charleroi."

A week later I was there and met a young engineer. She was about thirty years old, and her name was Sally McTeague. Her husband had died in an automobile accident about a year before and Uncle Walter told Aunt Cecilia to find her a husband because he didn't want her leaving his Pittsburgh research labs. Sally was a good-hearted gal. I told her I was about to leave for California, and she said to me, "I'll drive you out there. I have a whole month's vacation coming, and I have got to get out of Pittsburgh. I'd love to drive you to San Francisco in my new Chevy convertible." I couldn't believe my luck.

We got on the road a week later; and when we got out to California, we started living together. To make money we grew marijuana and sold it to hippies. We traveled to rock concerts and lived in a commune. Mostly we lived off the money Sally got from her husband's insurance policy for the next fourteen years. What a life we had in Big Sur, Monterey and then San Francisco. I finally had to go to work and found a job as a painter on the Golden Gate Bridge. Sally opened up a flower shop and I came home from work everyday and told her about the tourists I had met. They came from all over the world to see the bridge, some French people I met said it was California's version of the Eifel Tower.

One day I was on top the Golden Gate on a painter's platform, and a co-worker told me that some big wigs were going to have a retirement party on one of the towers. I had to paint a section of the floor so it would be neat for the occasion because a bunch of government dignitaries were scheduled to show up. I couldn't help wonder who would have a party on the Golden Gate Bridge. When I asked the painting supervisor, he didn't seem to know anything about it. All he had heard was that the Mayor of San Francisco and the Governor of California were both going to be there with their wives. A few days later I got to hoist a bunch of cases of champagne up to the top of the bridge on the day of the party. It was supposed to start at 6 o'clock in the evening. Right on schedule everything began, even the weather cooperated. That evening the sun had the bridge sparkling like a red jewel; it was absolutely beautiful. It looked like soft red clay and the dull silvery sheen on San Francisco Bay made me dizzy with the delightful scene strewn with white and aluminum banners, balloons and bunting.

I was pulling on a heavy rope to bring the painting platform to the top of the Bridge where a great surprise appeared. The retirement party was being held by US Steel for my own Uncle Walter. Aunt Cecilia and Mom and Dad were there. They came running over to me laughing and carrying on as Dad said, "We thought you ought to help see Uncle Walter leave US Steel in style, so Aunt Cecilia got you hired to work the party tonight." Mom's face was glowing like a happy balloon, and Father was as content as Sally and I looked on. He explained how her research project was finished after she left. The crowd was full of life, and the people there were all engineers who worked on the Golden Gate Bridge during the 1930's. Uncle Walter knew all of them and with their wives.

Poor Aunt Cecilia did not look good at all; she was a a shadow of her former self. She was a silent, sullied wife; a prostitute of the corporate paycheck that came in on one day every month on one day and went out the next to pay for the department store bills where she bought silly rags to hide her sagging, alcoholic fat. Aunt Cecilia appeared to be the wine cask that was now out of wine, an empty somewhat beautiful thing waiting to get it over with and just die. I tried to conceal these thoughts but the truth of them could not be denied as I looked out at the eternal bay and the lights on the horizon.

The little town of Sausaulito was off in the distance; Uncle Walter's roving eye was as usual going over the tanned women as he looked around at the guests. Aunt Cecilia wobbled over, tipsy on her alcoholic heels. Her cigarette smoke-scarred face had the same pathetic look of misery on it I remembered from over fourteen years ago. Lively and yet in a certain sense lifeless, Aunt Cecilia stood atop the windy bridge platform with the tragic inner truth of those endless glasses of whiskey and water; they had slowly worn her down. Her Florida- tanned face had aged and resembled my wrinkled brown leather work shoes; it was devoid of any happiness. It looked as if she was hoping that the night would soon be over. Aunt Cecilia had lived out a life hiding from all her wretched sadness. The sagging bags under her eyes were evidence of all the girlfriends, arguments, and passionate demands for the new Buick. She always dreaded seeing the next new car in the driveway. Aunt Cecilia's capped, smoke-stained teeth and false smile were witnesses to the misery of her hypocrisy as it had been lived out as a big company widow. It was conducted with superb aplomb, the carefree confidence of an accomplished corporate socialite, silently on stage every Sunday in a pew of the East Liberty Presbyterian Church. Those sad days were behind her now.

Aunt Cecilia and I found comfort in one another as always, we were friends, and we talked about the Pittsburgh we once enjoyed together. We danced a few Polkas around the platform atop the Golden Gate Bridge and enjoyed one another's company which turned merry after a few drinks. We got along like old pals, "You were my great hope, Jimmy. I wanted so much for you to be happy. I am so glad to see you are. You cannot know how good it is to see one of my few friends in this world. You always loved me for who I was; my many faults meant nothing to you. All the false people and all the shallow consumer souls who came to our home were merely there for promoting themselves or conducting business deals with Walter." Aunt Cecilia and I looked at one another longingly and then she whispered to me, "Whatever you do, never give up your happiness for it is the only thing worth having. Love always, for it is the only thing worth doing." She said all this to me very quickly and then turned away to forget her misery; she brimmed with whiskeyed laughter. Her words were consoling to me for it was clear that all her alcoholic delusions about life had ceased forever. Her liver cancer had finally woken her up to what her life with Uncle Walter was all about. The fear of facing it was now killing her. Aunt Cecilia and I remembered the grand old days in Pittsburgh. She sorely lamented the fact that the great steel mills in Homestead, Duquesne and McKeesport were all closed down. We felt a deep pang of regret for we wished with all our hopeful hearts that the great industrial city and its fine citizens had never come to see its own destruction. Life had to lived but our Pittsburgh would never be the same. After death our life had to go on, but our memory first had to be savored. We sang the Pennsylvania Polka and talked about her girlfriends I had danced with during all the parties at her home. I told her that I had taken more than a few of them to bed. She laughed; and when she started to guess who they were, I was struck by the accuracy of her knowledge. She knew each one for they had all told her such wonderful things about me. "Don't worry, I won't tell your mother. It'll be our secret, and it will go with me to my grave."

Then the snooty publicist for US Steel pulled Aunt Cecilia away from me; spots were marked on the floor where everyone was supposed to stand for a photograph. Aunt Cecilia hurried over toward the dais to stand next to Uncle Walter and the Governor. A balding press photographer was summoned from the drinks table. The Mayor of San Francisco made some stupid remarks, and the Governor of California chuckled idiotically—bored grimaces encouraged him to cut short his remarks. People were hoping to get back to the food and drinks soon. Before I knew what was happening, people swirled around Uncle Walter as he raised his glass of champagne to the heavens above. It clinked with my own as he offered a toast to Aunt Cecilia, who toasted in turn with her whiskey glass. Older but no wiser, her wisdom was always broken on some rocks with whiskey and water. Uncle Walter, the perennial pompous smiler, dedicated a fitting tribute as his winey imagination stumbled upon some gratitude for once. "To the great industrial capital of the world that was once Pittsburgh, and to United States Steel and all of its good men in the Monongahela Valley who have made us the finest steel producer in all the world."

UNCLE ART

Little girls often have the most remarkable memories of their childhoods. Every summer that I spent as a young girl in Pittsburgh was announced on the 4th of July by the arrival of my Uncle Art at the family's annual Independence Day picnic. Mother said that for almost fifty years the picnic was held on the river upstream from the Homestead steel mill. Mother told me that for all that time, the children and teen-agers would be massed in the shallows, under the trees along the Monongahela River not far from Homestead where the United States Steel's great mill loomed above us. In the distance, like a magnificent cathedral surrounded by train tracks, barges and train cars full of coke, the mill grew in our hearts as the men there worked day and night. My Uncle Art taught us that working with steel was hard and that the millworkers were all good men. Father worked as an engineer in the mill there, but he didn't like to tell us too much about what went on. We felt as though the steel mill loomed over our lives and that we were nothing more than ants living in its great smoky shadow.

Uncle Art loved to tell us all about what happened around the steel mills and the towns along the Monongahela Valley. Not far down the river the Jones and Laughlin steel mills were connected by a railroad line. Uncle Art explained how steel on the South Side of Pittsburgh was poured into large railroad cauldrons and wheeled over the hot metal bridge to the rolling mill on the opposite river bank not far from Pittsburgh's Oakland section. Uncle Art said this was where molten liquid was cooled and made into steel sheets. He worked on a crane there. It was enough for us to know that J&L must be a great place in Pittsburgh since everything Uncle Art did was immense and important. His role in the life of the steel mill went far beyond the limits of our childish imaginations. This was proven to us on the Fourth of July when all the boys and girls of the family waded knee-deep into the murky waters of the river. We were biding our time and saving up our energy and enthusiasm as we anticipated the arrival of Uncle Art around noon. Since he never appeared before then, Mother and Father always argued about what he was doing with the Union, where he was doing his organizing in the Monongahela valley. All their arguments always ended up at the same place, and it had to do with why Uncle Art drank so much.

Mother adored her brother and Father's opinion was the opposite. Mother usually started off by saying something to the effect that "Art is all sweetness and light, and he creates his own life. He is an example of what everyone of us could be if we were wiser." Father would snicker and then go on the attack; his criticism was always harsh, relentless and unforgiving. "Your brother is an overweight lush whose roving eye has never missed taking in a pretty woman whenever she walks by." Mother would chase us out of the room and then get defensive. She resolutely protected the great man we loved as much as life itself, "Our Art loves beauty and that is not a crime. Everything he does is good and kind." Father would not let up, "He's a dirty man. His work pants never change—they are worn everywhere, and their gray, metallic sheen is full of iron filings and cutting oil from his cluttered up work bench down at the mill. His pants look like they were hammered out of some old dilapidated piece of lead and then set out in the sun to soften up. God only knows when they were washed last. His khaki work shirt may look clean, but it is so old he could have been born in it, I am always afraid the shirt buttons are going to fly off whenever he starts laughing. His bulging beer belly strains those buttons so much. When those buttons let go I don't want to get hit with them. And the rolls of fat on his stomach are almost as big as the rolls of steel down at the mill." Hearing this, mother would walk away and not talk to father for the rest of the day. This was their usual routine on the Fourth of July. It always started in the morning when they were packing up the picnic basket before we headed down from Hunky Hollow to the river in our old station wagon.

Uncle Art was a much-awaited man, but he could never get there soon enough as far as the children were concerned. Father used to say he had to sober up first in the morning. Mother got angry and hushed father when he said this in front of us. "Art is my brother and I expect you to respect him like everyone else in my family." A tense moment developed whenever mother and father talked of Uncle Art. Father held him to be lazy, and Mother defended him with a series of blows always hit upon the truth regarding Uncle Art. Mother would say, "Art teaches people how to live and love and work with one another. His United Steelworkers Union has done more for the poor men and women in the valley than any of their churches will ever do for them. A good many of these preachers and ministers are controlled by the millowners and Art attacks them. Before the rotten tyranny of their lies he fights for the workingmen; and they know it." Father stood there motionless before Mother, and her tirade went on and on in preachy defense of her brother.

"My Art is the friendliest man in Pittsburgh and you resent that fact. Why do you think the men at Jones and Laughlin or US Steel's Homestead Works always reelect him as the Monongahela valley's Union leader? I'll tell you why. It's because every foreman in the steel mills of Pittsburgh calls them Pollocks and hunkies. Art is the end of chaos; his Union created human beings of these men. They finally got a decent wage that could support their families. The Union stopped the enslavement of the Hunkies in Homestead and Aliquippa. Art almost killed a foreman in one of the mills for using the word "Hunky" to a guy. They wanted to fire Art, but he fought the company and won. That is my brother, and his own mother doesn't even understand him; but all the working men in the mills do. All of the men up and down the valley know he looks out for them. He'd lay down his goddamn life for them, and they know it too. Why is it that his own sister is the only one who understands him in this family? Why is it everyone in this rotten religious family of frugal self-haters believes he fights for the Union because of money? It's not the goddamn money he's fighting for. It's the men themselves; he cares about them—they're not a bunch of dumb Hunkies and Pollocks to him. And don't think they don't know it too. He loves them the way their own mothers love them. That is why they are so loyal to him and his Union."

Father cowered at these words, for the truth of them could never be doubted. Uncle Art had hundreds of friends. Thousands of them and his admirers formed a legion among the workingmen in Homestead, Duquesne, Braddock and the southside of Pittsburgh. Art's Union finally took hold in 1937 and United States Steel had to march to a different drummer. Mother was fired up and growing quickly into a foul mood, which further convinced her that she was right, "Art is an irreplaceable part of this rotten family of Church lovers. He at least has a voice. Everybody in this family hates him for it. It's only because he is willing to use it for others. His mother and her sons fear him and his boisterous proclamations about the Union. His own brothers are afraid of losing their jobs. They'll work for nothing just as long as they can go to Church on Sunday. Well, the Church ain't going to put food on the table for their children, and Jesus Christ doesn't give a damn if you eat today or not. It's up to you to go out and work for a living. That's what I'd like to tell that rotten family of ours. Their miserable, greedy faces that fear everything that doesn't put money into their lousy pockets. Art's courage will knock fear on its ass. He will always be fighting for his Union, his workers and their struggling families. He'll raise hell cause he wants justice for the men." Father's face looked hurt and then sour, but mother refused to give up. She went on and on like a runaway train. "My Art is not quiet, but he's sincere and you can't engineer that. You can't put your slide rule to his love or his Union and its workingmen. His kind of loyalty is that which no man and no money can ever buy and you resent that. I'll take the drunken concern of my brother over a thousand sniveling and apathetic engineers like you . . ."

Mother now went after Father, "You resent Art and the men he leads because you don't have half his happiness. You don't have a tenth of his willpower and courage. All you care about is what your damn accountants at US Steel tell you. Well, my brother's made of steel, He is the heart of that steel mill. It can't function without him and his Hunkies. His Pollocks are greater than dozens of you silly college boys with your fraternity parties. My brother's drunken humanity is worth more than a mountain of your slide rules." Then mother paused amid her ranting, she took a hard breath and tore into father again and again, "God damn it! Why are you always arguing with me and picking on my damn brother? Goddamn you to hell anyway. You are no better than he is. You hate him as much as my own family despises him. I am the only one, the only one who loves him, I am not even his own blood. He's your own blood and you do not even care about him. You condemn and mercilessly seek to destroy him. Well, I won't have it! I will have nothing to do with it. I sometimes wish to God I had married him instead of you."

Father's face reddened, and he turned away. But he wouldn't give up, his angry voice roared and his screaming scared us to death. He fought her again and again, he cried out that Uncle Art was always late for every family picnic, every wedding or every funeral. "It is a lousy fact," his voice shouted back at Mother, "Your no good brother is always late because he's always drunk, and you defend him. You are that damn stupid. You defend every damn thing Art does. He'll have our two little girls working for next to nothing as stenographers for his Union before long. He will impoverish us. If that's what you want, then fine. If you want them scraping around for money all their lives then fine. But I want something more for my girls. I want them off Hunky Hill forever. I want something better for them. You and your Art are foolish dreamers. Your heaven is a lost eternity. If it has anything to do with time, then Art will for sure always be late. Ask anyone down at J&L, and they'll tell you all about your rotten brother because they're always complaining that he's never on time." Mother could never counter this for she knew Uncle Art was never where he was supposed to be when he was supposed to be there. Father railed that it was because he was lazy and drunk, but mother fought back. As children we often sided with mother for a simple reason—we didn't know what a fact was. All we knew was that we loved Uncle Art more than anyone else.

*

* *

The foul, sulfurous air of the steel mill in Homestead was soon forgotten every Fourth of July as we waded out of the river when Uncle Art arrived in his old car. Its rusted bumpers and dull paint soon disappeared in Uncle Art's smile and his wonderful lightheartedness. All the children rushed from the river to greet him. We gathered around to listen to his early morning exploits as he sat down and poured himself a beer at the picnic table. Uncle Art's voice flowed slow and smooth as we watched him drink down his beer. His great big beer belly laughed in league with us as we were mesmerized with his jolly talk. "First of all, I had to go out to Duquesne and wash down grandpap's tombstone with a scrub brush. Then I had to dig holes for Aunt Mary's geraniums and we had to go scrub her mother and dad's tombstone, then we had to plant more geraniums. Nothing in this world is so sweet as planting flowers for those you love."

Uncle Art took a long drink of beer. A child could barely wait through the span of time it took him to drink down his bottle of Fort Pitt Beer. We eagerly waited a long time as he picked up the bottle and sent the rusty liquid down into his large body. His throat trembled before us in huge gulps that riveted our eyes to his great neck. His whole being was huge and it ran on beer held inside his big beer belly.

We anticipated what was to follow but we already knew, "Next we went out with a few folks from the mill and had some whiskey and some sandwiches. By 9 o'clock we were off to Arsenal Park over in

Lawrenceville where Aunt Mary is from—she had to visit her Slovak friends over there and they took me down the street to the baseball field. I ran with an egg on a spoon across the grass field in a race with a bunch of other workmen from Heppenstall's, Blawknox Rolls and National Valve." Uncle Art always lost these foot races. We loved to imagine how he might have looked running across a field with an egg balanced on a spoon at the end of his meaty arm. Mother would be there looking up and admiring her brother. At that moment Uncle Art became the finest human being any of us had ever looked upon. His jolly laugh swirled about inside our childish hearts that soon resounded with joy in being in his company. Mother's eyes would be full of this glorious wonder that she could hardly contain as happy tears slid from the corners of her eyes.

Uncle Art had grown up on 43rd Street next to a jail in Pittsburgh's Polish neighborhood. As children we were convinced this was surely what was at the heart of Uncle Art's greatness. We fondly mused that it must be wonderful to grow up in the shadow of a jail that had been turned into a Polish beer garden. We didn't even know what a beer garden was, but it had to be wonderful because Uncle Art told us how sweet and beautiful it was at sunset. The sumacs in the alley draped over the summery world was a dream of pure goodness. The old brick jail with the heavy black metal bars on its windows rose up in our imagination and became a childish ideal. We knew that there was no greater place in all the world to grow up. We all wished we could have been Mother who grew up with Uncle Art and Dad. Mother loved to talk about her brother; she told us that Uncle Art and his United States Steelworkers conquered life inside the steel mills. Our eyes sparkled with wonder and hope when mother said, "Your Uncle Art is a great labor leader, and he's probably the greatest Irishman in all of Pittsburgh."

Mother said this to us over and over. She believed that Uncle Art was a thing of beauty and a joy forever, and we knew it was the truth too. Father would look at her like she was crazy when she talked that way. He said to us that we better learn our lessons in school and not get too caught up in a bunch of nonsense. "Don't you believe all the damn silly things your mother is always telling you because she ain't right half the time and she's pretty damn wrong or misleading the other half." Then their eyes would look hard upon one another. They would get into an argument about Uncle Art again and again. He was the heart and soul of their arguments, their favorite reason for fighting with one another.

Before long we were just sent to bed where we could hear their voices yelling as we gently fell asleep looking out at the soft smoke drifting away from Southside's Hunky Hill. Our life revolved around the stories and the arguments, the drunken battles and family feuds. It went on and on, and the issue never varied. It was always Uncle Art, the Fourth of July, independence and freedom. Father swore about him and mother cringed when he angrily announced, "Uncle Art is a goddamn nuisance. All he wants to do is fight the steel company. Every time we make a profit he's there with his hand out asking for more and more money." As children we didn't understand what a company was. All we knew was that come the day of the picnic, we would witness what was to us the greatest thing in the whole world. Its name was Uncle Art. His eating and drinking and swimming were all the proof we needed that he and Mother loved life like no one else to be found in all of Pittsburgh.

At the picnic, after finishing his beers, Uncle Art had a routine planned which we had memorized over the years. Uncle Art got up, strolled over to the other side of the picnic table and placed two big shopping bags on top. From one he retrieved the supplies of the day around which all the men gathered happily. They loved Uncle Art as much as we did. That was even more proof of how great he was. I looked up at the men's eyes and they sparkled when they were with him laughing and joking. He inspired them and sent a new kind of life into them all day. Uncle Art lined up a series of shot glasses and poured out whiskey that he hauled from his other brown shopping bag. He lifted up his own shot glass to the Union men who toasted him in turn. Together they celebrated America's Birthday. This may have been the greatest moment of our lives for we were silently amazed that they could celebrate the country's birthday as though it was their own. I was sure there was something special about the whiskey they drank, too. It made them happy and cheerful. I promised myself that once I got to drink whiskey I was not going to be like some of the younger men. They would always wince and cough when they drank it down too fast. Uncle Art laughed with them as they all staggered back toward the car as he got ready to go swimming.

He would get another bottle for them and then start thinking about all the impatient children. A moment later he would slip behind the car and put on his swim trunks. Within an instant he would quickly run like a madman down to the edge of the water. In wild pursuit all of the children gathered about would now chase him frantically into the river. At the last second before reaching the water, his great muscular bulk would halt, and the children, driven by their own momentum, would plunge into the water pell mell as he stood on the shore laughing as gleefully as only a great man can laugh. Each and every year it was the same and each and every year he caught us up in the swirling giddiness of this spectacle. His flabby chest and big beer belly then turned into the happy mass of a man as we screamed for him to jump into the river and make the big splash. Nothing was greater than seeing Uncle Art laugh. Mother said he could laugh better than anyone she knew. She said it was an Irishman's laugh, and it ended with a great flurry when Uncle Art's arms would be swirling like propellers as he dove into the water for the big splash.

Within a few minutes Uncle Art had suddenly turned from a self-propelled twirling man into our favorite water buffalo who would now cavort with us in the river all afternoon. Uncle Art took us for rides into the deeper water atop his shoulders. His immense white shoulders felt like huge soft cushions to the anxious initiates who waited for their turn. Uncle Art got to everyone, only everyone had to wait, his booming voice would soon bring order to our childish pleas as he called out to us, "The smallest to the tallest." We were taken in turn and each felt special for a thrilling moment. It felt like eternity to be atop the big man's shoulders on America's birthday. This was our reason for living, for doing our schoolwork, for finishing our chores, for saving ourselves up all year; this was what we waited for all year. Uncle Art waded along the shoreline with one child and then another as sultry and jealous parents pouted about his boisterous laughing.

Father said he was drunk, and Mother had nothing to do with Father for the rest of the Fourth of July. In our childish eyes Uncle Art was infallible, joyous and fun loving as a child. He could do no wrong and nobody, not even Grandma, sitting under the trees with her stern wooden cane and her two crabby sons, Uncles Al and Tom, could convince us otherwise. Grandma called him a drunk who never went to Church. Mother would argue with her every year at the picnic when she said this about Uncle Art. For the whole summer long, we might not visit grandma's house until school started or even until Christmas. It all depended on how angry Mother got with grandma and whether or not there was a good reason to make up. Usually if one of us got sick Grandma came down to the house and they made up, but this usually took a telephone call from Father and some yelling and screaming. This was done when we went to bed at night. When mother got too worried about how sick we were, she gave up being mad so she could let Grandma help us get better so we could go back to school.

After swimming all afternoon we children finally tired. We then huddled around Uncle Art and were mesmerized as he showed us his rabbit's foot. He had won it in a potato sack race with a little Italian boy only a few hours before. Josephine had a crush on the boy and said he was the most handsome kid in her school. Uncle Art adored his two little girls. They hugged onto him jealously. He went into the back pocket of his pants where he retrieved the prize he won. "Feel the rabbit's foot, " Uncle Art would say as he pulled it out of his pocket. "It's still warm. It just came off the rabbit this very morning." The kids would pass it around and their hands would clutch at it as though it was a part of Uncle Art's greatness. We were all amazed how warm it still was. Mary and Josephine looked upon their father in profound wonder. Their big eyes saw him as a huge boy who loved to make them laugh. They clearly had the best dad in the whole wide world and a lot of us felt jealous of them. Deep down we knew we were just lucky to be at a picnic with Uncle Art once a year when summer started. Mother told us that Uncle Art was also the best uncle any little kid ever had—and we all knew it too.

When Uncle Art sat down and drank beer or ate sandwiches late in the day, he always sat at a picnic table set aside for the children. We sat there in awe of him. He was a giant among us, and we watched his every move and listened to his every word as if they were the source of all goodness and light. Uncle Art's laughter was the sweetest thing we had ever heard, and the whiskey he drank from a pint bottle made him fun and joyous. Grandma would usually look over at him and grimace, grind her teeth and scowl. Uncles Tom and Al told everyone they had to leave early, I could never figure out why they left before the fireworks. Mother said they had to go home and take care of Grandpa, but I thought they told me he had died a long time ago in a coal mine.

On the evening of the Fourth of July picnic, Father would arrive home and tell mother how Uncle Art had passed out watching the fireworks. Or that he had taken in half a bottle of whiskey during the course of the day. Mother's reply would always be the same, "I doubt very much that there is any man alive who could drink half a bottle of whiskey in one day." Father would angrily protest mother on this point, "Well, I know someone who can do it, he is your own brother and he's a damn lush." Mother got stone-faced and she said that it was now time for us to go to bed. As we crawled slowly under the covers after a long day mother tucked us in, we asked her tiredly, "What is a lush, Ma?" She bit her lip and say slowly; "I'll tell you in the morning." But of course we always forgot to ask her about it then because we were so good at forgetting.

We never tired of thinking about our family picnic where we

went swimming, jumping and playing in the Monongahela River all day with Uncle Art. His immense body floated out into the river of my watery imaginings as I snuggled up next to my little sister who was quickly falling asleep. We hid together under the bed covers from the darkness of the summer night where the noise from the fireworks and the steel mill down the street frightened us to death. When the mill whistle rang out for the night shift in Homestead, we felt safe and more secure and became lost in our wonder. We whispered to one another about how much fun we could expect now that summer was here. Uncle Art had kicked it off with a joyous start. When we finally dozed off, a vision of beauty enveloped us as a dream. The children we had been with all day were now huddled about the riverbank holding a long rope from the mill. Uncle Art was seen pulling all of us into the river in a tug of war. His great arms reached out to us as our screams echoed off the old steel mill where a yellow flame was burning brightly into the darkening sky. Uncle Art loomed immense and friendly over the scene where time and the river flowed endlessly on into eternity. We could see Uncle Art and his greathearted goodness. Within it he gave us something that could not be found at home. It was a certain truth; somehow we understood what we had forgotten from the last Fourth of July. Uncle Art would always be there and as long as the summer lasted, all the world was gloriously ours forever and ever.

ANOTHER FIXTURE AT THE MILL

Joachim Capek
Laborer
McKeesport, Pennsylvania

I had been in prison for only a few years. It was worse than I thought it could be; but once it was over, I was determined to be finished with it for good. I made up my mind that I would make a new life for myself in one of Pittsburgh's steel mills. When I left the penitentiary on the morning of my release, I stood before the prison wall a long time. I felt as though the prison door had just spit me out onto the street. I was alone and I wondered about what I should do. Then I remembered something that I told myself over and over for years; my life in prison was one side of a coin but once I got out, my life outside the slammer would be the other side of the coin. Though indelibly welded together, different and ignorant of one another, these two sides were a reality I could not run away from. Fused into one coin, they made me who I am. I told myself, however, that one side would be better than the other, I resolved to reform myself. The prison life I lived would be a part of me but my memory would only be a link to something absent, gone.

I can barely remember the day I got out. What I do recall is as much a part of me as leaves are a part of a tree, a man is essentially a series of partial memories that form the whole basis of his future life. This is what I recall. It is a part of me just as the bones in my legs or the ribs in my chest are a part of me. After my release, the big iron gate of the prison opened and I stepped outside and onto the sidewalk. It was then that I suddenly seemed to be out of place. The immensity of the world swiftly overwhelmed my senses; it was too much and it made me afraid. As long as I was in prison, the world was contained and manageable. Every object inside the penitentiary had a certain meaning and it couldn't be changed. A guard, a cup and a window were only their identity and nothing more; outside things changed. When I heard the prison door close with a metallic echo, a great leaden thought grabbed hold of me. I was now condemned to freedom. The world was foreign and inert; incomprehensible as the stone prison wall that now loomed up before me, it was beyond me. My senses were dwarfed by the immensity of the landscape flowing out from my little view of things.

A state road in front of the prison rolled out toward a hill before me. It felt as though it was made to be quiet so that I might listen to the sound of my footsteps as they fell upon the hard road of life. Off in the distance a plume of smoke from a coal mine blew silently in a white drifting streak over Shippingport. I found the silence comforting, consoling for the prison was nothing more than the noise of lost and lonely men. Rain from the overhanging tree branches splashed onto my forehead. In tiny steps on the wet pavement, I slowly overcame my fear of the outside world; I started to walk with more certainty. The prison within me echoed off my footsteps, reminding me of the silence of a nearby shaft in a coal mine. I once had a work release job in the mine till the coal mine closed down. I looked around timidly as I went along the road. The scene before me stretched endlessly in every direction, it was beyond my tiny comprehension. The freedom of the clouds up in the sky seemed to be flowing everywhere without any purpose. As I walked along the wall I saw the prison towers with their peaked roofs. Their windows looked down on me, and I felt as though the men in the towers were omnisciently poised so they could watch every move I made.

I put out my arm to touch the wall to test its brute reality. I tried to convince myself that I was now free, or that the wall was only a part of my past—but the thought wouldn't hold; it was impossible to believe. I could not leave my past behind and simply walk into the future on my own without a guard's permission. I believed this for a moment, and then I got a grip on things. My fingers found the solidity of the prison wall to be hard and impossible. It was too much to understand all at once. I could not have spent the last fifteen years behind this wall. And yet it was so. The wall was the sole obstacle to my freedom, and now it meant nothing to me. It was no more than a bunch of stones fitted together and owned and maintained by the Commonwealth of Pennsylvania.

All the familiar moments of my daily routine evaporated and were gone. They disappeared into a nowhere that was now as smooth as the road or the sky or the stone wall. The prison mess hall at dawn, the prison laundry where I worked all morning and even the prison yard itself now dissolved into nothingness and became empty of meaning. And yet thanks to the State, these were the very things that held my life together for years without exacting any effort. The stern, lawful and familiar faces of the guards were nothing to me now. I had a difficult time even remembering some of the ones I had seen everyday for years, I had been a slave to the image of their faces which were now gone forever from my memory. What I did recall was one thing; they looked at me jealously when I left. I could not conceive of where I was or what I was doing out on the road. The prison dissolved in rain behind me. A horrible feeling of where I might go entered my thoughts and haunted me. I suddenly came to believe that we are never alone; we are always hunted down by thoughts that can either make or break us. Consciousness is always consciousness of some damn thing.

My feet went on of their own accord as I walked along the road. Farm after farm went by slowly as the clouds dimmed the sun overhead. I was tiring. Before long I was in a small town tavern where half a dozen men were talking among themselves and drinking away the afternoon. I mounted a barstool and drank a cold beer. The taste of it was so new that I realized I would be drinking it every day; before too long I would be saturated with the taste of beer. My prison wages were in an envelope. The feel of the money in my hands felt odd and unreal—it reminded me of the wafers they put on your tongue at communion. I put a dollar bill on the bar and the bartender brought back change and set it down in a neat pile. I fingered a quarter for a moment, and said to myself, "So this is why I robbed the bank, to get money like this. It was the stealing of money just like this from a bank down in Pittsburgh that got me sent to prison in the first place." It all felt so odd now. I suddenly realized I had to do something. I finished my beer and went outside—then I went along the two-lane highway that led to the city.

I hitchhiked to Pittsburgh and ended up on the South Side where I grew up. I went along East Carson Street and then strolled up into Hunky Hollow where an elderly woman had a sign in a window. She was renting out a room in her house. I knocked on the door and had to listen closely to her while she spoke. She didn't speak much English. She didn't ask where I was from or what I was doing. This situation slowly warmed my heart and made me feel good about this old woman. All she was interested in was whether I had money to pay the rent on time. I pulled out a thin wad of dollars from my pants pocket, and she immediately smiled at me as if we were friends. She hobbled into the hall and showed me upstairs to the front room that had yellowing wallpaper with faded red flowers. The curtains seemed to hang in long lifeless sheets against the windows. When I looked out a side window, there was a jumble of long train tracks that reminded me of a pile of metallic spaghetti flowing around a big dirt hill; it was cloudy with smoke. She said that the train tracks ran into the Jones & Laughlin steel mill. You could see it from the front window of the house.

The mill was the largest thing I had ever seen in my childhood. It had black smokestacks and bridges and catwalks running all over it from every possible height, angle and direction. I got the notion that I could just go over there and get a job. The landlady thought that was about right, too. We finished the business about when I would pay her again next week. She counted her money a second time and she left me alone in the room. I took off my shoes and lay down on the bed. My eyes closed and I felt as though I was absorbed into the soft mattress and pillows that smelled clean and starchy. I had walked over twenty-two miles in one day, and I was absolutely beat. My mind seemed to be flowing off to sleep; in a few minutes I was out.

I awoke around dawn when the loud burst of a train whistle rattled me back to life. The lumbering of coal cars seemed to bear down on the rickety old house whose windows started to shake gently in their frames as the train approached. The noise of the train was so great that I was sure it had jumped the tracks and was bearing down on the little house. I was certain I would be crushed to death at any moment. Then a whooshing sound combined with the pounding of metal wheels on the train tracks consumed me. As an echo bounced off the brick row house, the chattering windows seemed as though they might rumble right out of the wall. While coal cars slid quickly by, I jumped out of bed and ran to the window to watch them pass. The rapid flow of black, rough metal train cars loaded with coal looked like a scene from underneath a Christmas tree stolen from a holiday in my youth at the reform school. For a long while I saw the cars flow on and on and then around a curve and further on into the mill. I watched the dull red wooden caboose disappear into a shadowy curve, and then it dissolved in a hazy fog of uncertainty. The dull grayness of the window comforted me, and then I saw something moving. Smoke was billowing in immense gray and white plumes. The sky seemed to be rainy and rounded; it was a bowl made of solid gray lead. I heard footsteps of workingmen on the stairs and felt the sharp knife of hunger cut into my stomach; I had to get something to eat.

The gray sky at dawn was coming up gradually over the steel mill that loomed like an immense black anvil hard upon the windowpane. I put on my shoes and took the worn steps that led downstairs to a dark wooden hallway painted with shadows. I went out the front door and walked toward East Carson Street. I knew that after being out of prison for just a single day I had to find a job if I was really going to make it. I had to get moving before the landlady got suspicious and put me out on the street. I had only twenty-eight dollars left, and that would not even hold me for a month. I had to get a mill job. I met different guys on the street but nobody talked to me, nobody seemed to know how I could get a mill job. I walked the streets of Pittsburgh's South Side like a pacing man on death row who knows that time is limited. Once the twenty-eight dollars were gone, I would have to move out. The landlady had a son who was a policeman, and he was supposed to be a real tough guy. If he knew I only had twenty-eight dollars, he would probably have had me out of there by now. I couldn't figure out what I was going to do, so I just decided to spend a dollar for breakfast—I had to eat.

    I found a Mom and Pop restaurant run by a Ukrainian guy with a scraggly gray beard. He was the cook, and I could tell just by the way he looked down at me that he felt sorry for my situation. I told him I had to find a job, or else I would be out on the street. "I know the feeling. About ten years ago I came here from Russia and I was in the same damn fix. Unless you got relatives here nobody can prepare you for America," he said. He looked around the restaurant for someone, and then he told me the J&L mill on the South Side wasn't looking for laborers right now. But I was sure to get a job at a steel mill up the river in McKeesport. He called a guy over from one of the back booths. The people at the restaurant counter said they were hiring at the McKeesport mill, and they sounded hopeful about my prospects of getting something. The man who came over from the booth was wearing a railroad hat. He was friendly, and he shook my hand real hard. He said I should look up this guy named Smitty. Smitty would see what he could do. He said Smitty was always willing to help a guy out if he was willing to work. Another railroad guy sitting at the lunch counter handed me a slip of paper with Smitty's name scribbled on it in pencil along with the words **US Steel-McKeesport**. I put the slip into my pocket and felt a little happy for once. Maybe now I had a chance.

    As I wandered about the streets and looked into windows, the whole world seemed to be busy. It was passing me by. I had no idea where everyone was rushing off to, but it didn't really matter that much after a while since they had places to go that I wasn't supposed to know about. I had no idea of where I was going. I walked over a long black bridge that hung out over the river. A man I met there told me where I could get a number 61C bus to McKeesport. I took the bus along the river through a bunch of grimy little neighborhoods, and then I got off at the end of the line on Lysle Boulevard.

I walked along the street and down toward the Monongahela River to an office. I mentioned to a man there that I was supposed to contact Smitty. "A guy from the Pennsylvania Rail Road gave me this piece of paper, and said I should talk to Smitty." The guy looked at the paper and then said, "Smitty ain't in right now, but I'll take care of you. If the railroad sent you over here you must be all right." His hand disappeared into a drawer and came out with some papers. He handed them to me and had me fill out some clean white papers that had black printing in big bold letters on the top of them:

United States Steel Corporation

Everything in the room seemed official and solid. Nothing seemed to move in the hard wooden office, its silence announced one clear fact: this was a no-nonsense sort of place where nothing but hard work was expected. Anything less was not going to be tolerated. I played it smart by keeping my mouth shut most of the time. My eyes looked at the lines on the white paper set before me on the table where I worked at the application. The pencil they gave me to fill out the form felt odd in my hand. I couldn't remember the last time I wrote anything down on a piece of paper. As I nervously pressed down, the pencil point broke off, and I was sure I was a goner. I broke into a sweat—I figured I had just sealed my fate, and they would now throw me out onto the street. I wanted to stand up and bolt for the door before they found out, but I waited.

The silence of my writing must have announced that I was having trouble with the paper. The man behind the desk came over to the table with a look of sympathy on his face, once he sized things up his features grew solemn. He retreated back to the drawers and became the man behind the wooden desk again. Then he just said in a blunt disgusted sort of way, "They don't make these damn pencils like they used to anymore. . . ." He reached into the drawer, and passed me another pencil and put the broken one in the desk drawer. He never thought anything of the broken lead. I gulped nervously; it was as if the pencil was the greatest mistake of my life, and he didn't even think it was worth bothering about. Then he mentioned he might sharpen it later if he remembered. I felt that it was gone for good, so I relaxed a little. What had I been thinking? For a moment I was sure they were going to tell me to leave because of the broken pencil; but nothing happened, and this utterly dumbfounded me. I couldn't believe how powerful this guy behind the desk was. I knew that it was good that I had played it smart from the beginning. When I got back to work on the papers I was calm and assured. Once I was finished, I handed the sheet over and he smiled at me. I swear to God I never felt so happy in my life as when I saw his teeth grinning at me. Then I got to thinking that the twenty-eight dollars might even be enough to hold me over for a little while longer.

    Some other people in the adjoining personnel office appeared and they told me to go over to another place not far away. It was all wood and had dirty windows. I sat in a waiting room on a wooden bench with a bunch of somber high school kids who looked unhappy about the fact that their mothers had sent them down to the mill office to get a job. Each of us waited our turns in a dingy, unpainted room. A November drizzle began as the time slowly passed inside the wooden office.

    I went into another drab room where I saw a seated man with an ashtray brimming with old cigarette butts. He had a mean and wily face that was pitted with scars, the hardness of his life could only be imagined. His whole attitude was one of death and destruction, he had no time for small talk. Soft swirls of cigarette smoke twirled from between his fingers that held my fate in the balance. This man would make the final decision of whether I would proceed. My future was in the smoky hand holding the cigarette. His hard, steely eyes and wire rim glasses were a piece of the mill's grayness that was as still and as rigid as the metal desk behind which he sat. I could tell by his attitude that he was a company man, he had US Steel written all over him. I thought I could see it in the tough-minded sharpness of his mind and the hard iron wrinkles of his hard sober face.

The cautious head held two beady eyes, and they were pointed at the paper and reading up on me. The man was curious, but he looked as though he wasn't happy at what he found. I cringed inside every time a big boom from the steel mill sent a shock wave through the tiny wooden office. The dirty smoke-colored windows rattled like chattering women on the bus ride to McKeesport. The mean-looking and careful man didn't even blink. No kind of noise and nothing in this world of industrial grit and smoky grime could bother him. His heart was an alloy that could not be fathomed or understood; he was made of a metal that nothing could budge. His hard-bitten life was greater than gravity, his tough muscled arms ruled over McKeesport's steel industry. This was Mr. Kopek, and it was immediately evident he tolerated no fools. He was the plant superintendent and his word was the way it was, and nobody doubted it.

Mr. Kopek roughly beckoned to a woman who moved briskly across the wooden floor as if his iron hand was tied to a string that jerked her one way and then another. Her sharp face was as hard as his only it moved faster and seemed not to be cast in such stony silence. Her white stockinged legs told me she was a nurse. She summoned me to the exam room with a curt motion of her skinny arm and said, "Take off your clothes." She uttered the words as sharply as the steel that was being cut by shears in the busy mill not far away. I was nothing more than an automaton in her eyes. A minute later she had me standing on a scale. My weight was scribbled on the white paper that held the history of my life.

A doctor arrived and talked to me in the clear, kindly voice of a friend, a friend of man. He had a Russian accent and he asked me about my health. I told him what I knew, and it wasn't much, "I coughed up blood once in high school after a baseball game." His head nodded in acknowledgement that he had registered this fact and found it unimportant. Then he listened to my heart with a metal disc he warmed in his hands. When he was done checking my pulse and my eyes and ears, he picked up a big wooden handled rubber stamper on a nearby table. He pushed it down on an inkpad and then onto the paper which bore my name. A big solid black word appeared on my paperwork:

APPROVED

It felt good being found fit to move along down the assembly line of the process. Only I didn't really know what to expect next. I had no idea of what these people wanted of me. I went out into a hallway where they told me to go see a skinny man with a thin pea-green tie. His thin mouth was missing a tooth. His dull suit pants hung down on him like the long iron curtains on the windows in my bleak bedroom. He looked suspiciously at the paper. He abruptly took it from my hand as if I was a machine handing a piece of sheet metal to another machine to be rolled, cut and pounded. The man became a hand—he didn't look at me but his voice was absolute as a loudspeaker. It told me in a stern hard tone, "Report here tomorrow night at 10:30. You'll be working the night shift. Here are your Union papers. Sign them, and bring them back to the office tomorrow night." The hand shoved an envelope with Union papers in it at me. I stood there waiting, not knowing what I should do next. His anger caught me by surprise. "What the hell are you waiting for?" The mean voice called out; "You're through. Now go home and get outta here." I stumbled through the wooden door. I felt terribly odd and out of place as I left. How was I supposed to know what to do? The bundle of papers in the envelope was put into my coat pocket. I left, wondering where

I was as I drifted outside into the cold afternoon air. Gusts of cold, sharp wind were blowing up the hill like shrapnel from the Monongahela River.

At the mill gate a great brick wall seemed to rise up in front of me. When I looked around again, a wooden wall was now flowing by on wheels that were made of metal. A long row of black train cars loaded with black coke scuttled by into the gaping mouth of the iron mill gate. Things were in motion and went in every direction. I could barely understand the smoky mirage of it all—men, trains, cranes, coal cars and smoke stacks. They crowded out the sky, which was eclipsed by the mill smoke rising up against the grey and brown scene above the hills. The syrupy slowness of the dark brown river nearby made the landscape look as though it was flowing in time and before long it would all disappear into the night. I saw an overhead crane, tugboats and more mounds of coal in train cars. Barges moved slowly in the water, they were going every which way, but they all flowed toward the mill. It could easily consume everything and everyone in its motionless inertia; iron ore, coke and limestone were gobbled up greedily. A tall, tireless man in a tugboat was intent on aligning the barges just so like long black dominoes shining with pyramid mounds of coke. A massive shovel reached down and brought up shovelfuls of coke into the bowels of the mill's blazing furnaces. Men tended funnels with hand shovels, iron bars. These strong workingmen were sweating, some of them looked as if they were encased in gray asbestos-like armor. I was sure they could take on the anything thrown to them from the furnace, the fiery hell inside the mill.

Flat cars were loaded down with coils, beams, rails, billets and bundles of wire, thick steel sheets, iron scrap, ingots, compressed boxes of corrugated steel. All of these were lifted by a magnet onto a steel mesh conveyer belt. Men pushed around wheelbarrows, trucks, shovels and rolls of steel. Their thick arms glistened with shiny sweat. They rode around in trucks and handcars and on the backs of coal cars. As much as I looked around at everything going in every which way, the more it appeared impossible to understand.

Everything was moving too fast for me. There was too much motion, manly movement and mill noise; machines ground out a metal noise which formed a vacuum of pounding that soon sucked me into itself. The chaos of work was everywhere taking shape anew; a purpose was seen in everyone that moved one way and then the other. A man standing by a door smoking a cigarette and laughing among his friends made immediate sense to me. In front of him vehicles wove in and out, activity came from every direction and overhead a crane was swung big plates of steel. In the distance the clanging of another train on the tracks seemed to be approaching the mill from an odd angle up the river. Not far away I saw pig iron glowing red and bright orange. A guy waved me toward the mill gate. There, a bunch of men were on their way to lunch at a nearby bar. Then I felt I was being pulled along by a metal hook in the sky. Something greater than myself was organizing things. I flowed with the crowd of men and then my feet stopped moving. I came to a complete stop all of a sudden in order to catch my breath.

When I recovered from all the motion swirling in and around me, I went down a street and bought some cigarettes at a corner store. People were in motion and walking rapidly in and out of stores buying potatoes, shirts, walking canes, a package of snuff, pipe cleaners and a bunch of bananas. A big Italian grandma held onto two little girls' hands as she walked them across the street to talk in Italian to one of her paisans. The happy faces sitting on a bench welcomed her and spoke in a friendly congenial language from the Old World. It announced that each person changes things for the better by leading a good and happy life but this was almost impossible to do. Then I watched this small scene of contentment for a while; it was framed on the periphery by a rag tag flock of pigeons circling the sky in a great arc above the corner store. They took refuge on a porch roof where an old portly woman in a housedress was throwing them bread from underneath a big gabled roof. Then her husband came out and started yelling at her. She told him to go inside the house before she murdered him, the Italian women laughed at her and she called out to them to come up to see her with their children, she had cake for them.

I loitered around a while on the street in front of a big granite bank on Lysle Boulevard. It had massive granite columns from an ancient world about which I knew nothing. Those columns soon convinced me that my money would be safe inside its vaults. I waited patiently for a ride home. I got on board a slowly lumbering bus with 61C on it. The driver told me it was headed to Pittsburgh. The bus crawled up a long steep hill as though it was a big brown caterpillar lumbering along a black limb from which I could see where I had been. I looked back at the McKeesport steel mill. At the base of the valley, the mill was a vast assemblage of buildings and pipes. A sulphurous fog was flowing into the valley below me like an immense smoky painting smudged with mud, grit, steam and hard times. I came to think that each scurrying man I saw down below on the grounds of the mill yard was a stone in the great wall of society. I would soon be one of them. Society was like a beehive I had seen at the prison one time. It was a place where everyone worked to make honey. My thoughts drifted down through the Monongahela valley. Not far away in East Pittsburgh was the Westinghouse Electric and Manufacturing Company. It was proof that all men and women were alike and all were the same. I was comforted by a fact, I was now alone and a part of them, a man without qualities. Being the same as everyone else was a comforting thought that almost put me to sleep as the bus bumped along a rutted road toward Pittsburgh.

As the bus paused now and then on its climb up the steep hill I felt the impression of the steel mill on my memory. My eyes and ears created a new image of existence that I had never understood before. I was a free man, free of prison, and I was on a different road. It felt like it was really going somewhere. It was opening up before me as an endless series of tunnels, turns and traffic stops. I overheard a guy sitting in the seat in front of me say that McKeesport had the best Slovak and Hungarian priests in all the world. A little flame of hope lit up my inside my heart and a gentle stream of light and confidence flowed from it. I told myself that someday I wanted to live here among these people. They were good and generous, and I felt as though I was one with them. I knew that I could make something of myself. It took a while for this thought to settle in. I felt quietly content to be among my people. The feeling was purely my own. It was a discovery borne of my inner yearning for a life that would be strong and beautiful. Money would make a different man of me. Now that I was no longer a thief, I would be a working man at the steel mill.

I glanced at the calm, tired working people who sat there on the bus with me; they looked as though they believed that such an existence was possible. Locked within their solemn and tired faces was a secret kind of knowledge that told me a simple truth— working in the mill could merely be another form of prison. I cringed before them and didn't want to believe it. And yet their hard hands and tough-minded resolve made me think that this was the way it was and nothing could ever change it. The facts of life were written on their tired faces. Their hard experience told the sweetest stories where faultless eyes looked out at me with blank stares, it seemed as though I was barely alive. Deep down I sensed that I was among my own people here in McKeesport, we were all equals on common ground.

I can't really say what happened next, I was on the bus dozing off. I felt myself moving through different places and saw colors, lights and people washing by the bus windows rolling along before me as the sun set. I dozed off again and again, and then I was in downtown Pittsburgh. The bus driver announced that we were at the end of the line. He said I had to get off because he was going to take his dinner break. Old women wearing babushkas wished him well and spoke noisily about getting to work. They were off to clean the offices in the skyscrapers that loomed in the sky like tall, industrial granite tombstones. I was unsure of what to do so I just followed all the people out the door of the bus. I remember stepping down onto the sidewalk and feeling how worn out my prison shoes now felt on the hard Belgian blocks of a Pittsburgh street. I tried to get my bearings, but nothing looked familiar to me. I was a stranger where nobody knew me. The smoky city was a blur in the November drizzle as it wore on amidst tired people heading home from work. I wandered around alleyways and avenues and half-deserted streets, then I bought some work clothes at a Murphy's 5 and 10. I walked back to the apartment to hide out in my room and rest up for tomorrow night's shift at the mill, but my feet wandered away. I walked by houses; the rainy air mesmerized me as I listened at windows. I heard the clinking sound of silverware and dishes, and this made me hungry. I promised to go out and get something to eat once I got back to the house and took a rest.

When I arrived at the brick row house, I told the landlady about the job. She said something selfish and hardhearted: "Good, now I don't have to worry about getting my damn money every week from your dirty hands. I know I will get paid from you. And you better not pull any funny business here either. No women upstairs or I'll call my son the policeman." Nothing kills so surely as mean-hearted words, and this lady's tough talk meant business, I glanced down at my hands and they were filthy from the grime from the mill where I had spent the whole afternoon. Dirty and clean were absolutes, and this old woman's eyes saw everything in this light. The little joy burning within now seeped out of me all at once. My heart quickly slid down in my chest like a lump of coal disappearing deep into a dark abyss of her hard and callous red hands. Her arms went back to work, pushing a mop across the grimy floor where most of the dirt collected as grit from the J&L mill across the way. Then I was distracted by something like a vision of a policeman's badge marching angrily toward me with a summons and a district attorney. She complained about washing down the walls of all the mill smoke deposited in the house. Spring-cleaning was the worst time of the year for her. I walked toward the stairs and the old woman dissolved in the dirty bucket of gray water at her feet. I climbed up the wooden steps thinking about my lonely room.

The thin wooden banister felt flimsy in my strong, willful hand. I trudged to my room and the wooden railing along the top of the banister felt cold and odd in my poor grip. I felt like I was back behind the prison walls. I felt down and out, worried and as afraid as when I left the lonely prison gate. Only now it was the mill and the people and the streets of the Pittsburgh, and I didn't understand what I was going to be doing tomorrow at the mill on the night shift. Nobody had really told me anything, and I was afraid to ask. I thought I heard somebody in one of the wooden offices tell me that I would be a laborer in the raw materials department.

I was the same man only all the things around me had changed all of a sudden; I wasn't sure what was what. I had no idea of where I really was or where I was going or where it all would end. Anguish was coming from out of nowhere toward me in the little room where the wallpaper was coiling from the wall in the corners. Scrolls of it formed eyes that looked at me with their guilt. I could feel it rolling over me like a piece of steel at the mill. Before long I would be pummeled like a soft piece of iron and then rolled thin and flat and finally laid to rest. The anguish in my heart had a sound like that of a train whistle passing by. I was now concerned that something was terribly wrong inside me.

I climbed into my cold bed and this immense thing suddenly came over me—it was a feeling that everything outside was too much for me to bear. Traffic on the street outside had cars honking their horns, trucks and buses with exhaust pipes blowing out dirty lead-gray smoke to choke me. I smelled diesel fumes and realized they were seeping into the room through the rotten, wobbly windows sitting loosely ajar in the walls of the flimsy rowhouse. The mill across the way was spewing some sort of dull yellowy plumes into the air that made my every breath smell like warm sulfur and old rotten eggs. I cowered and dozed off to sleep but the anxious flow of noise outside woke me up again and again. I heard a distant locomotive; the rumbling train with its coal cars approaching scared me. The hard grinding sound was made of metal against metal. Loud and rumbling, it bore down on me. I fell deeper and deeper into my bed in order to hide away from the world outside. My mind tried to get ahead of the dull grinding of the train, but reality could not be stopped; it was just going to run me down and keep on going. All the metallic railroad noise just kept going on and on until it turned a corner and charged into the mill across the way.

Shadowy dreams, thoughts and feelings suddenly crowded into me like the old plaster wall I was wedged up against, I immediately fell into a sweaty panic. I was sinking into a vortex of ambiguity that I didn't understand. Another train coming down the railroad tracks behind the rowhouse wouldn't stop. The squealing noise of the metal wheels screeching along the curved track suddenly paralyzed me with fear. I was frozen to the cold iron sheets of the bed; I couldn't move. My heart was racing in terror. Stilled by death's grip, I was stiff and motionless for what felt like hours and hours. My mind became a steel trap that refused to open up. Its hinges were fused together like melted metal forged into one piece by a fire.

Time slowly disappeared. My mind rolled out like sheet metal back and forth upon itself to form a cylinder. I was a silvery sink faucet that had not been completely shut off. The slowly and gently rounding drops of water formed on the lip of a dripping bathroom faucet became a soft distraction whose plinking noise sought out my silent ears. The watery drips brought me slowly back to my senses. Something made sense to me for a moment. A long second passed before I gradually grew calm inside as order returned to the bedroom. Everything was different. I knew I would never get over this terrible feeling of nausea creeping up inside me like a silent disease. I just lay there without moving for a time. I tried to figure out where I was and what was happening to me, but it was useless to strive for understanding of the unknown darkness. The roar of the city with its pounding hammer noise, mill and tugboat whistles overtook my hearing. The screaming voices of lost people wandering about like fish in the ocean not far from my window went on of their own accord. Beneath the bedroom window there was a street sign advertising The NY Bar and Grill down in McKees

Rocks not far away. I heard working men talking about going there, then they decided on a beer garden that had a new young waitress. They wanted to go see her and then they would play poker. My head was an echo of every kind of hidden madness in the leaden city as I drifted in and out of sleep where steel encased every dream. To hide from all the city noise I buried my head in the pillow that was wet with cold iron tears.

My being in the world now seemed to me to be too much for me to comprehend. I had no idea of how I could deal with the loud and harsh free world outside. Reality moved so hurriedly toward me that there was a constant and insidious humming inside me. It had gotten lodged there during the last couple days of frantic city life. I knew now that it was too much for me to handle, but I didn't know what to do; the present had me locked-up in the iron, vice-like jaws of the past and the future and there was no way to escape. My thoughts drifted around a thing called tomorrow when I would become a laborer at the vast steel mill where railroad tracks wrapped around the earthen hills. They rose up from the world of all eternity. Within a few minutes, I was lost in a vision of a great steel gear; it wound me up and up into the air and then upon a rough, mechanical armature where I was a tiny strand of wire cable. As the cable wrapped about the armature tighter and tighter, I cringed ever more tightly into myself. Deep down within me I could feel the pounding of the mill—its was relentlessly hammering away at my life. Its pounding would make me thinner and thinner, and I knew that before long that the memories of the prison would be hammered away into a paper-thin sheet. Its terrible reality would be nothing more than a worn down faceless coin of an old memory. I would turn gray haired as the face on the silvery coin whose features faded into a blurry image that would be lost and gone and finally forgotten.

A PROVINCIAL POET

Looming up over the Ohio River on the watery edge of Pittsburgh is an enormous red building on which the yellow bricks are emblazoned with words resembling a Renaissance mosaic:

**Colligan Brothers Brick Works
~Established 1889~**

Less than a mile away the H.J. Heinz Company's many voluminous buildings tower over the Allegheny River on Pittsburgh's North Side. Nearby is the solemn and compact red box of a building on which is painted in tall block letters:

Pittsburgh Wool Company

All these factories were erected over a century ago using bricks produced by the Colligan Brothers. The legacy of these Pittsburgh families harkens back to the beginning of industrial Pittsburgh. The clay for these bricks was dug out of a rich clay vein from a hillside in Pittsburgh along the Monongahela River. The raw clay was then loaded onto long barges in mounds resembling the many surrounding hills of the city and floated downstream where its clumps were broken up, processed and shaped into bricks. Once these clay blocks reached the kilns, the bricks were baked overnight in immense fiery ovens blazing like smoky bonfires along the riverside.

The fires from the smoky kilns still illuminate the night; they have always been in smoldering competition with the city's steel mills. Their bright sunlit smoke, cinders and soot come down in grimy streaks upon the citizens of Pittsburgh as soon as it rains.

The source of this airy dirt is not far away; its origin can be found in the great steel mill furnaces in Homestead, McKeesport, Duquesne and Braddock along the Monongahela River. The firebrick inside these vast steel mills was manufactured by the Colligan Brickworks. Once the mills were busy producing molten steel these kilns were put to more ordinary work. It was within these beehive-like kilns that virtually a half of the city itself was built. These squat iron-reinforced kilns produced the bricks for thousands of row houses, hundreds of middle class homes and dozens of mansions throughout the city. The Colligan company now produces all the brick for the city's burgeoning and anonymous sterile suburbs, dull government housing, dreary high rises and the city's many uninspired and lifeless municipal buildings. As facts are the blocks of reality, so Pittsburgh itself is a city of brick houses, sidewalks, streets, avenues and thoroughfares. For over a century, virtually all of them have been manufactured by a family of poetic Irishmen whose fiery Catholicism was like the hot kilns of the company, the Colligan Brothers Brick Works.

All of the Colligans grew up loving the poetry of the nineteenth century. They brought this Irish tradition with them to America from the heart of County Cork. Along with poetry these Irishmen loved hard work, women, Irish whiskey and beer. America transformed their love of Ireland into a great affection for Pittsburgh once they settled into the business of brick making. During the last quarter of the nineteenth century, the firebrick used in Pittsburgh's great steel mills, situated along the Monongahela and Allegheny Rivers, soon hastened the local manufacture of house bricks by the Colligan Brick Company. Great grandfather Colligan began to manufacture house brick and before long his firm was the largest producer of bricks east of the Mississippi River. He wisely steered the company into the production of bricks just as the industrial capital was rapidly expanding at the turn of the century to fulfill its great destiny. Immigrants from all over Europe were coming to America to work in Pittsburgh's steel mills. Since the outlying mill towns around Pittsburgh needed brick for factories, schools and houses, the Colligan Brick Company supplied the regional need for brick, it was soon shipped throughout western Pennsylvania. With the wealth that came from this enterprise, the Colligan family moved into the fashionable Highland Park section of the city. Here they leisurely enjoyed Sunday afternoon excursions to the zoo, the city's reservoir and the ambling, urban paths located near their sprawling twenty-room mansion.

Two generations later, Charles Colligan III grew up loving silent movies, French novels and the eternal beauty of American poetry. The young Charles Colligan, named after his great grandfather and father was a large studious boy who loved to dream of faraway places. The first thirty years of his existence could be summarized as becoming a man who always kept promising himself that one day, he was going to become a poet and stroll along the magnificent boulevards of old Paris.

As a way of reminding himself he wore upon his right hand a gold ring with an ancient Greek coin that turned in Janus-face fashion. The one face was Apollo's, and the other had a calm and patient man sitting quietly in the bronzed solace of his eternal wisdom, Homer. Colligan used to tell his mother that this was his ideal poet. To him he owed all the beautiful allegiance that his poetry sought to comprehend. She smiled at this thought, and her heart was set forever upon her son's goodness and faith. She never worried about her little Charlie for she was comforted by a simple idea, 'What a good boy he was. He had been a fine baby, and with time he had become a fine man.' Her thoughts were always the same true thing, she knew that any boy who is good to his mother is a fine and noble thing on this earth.

The young Colligan often liked to tell his mother, "One day I am going to read all the books on Dad's bookshelves and know everything that is in them." His shy Slovenian mother smiled warmly upon him. She wished it were so, but she noticed a lazy streak in her son and this contradiction worried her. She said to her husband, "He is always planning, to do this and do that, and yet he cannot even look after his high school homework. It is never handed in on time because he has virtually no understanding of deadlines. School schedules mean nothing to him and his poetry everything."

Colligan was always telling his mother that by the time he was through college he would possess an understanding of men such as Plato and Aristotle, Flaubert and Maupassant, Dostoyevsky and Tolstoy and maybe even Gonchorav. "The year I graduate from college I will read a Balzac novel, for one of my classmates told me that his work is essential if you truly want to fall in love with Paris. Once I have mastered one of his books, I am going to travel to the city of light to see this great capital and all of its mysteries first hand. I will embrace the French soul and make it an integral part of my self." He looked at his mother with a great sincerity and then confidently announced, "If I read Balzac, I will be superbly prepared for the Paris of my dreams. Balzac will be my guide and my reference and from him I'll take my example." Colligan, however, never got any farther from Pittsburgh than the trucks that delivered the bricks from his father's grimy brick factory. His whole life seemed to be nothing more than solitary and poetic plans that never became more than a series of lost and idle illusions.

When Colligan went off to college, he detailed his travel plans to his many literary friends in Pittsburgh who were all devoted bibliophiles. They would smile at him, suspecting that he was no more likely to leave the city than he was to take over his father's brick factory. Colligan was a young idealist perennially engaged in literary and philosophical debates with his fellow man. He loved debating with a select few of his college friends, and they thrilled at witnessing his fiery wit. He was truly a fine, if rather shy, debater who mixed poetry and common sense together in a way they had never experienced before. It almost seemed to them that irony for him was a way of life.

*
* *

Now Pittsburgh is a very literary city that keeps its greatest secrets to itself. While some places boast of their achievements, Pittsburghers sit back comfortably paring their fingernails assured of their place in history. The city's great families and its diverse and ethnic citizens are never confused and yet, if it has ever known a debate, it is always the same one that has gone on for many decades. The controversy centers on what city neighborhood is the most literary. Citizens throughout the city are often divided on this issue, so there has never been any sort of agreement in over a century. Some say it is Highland Park, others say Lawrenceville, another claims Squirrel Hill and the three other groups who are always doing battle with the former ones are the Southsiders, the Northsiders and the people of Edgewood. Every year or two angry booklovers who once shared evenings of poetry readings, book reviews and short stories do battle arguing with one another at a local tavern called the NY Bar and Grill in McKees Rocks. The results of these debates have not varied for over half a century. Inevitably the Northside book club will not be speaking to the Squirrel Hill crowd of bibliophiles. The Southsiders, dominated mostly by old men from the Slovak Literary Society whose members are mostly retired policemen and schoolteachers, refuse to get along with the Lawrenceville book lovers. The Highland Park Book Readers Association simply bands its members together in stoic, stony-faced confinement if a worthy opponent is unwilling to admit its preeminence. Pittsburghers love their literary life and conduct it with an absolute fervor that no boring academic will ever fully appreciate. The book battles are venomous, long standing, stuffy and infinitely amusing to the outsider unfamiliar with the provincial opinions most city dwellers enjoy. Like provincials generally, Pittsburghers often seem utterly unaware of the outside world. Their literary life is their own, and no tourist or foreigner to the province can ever fully understand, appreciate or interfere with it.

The Mayor of Pittsburgh has occasionally sided with one book group over the other and alienated all the other neighborhood bibliophiles. Annually he submits a proclamation to city council, showering each neighborhood with a certain Book Day, but the day itself always ends up in an argument. The Lawrenceville group wanted to have the first book day last year, and they ended up second behind the Highland Park group. A scuffle in the city council chambers ensued, and the Southsiders got evicted while the Squirrel Hill group threatened a lawsuit. Since most of this group's members are lawyers, they are always trying to drum up additional business in spurious legal pursuits for some of their less than successful attorney-friends. Nobody ever seems to take their threats seriously. Pittsburgh suffers from these scholarly scuffles in the book trade to such an extent that antiquarian booksellers in the city occasionally refuse to let the members of the Southside group to enter their establishments until all the Squirrel Hillers or the Edgewood clan have left the store.

Boycotts of the second hand bookstores have now become a commonplace event in the literary life of Pittsburgh. The infinite book battles will probably never cease anytime soon. Recently, the Mayor published a statement that none of the neighborhoods would be given their own book day next year. His admonishment to the city's bibliophiles was printed in the afternoon edition of "The Pittsburgh Press" and read in part:

> *Since our dear learned librarians and book-loving friends in the city refuse to get along with one another, none of them will have their own book day. All must be punished because of a few trouble makers who are to blame. They have ruined it for all the city's bibliophiles, and I deeply regret that I have to take this action. It is necessary to prevent violence which I fear could happen at one of these annual book fairs.*

The spineless newspaper, unwilling to take sides for fear of losing readership, has been unwilling to intervene for one neighborhood over another. It has retreated to support the clever Mayor, who has said he will cut the city's schoolbook budget if the matter cannot be peacefully resolved. Amid all the literary hubub, the private libraries in the city flourish and the largest one is owned by the president of the Highland Park Book Lovers Association. He is a devout Roman Catholic; an Irishman named Mr. Charles Colligan II.

Anyone who knows Pittsburgh industry is familiar with the Colligan Brick Company on the Northside of the city that came into even greater prominence in the 1960s. When the Roman Catholic Church was building a series of new schools throughout the city, the Colligan Company supplied all the bricks for schools, rectories and playgrounds. Even the streets leading up to these institutions were made of brick, since Colligan Sr. not only had powerful friends in the Church but in the Mayor's office as well. Virtually every government building that went up in the twentieth century is made of Colligan Brick.

It was in the 1960s that Charles Colligan, III was born to Mr. Charles Colligan and his wife, Annie. The Colligans spoiled their little boy who, unlike his father, spoke clear, unaccented American English. The Colligan Irish brogue and his mother's Slovenian accent were lost on the young boy who humbly prided himself on being the center of attention in the family. Never having worked a day at the Colligan Brick Plant on the Northside, Charles Colligan Jr. became a bibliophile the likes of which Pittsburgh has never seen. He read both Latin and Greek and finished his undergraduate philosophy degree at Duquesne University, the city's premier Catholic college. He tried to learn something about speaking French by haphazardly skimming Balzac in the original. Poetic dreams flashed through his heart like scenes from a movie or pictures from a magazine. Charmed by the French language, a paper he wrote in 1980 was published in *Les Temps Moderne*. Local people who came from the poorer literary families liked to say that with this scholarly work, Mr. Colligan undertook his first and last effort to do anything with his own hands. His own mother used to tell the Bishop of Pittsburgh that, *If a thing is heavier than a fountain pen, my Charles won't lift it.* Old man Colligan constantly mulled over this stubborn fact which ended by giving him high blood pressure. Arguments with his son about the sloth that he had become meant nothing to his plump offspring.

There is always a chance that Charles, Jr. will awaken the city's literary spirit with some sort of poem, proclamation or pamphlet. Yet nobody knows why anyone should anticipate such a lazy man to produce anything worth reading. Pittsburghers to date have kept an attentive vigil in the Saturday issue of the *Pittsburgh Post Gazette* in anticipation of some poem worthy of their attention, but their hopes for over a decade have now fallen into nothing more than idle gossip. Rumors that Charles Colligan lives like most men—in a world of his own words, now circulate throughout the city. He is said to be working on a history of his father's brick business, and that it promises to be an important work. People in the book trade always chuckle knowingly when they hear this story. They have been hearing it for years, and as much as people may live in brick houses they rarely read books about brick making, "Brick-like poems fall awfully dull and hard upon gentle hearts yearning for literature. Such poesy deadens the senses and stifles the passions, it trips idly off the tongue into odd inflections. Their thoughts are so intricate and leaden that not even Sisyphus could move them more than a millimeter up the steep hill of human knowledge."

These wily Pittsburgh booksellers regularly tell their loyal clients that there is no market for a good book on brick manufacture or poesy, but the rumors and stories about Colligan and his upcoming treatise on bricks persist. Perhaps one day Charles Colligan Jr. will capture the hearts of the people of Pittsburgh by writing some new poems about his grandfather's and his father's brick works. The calm and patient and ever shy Charles, however, refuses to admit he is busy at work on anything whatsoever. He collects books by the hundreds and makes promises about nothing. Deep down he secretly confides to himself that eventually he will read Balzac and travel to Paris. Nothing much more is known about his dedication to this formidable literary task since he has avoided all the book stores in Pittsburgh for several years. The only other rumor is that Colligan sleeps so much that he has gotten to be called Rip Van Winkle by his neighbors in Highland Park. In twenty years when he wakes up from his poetic dreams all the world around him will have been changed by progress, which he will consider useless to his poetic soul.

What can be ascertained about Charles Colligan with any certainty is that sometime during his thirty-fifth year, he read America's most loved literary works and his head was completely occupied by the poetry of Walt Whitman and Emily Dickinson and the essays of R.W. Emerson. This literary experience had a profound effect upon his understanding of the world around him. For years he repeated to himself, "My soul selects its own society." And with these words Collgian began to winnow away who was important to his work and who was not. Only the vital ones would be included in his sphere of poetic influence. Every human being came under his scrutiny and his critical eye was ever awake to men and their flaws. His own father was its first subject.

Colligan newly observed the monstrous nature of his ambitious father and saw him in a hard, new light. At the brick factory the man was a skillful manager for whom language was a tool. His words ordered men around as though they were no more than ladders and hammers, buckets of nails or shovels of clay. Smart businessmen like the elder Colligan knew the ins and outs of getting things done and his words were purely utilitarian. His words made him money, and that was the only precious thing to him. The enormity of the brick mill captured the poet's aspirations in a way that couldn't be shaken off. Surely he could write poems on the ever expanding and fascinating world of bricks. What crazy dreamers poets are! They are completely taken up by the beauty and goodness of their words that they actually believe in the ultimate power of their truth. To them, reality is made up not of men and women but words, phrases and well turned thoughts. Words consume the poet in the same way that their moment on this earth is eaten up by the tiny grains of sand falling through the glassy funnel of an hourglass. To Colligan, each man was a clock who knew and understood a certain time. The poet ought to patiently understand the intricate gears working within them all. It was thus and only thus that he could truly come to show others a portrait of Pittsburgh, its three rivers and the mills and mining towns scattered about its landscape. Through the lies of literature he sought to learn the whole truth about the place.

The scrutiny of his father now became a part of this society he strove to collect within his soul. When his father asked him if he would like to work at the brick plant, Colligan's response was immediate; it sounded somewhat cowardly and mysterious but it was honest. "I could never work inside the vast caverns of brick, clay and kilns. The place is too immense. I would lose my way among the many paths and the alleyways between the kilns. The whole floating world of brick-making would collapse all around me in a ruin. It would crush me for sure." His father did not now comprehend his son one bit. "What did he mean by this?" he asked his wife who simply shrugged it off in defense. Mrs. Colligan came to the rescue of her son. She supported him more and more as he retreated to his dreary bedroom every evening after dinner to read about his immortal friends and their dusty books of American poetry.

A year and then two went by, and Colligan came to understand Walt Whitman to a certain degree. Within a few years, his whole existence revolved around poetry. His mornings were spent in reading. He enjoyed whole afternoons that were idled away in Highland Park where a reverie of couplets linked him to Nature, language and all of the seasons. He was a walking poet who lived among the grassy urban meadows. This was his life, and he drank it in leisurely as he lounged next to the maple trees reading dusty volumes of verse and the histories of his favorite poets.

The soft, quiet evenings slipped away in readings along the boulevards of the university. Charles walked home in the night in a soft ether and then became lost in dreamy comparisons. The night sky over Pittsburgh became a blaze of orange and yellow steam clouds above the steel mills. Colligan's musing went on uninterrupted amid the industrial whir of factories, rolling mills and tugboat whistles that echoed off their barges mounded with coal. When Colligan reached home he had to enter the house without waking his father, who now looked down with angry regret on his only son's self-consuming bibliomania. His mother, who worked as the brick company's bookkeeper, had secretly begun to save money for her only son.

The mansion where the Colligan's lived was in danger, and Mr. Colligan knew he had to do something about it. The floor of his private library was sinking under the weight of all of his son's books piled there. They reached up to the ceiling and the cleaning lady now refused to go into the library for fear that the walls or one of the tall piles of books would fall over on her. Mr. Colligan argued with his wife constantly about the fact that their house was crumbling. He had noticed cracks in the bricks on the exterior of the mansion and this worried him, "Ann, the whole house will fall down on us if we do not get the books out of the library. Charlie has them stacked so high that the walls are buckling. Go outside and look, the bricks over near the fireplace have hairline cracks. If the sagging floor gives way the whole damn room could implode and pull our bedroom upstairs with it, we could be killed." Mrs. Colligan was worried about it too, but she tried to remain impassive while her husband pleaded with her. "Ann, years ago my grandfather and my father both entertained the Chancellors of the University of Pittsburgh and the Carnegie Institute right here in our grand library. And look at it now, it's a dusty mess piled with books that are grinding our oriental carpets into paper thin sheets. The carpets are destroyed and utterly worthless. Just open the doors to the library and look at the mess your son has made of the room. There are stacks of boxes loaded down upon one another. It's out of control. Charlie's mad, and you refuse to say anything to him. Just go into the library and look at the bundles of newspapers, journals and magazines he's collecting. He goes to books sales and thinks nothing of spending $15-20,000! For God's sake Ann, it's out of hand. Something has to be done or he'll destroy our home. Your son has books and boxes piled all the way up to the ceiling, on top of furniture. Two library tables collapsed under the weight of books last week and the room is literally sinking under Charlie's bibliomania. He's a vain and selfish human being, a boy who we've both spoiled rotten. Something has to be done before our library is destroyed by Charlie's books, you're going to have to stop procrastinating and tell him. He's got to stop bringing books into the house. Before long his overfilled bookcases will be toppling all around us as the house collapses and the name of Colligan is dragged down with them and made into nothing more than mud."

Colligan's father now wanted his son to move out of the mansion, and he demanded immediate action from his wife who resisted. For a week he ranted and raved about his son's reckless spending, his laziness and his sickening affection of books. "I've had a good long talk with a few expensive psychiatrists in Pittsburgh, Chicago and New York and they all agree on one thing. Our son is suffering from bibliomania, his poetry is going to drive him to ruin and we might be swallowed up with him. He needs help and the doctors have all told me the same thing, he has to go into psychotherapy, and he'll probably have to be hospitalized. We have to do something now . . ."

Then his anger got the better of him, "He's thirty-four years old and he has never held a job in his life. He's never done an honest day's work, and unless we force him to carve out a life of his own he will be nothing more than a leech, a parasite, a rotten lazy loafer. After I paid $17,000 for his college tuition and his books and all of his credit card bills and his damn marble busts of Horace and Dante, he is ungrateful to me. He tells me I haven't done enough for him, and then he is sullenly self-possessed. He is a self-satisfied worm. He's nothing more than a parasite to me anymore. He's a hopelessly poetic and lazy man that I refuse to support any longer. Charlie can justify an idle lifestyle better than anyone I have ever met. He is drunk with his poems, biographies and histories of the perfect rhyming line. Something has got to be done; our Charlie has to wake up now. He had better get moving because he can't spend the rest of his life lounging around in his dumpy bed, sipping tea and dreaming about Longfellow. I swear to God that if I hear one more silly thing from Charlie's mouth about Walt Whitman, I will jump out of a window. All he talks about are poets, books and novelists. I have had enough of them. If I ever see this Balzac or his precious Henry Miller he's endlessly talking about, I will go out and strangle them with my bare hands. They're set on ruining me and don't think I don't know it now. They'll be dead forever if I ever find them snooping around here wanting to see Charlie, I'll kill them I tell you, I'll kill them."

Mr. Colligan went on a rampage and his wife listened to him in fear, "He's a madman I tell you. He spent over $880 last month alone at the University of Pittsburgh Book Center and when I asked him about it he shrugged carelessly, "Knowledge is more important than money," he said to me. He's insane! What goddamn poet put this crazy crap into his head?" My hard-earned money means absolutely nothing to him. It is no more than water or air and he's supposed to be supplied with whatever he wants for free! Well, not anymore, this is the end of him and his poetry. He has to leave, he's gotta go and that's that and you have to tell him." Mrs. Colligan's face was scared, her eyes began to tear. She was afraid for her son as his father stomped out of the house in a rage. "If I face Charlie I might lose my temper and strangle him right on the spot. I swear to God I might. If his grandfather were alive our little Charlie would have been dead by now because my father would have dragged his lazy ass over to the Highland Park Zoo and thrown him into a lion's cage. He'd have had to fight for his life and it would have been survival of the fittest . . ." The yelling had made his voice hoarse, as he marched around the mansion. When he recovered he sat down in the oak dining room and looked at his wife beseechingly. His eyes were pleading with her to do something. He tooks his wife's hand in his and explained what had to be done with their son. "We have to stop babying him, Ann. Now you tell him he's got to move out from under my roof. I've had enough of his poetic crap, him and his poetry have gotta go."

The old man had laid down a mandate. It was done; there would be no delays or second chances. This was it, the time for patience was over. He now stormed out of the house and went to the Long Vue Country Club. There he would drink away his terrible temper.

His worries chased him angrily about in money concerns since he had to finance a new kiln, and it wasn't going to look good if he was always dipping into the company's reserves. Their revenues seemed to be decreasing; something had to change. His mental state was starting to adversely effect his brick business and it wasn't his fault, it was a disaster. His only son was nothing but a profound disappointment to him. When was this boy going to grow up and become a man, go out into the world and become a productive citizen for once? The only thought he possessed of his son was graven on his mind; its image was a calm and patient head. The studious face hovered in his thoughts like a ghost, and it lived in a sickly chloroform of delusion that sapped him of money. Charlie's vague and aimless eyes always appeared to be wondering about what no one could even imagine, the kid spent over $44,000 last year on books, walnut bookshelves, literary conferences and meeting of the Modern Language Association. He took all his poetry friends who he sees only once a year out to dinner and it cost me $6,700! A first edition of Frost and Whittier cost me over $4,000.

Charlie is going through money and books like they were nothing and his mother won't say a word to him! "She defends him, she hides him away from me but I always get stuck with the bills. It's my money! Poetry is eating me up and it has to stop. It's given me high blood pressure and I wouldn't be surprised if its done real harm to my poor heart." With each scotch and water his son's eyes slowly dissolved into the glassy sheen on the ice cubes. They gradually melted away and were slowly drown by an angry procrastination where nothingness soon took over. When old man Colligan finally passed out, the bartender at the country club put him on a couch where he slept there through the night in front of an immense and blazing fireplace.

Mr. Colligan's return the next day put him not so much in his own home but in the oppressive confines of his son's apathetic laziness. He was infuriated by the smell of his son's Parisian cologne. Charlie used it liberally to cover his bad body odor. As a child he was found to be allergic to deodorant and so cologne took its place. A large bottle of it sat on his dresser. The father was furious every time he looked at it, the imported cologne said Paris and it cost over $1100! What his son needed was a good, long weekend with a bad woman, that would cure his stinking ass of all this poetry nonsense once and for all. "That silly prick needs to go out whoring for a few weeks. That would deplete all of his pent-up passion for poetry. He'd better start pining for something other than his goddamn dusty books. That's what he truly needs to do. What he really ought to work on is finding some woman to clean his pipes out for him for once in his life."

Old man Colligan was now angrier than when he had set out. His hasty threats of disowning Charlie hovered about the house like impudent credit card bills with finance charges that were overdue. Charlie had hidden the bills inside his poetry books for fear of turning them over to his father. The father looked at the bills and was furious at the charges:

Schoyer's Books	$1999
The Tucker's	$ 46
The Bookworm	$ 30

"Why did I have to bring a poet into the world?" he asked his wife pointedly. She never had an answer. Who can say what men will be when they grow up? This thought was always in her mind, and she could never chase it away. She continually fretted about it. Colligan's worried but resolute mother was now compelled to take her son's survival upon herself; she had to do something to save the boy from his father. Within the next month she began to surreptitiously remove money from the brick business every week; she placed it into a bank account for her poetic son.

For the next few months, Colligan's mother took larger envelopes of money out of the company at night and deposited them into a bank account in her son's name. The profits of the brick company sank, and the old man never wondered why.

His own wife was helping to make his brick company struggle under more debt. Expenses were growing, and there was never an end to the bills. His wife was a trusted ally who now was forced to look after her only son, the only true joy of her harried life. She shared the plan with Colligan so that peace and quiet could be maintained in their Highland Park home. "You will soon have to get an apartment on your own, Charles. Your father wants you out of the house for good, and he won't wait. Now, I have put away some money, and it should supply you with all your necessities. Perhaps you could go back to college down at Duquesne and learn how to be a pharmacist or a poetry teacher."

Colligan for once in his life almost flew into a temper about his 'going back to college' but his inertia was too great. He just sat there patiently listening to his mother but the idea was absolutely ridiculous. He would never do anything to hurt her, but this idea of going back to the university was foolish. He had completed almost a half semester of graduate school but it hadn't worked out. He was utterly bored by the stupid professors. He harped on them to his mother when he returned home from his evening classes, "Their wormy and maggot-laden heads are bricked up against common sense, their lives are self-styled escapades in flummery. As soon as they get tenure they are smiling at themselves. Their seniority is a monument to their self-styled stupidity; and the longer they're in the university, the more foolish and cutthroat they become. The pedantic scholars among them are like lazy waiters in out of the way restaurants on back country roads, they are forever sweeping up crumbs from the table of Literature."

His mother thought her Charlie hard-hearted and even merciless at times, and she complained to her mother. "This attitude he has inherited from his Irish father; the Slovenians are a mild-mannered people. And his sort of tough talk is very surprising to me. My Charles is such a kindly man; he would never say anything to hurt anyone. I must tell him he should think about pharmacy.

Everyone knows that sick people will always need pills. He could do that and then write poetry in his spare time or on week-ends." Then her thoughts were distracted. She forever wondered about the word flummery and whether it was really and truly a word. She worried terribly about her son and his solemn, self-possessed and often stubborn disposition.

The sad eyes of Charles Colligan Jr. grew sadder and more serious and then became weary with all his worries about what was going to happen to him. His soft, heavy belly sagged like a sooty bag of coal under the weight of this trial of having to move away from home. He faced the prospect humbly without much courage. He had anticipated this ominous moving day for many years and hoped that it could be delayed. But the time had finally come. His father would not wait, and the word of the father was, as it is with all good fathers, an absolute. It was set upon his brow that was now wrinkled with worry. He was sure he would never conquer his poetry inside the confines of a drafty apartment building whose noisy tenants were sure to distract him from his meditations.

With his mother's help Colligan rented a cheap one-bedroom apartment on a back street in the Shadyside district. A French bistro was nearby if he needed food. La Charcuterie became his new hang out, and he carried packages away from the store in small paper mounds, each sandwich and salad wrapped like a precious jewel that soon would be consumed. Now and then Colligan promised himself that he would one day sit out at the cafe tables, sip wine and scribble poems in the hot summer sun. For the moment this dream was forgotten when the movers came to transport his bed. His bookshelves and the thousands of dusty books he had accumulated were hoarded in the same way a miser hides money. Books were under the bed, in his clothes closet, in wooden cabinets, on tables, chairs and even in his private bathroom. The texts were retrieved from their hiding places and put into boxes and taken for a ride down Highland Avenue where they were deposited in another place in a nameless alley behind Ellsworth Avenue.

The small old wood-paneled apartment was a fraction of the size of his bedroom suite at home but Colligan decided that it was for the best. His cranky father had grown increasingly dour and silently unhappy about his son; their existence together was one of mutual evasion. With little human interaction the young man became a recluse. His mother said he was drying up inside. She cried on the phone to her ninety-year old mother out in McKeesport, "He is sick in the head. All of his life is devoted to words. He lives only for poetry, ballads and the silly rhyming of a line. Sonnets mean more to him than the daily newspaper, he has utterly no idea about the world at large . . . Nobody can understand the life of a mother who gives birth to such a poet . . . I tell you this . . . it is a living hell." Colligan's wily maternal grandmother immediately took action; she went off to church that very day and lit a candle for the salvation of his soul. When she left the altar of catholic piety in which she was raised like a nun, she knew one prayer that was going to consume her and her daughter's intentions for the rest of their days; hope for the best but expect the worst.

The whole of Colligan's being appeared like granite; inert and immovable and upon it was inscribed the holiest words of the Almighty. From the God of the Bible he drew his poetic sediment, it appeared in the engravings of his steel pen. Long lines of rhyming wonder were whittled away, the world was writ larger than life in his mute poems. His blood flowed like ink from his black steel pen. It went this way and that and ever in a circuit. Harmony and balance directed his every move. Poems and words were his haven, his heaven; his Eden secluded away from the harsh realities of Pittsburgh. They fed him, nourished him and kept his heart alive. In the midst of the dead authors hidden inside a thousand dust covers, bindings and books he drew life. It washed over him and he fumbled with his dreamy love of the literature of the past, present and future. Then the future took a hold of him, and he formulated a plan which was gradually put into place.

Over the course of the next year he saved up enough money to have two volumes of his own poetry printed for his own private consumption. The poems were like water bottled up inside of him. Slowly a little bit of it was sipped carefully by his spirit and it then seeped ever so gradually back into his life. Colligan walked carefully and almost courageously along the avenues and the sidestreets, back alleys and boulevards of Pittsburgh. Lodged safely under his thick arm was the hardback volume of poems. He held onto it tightly as though it contained the whole of his dry existence. He wrote notes to his mother that always concluded with the same thoughtful line, "I am my poems."

Mrs. Colligan grew increasingly concerned about her son. She worried about him constantly; this to her was a mother's duty. She knew that, in the fashion of many fine men, her boy was an eccentric Irishman at heart, and nothing would ever change him. He loved his Joycean reveries every June 16. He read about them in the only newspaper that he bought once a year. On this one day of the year he would commit himself to complete silence and say to himself thoughtfully, "James Joyce . . . even the name of the man rings like sweet music upon the ear." Slowly and carefully chosen words became the soft and quiet bible of his dusty soul. Colligan walked about the city like a man on a silent mission of Poetry. He carried his brown and weathered volume of poems wreathed in laurels with him throughout the summer and autumn. He read from it continuously and reflected upon its words on secluded park benches. He huddled under bridges or in the darkened and recessed corners of the Cathedral of Learning where the students and the people driving by in cars could never see him. In winter, the volume of poetry was so worn out that the binding came off. Colligan buried it in the back yard with a shovel. A multitude of prayer-like poems followed, and the text was soon covered by a large, red brick paving stone. It sat upon the mounded earth like a thick tomb where the poems were sent off to rest forever in the cold and merciless ground.

He took out another of the volumes and proceeded to carry it with him anew; it was his source of self-reference. Refreshed and revitalized by reading his slim volume of poetry, Colligan now began another phase of his literary life where the previous poems had left off. He nestled the precious text under his flabby arm, feeling calm and secure in his knowledge that was always ready to hand. His whole being resembled the precious book itself, and it was stitched together like a sausage or a shoe. It gave him a calm and lasting sense of comfort; in it he found consolation. A spirit of self-hood resonated in his heart that was soon turned into more and more poems. They ran about his apartment like little brown mice and hasty cockroaches.

*

* *

The eternal fascination of the female form forever eluded Colligan; the feel of a fertile passion fell in dust balls about his tomblike bedroom. Its dull heavy furniture was handed down to him in Victorian splendor; his grandfather had slept in his bed. His father had been born in this bed and so too had Colligan. This bed had been the beginning of his life, and now it took on an even greater role. He slept in it for sixteen hours a day and even longer on the weekends; it was his comfortable home away from home. Women would never soil it with their perfume, their hair curlers and their rabbit-like lovemaking. It seemed it was made to sag solely under his heavy bulk. Colligan had utterly no interest in the charming beauty and the spiritual wonder of smiling women; their slender figures were a mystery to his obesity. Men were but shadowy stick-like beings in his corpulent thoughts.

By the time he was thirty-five years old, Colligan had spoken directly to fewer than a dozen of his own gender and even less of the other one. Hermetic and self-contained, he lived out his life in a purely literary way that few men are privileged to enjoy. It could be learned from his poetry that he liked to sit and read hour after hour in the Carnegic Library of Pittsburgh. Its long marble hallways echoed with Colligan's pacing as he slid along the open stacks like a curious beetle. He moved gradually behind the tables and slumbered silently in the library's comfortable reading chairs. He knew them all intimately and had given each a name. The wing chairs were Frost and Longfellow and the austere leather lounge chair was called Whitman. Within it he found a little bit of his soul awakened over and over. The librarians were much amused by this man about whom they knew one thing for sure—Colligan was a man of his own mind's making. He was a singular sleepy being whom the genteel library staff always woke gently at the end of the evening.

Closing time at the great main library in Pittsburgh's Oakland section put him out onto the street. The autumn leaves swirled about him like disciples in the bright, harsh streetlights of Forbes Avenue. All the world flowed dreamily out from him as he climbed the steps and stairways of the university's immense gothic skyscraper, the Cathedral of Learning. It loomed high and mighty into the sky over Pittsburgh and served as a beacon to the ignorant and the confused. It silently announced with its august presence, 'Here is Knowledge.' Pittsburghers revered it and Colligan often mused to himself that its foundation was built upon his grandfather's and his own father's industry. Even the great cathedral's basement was lined with Colligan brick and tile. Colligan often thought to himself, "I and my people and their abiding brickwork are to be found everywhere in this great city." He comforted himself with the thought that T.S. Elliot had emerged from a family of St. Louis brick makers, and he relished this thought as though it were a pure, poetic truth to which he alone was now cemented and forever linked.

Colligan's volume of poems and his small and certain steps made their revolutions about the vast gothic cathedral whose medieval interior was a refuge of warmth amid the impending winter snow. Colligan's favorite corner was habitually sought out. It always offered solace for his tired, greasy head that dreamed of making a pillow of his winter jacket. He often dozed in this one snug corner, his volume of poems tightly pulled to his side as though it held all the secrets of his poetically stubborn heart.

In the morning he would wake before the students arrived for lessons. He walked gingerly out of the massive cathedral and wandered home. As he drifted casually down Fifth Avenue, the mansions of the steel magnates rose up before him. He paused and became curious about the great steel mills. His spine stiffened as though braced by an iron rod. As Colligan walked on he told himself, "I am a poem rolled out like a piece of steel." As he headed home he went dreamily along the avenues, boulevards and shady lanes in the form of a dead soul wandering among the great steel mills as they crumbled into rusty-hearthed nothingness. He might eat a boiled egg and a sandwich at a sidewalk cafe in Shadyside and then take a nap on his couch.

Late in the afternoon when most of the city was sitting down to dinner, Colligan was like his hero Balzac—wide awake and getting briskly out of bed, washing up and dressing in his perennially wrinkled corduroy pants and shirt. These were his favorite clothes, and his favorite clothes never changed. They were a uniform, a badge, an act of courage against the cold, wintry winds of Pittsburgh. In summer he wore the same corduroy and the people who saw him on the street always wondered about him. They were headed home from work at the end of the day, and they saw Colligan walking down the street in his corduroy. He was going in the opposite direction with poetic determination, Poetry was emblazoned on his sweaty brow. His whole spirit spoke to them, here was a man going off to work on his poems. Soon he was making his way toward his writing desk in the dusty back rooms of the Carnegie Library. The map of Colligan's limited world never varied. Mostly he went out of his apartment, down Highland Avenue to Fifth Avenue where he proceeded to the great library. The path was reversed when he headed home in the morning. This, then, became his habit, his routine, his being in the world of Pittsburgh.

When the librarians started to miss him it was for a reason; the man and his poems were made invisible by his absence from the library. The poetic man who lived in a cocoon of the library staff's constant attention had retreated to his sick bed, from which he could not readily escape. Colligan reasoned that he had been taken over by the syrupy slowness of a certain kind of poetry from which he could not emerge. If the world of Nature tells a story with every infection, then Charles Colligan was experiencing it anew. He was in a warm wet fog where he copiously sweated, ached and was miserable for over a week.

The great sweaty heap of a man had come down with a fever. He then suffered relentlessly from fever and chills; they dominated his whole routine. He couldn't think, read, eat or function in any capacity. All the poetry from his happy heart had been stolen by sickness, which he failed to understand. His sick fingers paged through a sheaf of his poems with an apathetic dullness. Poetry suddenly meant nothing to him. The noisy world existed only to amplify his condition, he was now truly heartsick. Colligan wandered down the short wood-paneled halls of his apartment like an oily worm plodding through earthen tree roots; his hands gingerly balanced him against the walls. He steadied himself against their flimsy mass whenever he trudged to the kitchen, the bathroom or the front living room to warm himself in front of the carved wooden fireplace.

After a few days, he had finished all the food he had stored up in his kitchen. Now Colligan was confused about what he should do. The fever made him delirious. He often thought he heard a ringing in his ears. Then it would go away and the fever returned. He was confused by the sound of bells. Anxious thoughts about his unfinished poems continuously punished him, he had to complete them before he died. Colligan was tortured with worry, he lost weight and the sheets of his bed were so wet from his sweating that he took refuge on the couch in the front room. Colligan was logical for once when he figured out that he had to do this so as to let his bedroom dry out. His immense form flowed listlessly about the rooms in need of help, but there was none to be found, his condition grew ever worse.

Then the ringing in his ears was finally solved; it was the telephone. He picked it up late one snowy afternoon when the sun was pouring into his bedroom like yellow honey. He spoke into the telephone slowly and cautiously. His mother's voice was frantic, she said she was coming over to visit him. When she arrived her heart was nearly broken because her precious boy was in a state of utter exhaustion. Colligan promised her he would do anything she asked of him as long as she helped him out of the misery in which he fell deeper with every passing day.

Mrs. Colligan looked at her son and saw that her little boy was a man whose corpulent laziness had become a pathetic sight. "How long have you been ill in bed like this?" She said testily; she was now furious and raging inside with fear for her son. Colligan responded slowly with no real assurance, "Maybe it's been a week or a month. I don't know . . . I've been too sick to look at a calendar." His voice dribbled off into confusion; his sappy eyes were tearful and sad. His bald head, neck and shoulders were covered with boils that needed to be lanced. When he coughed a dull watery fluid that smelled bad was deposited in his mouth. It glistened in the handkerchiefs and tissues strewn about his bed. Mrs. Colligan's heart was rent. Her frustration was needling her again but she now resolved to do something.

She hastily brought in a doctor who spent the whole afternoon bringing her poor, sick son back to life. Pills, vitamins and bottles of seltzer were sent for. A stomach pump from a hospital was delivered to the apartment. Colligan suffered into the night with sweating and fevers—his hands were cold and then hot. His chest ached with raspiness, and he weakly took slow, unsteady breaths that tortured his expectant mother to no end. The pastor from St. Benedict's Church was summoned from the North Side. One of the neighbors in the apartment had called upon him to offer Colligan the last rites. Mrs. Colligan was now worried. She didn't have any money to give the priest; she had spent most of it on orders from the doctor. As the patient lay in bed looking up helplessly at the physician and the priest babbling Latin prayers, Mrs. Colligan went to East Liberty and fetched medicine, blankets and food. Late in the evening she began making soup for her little Charlie, telephoning her mother and praying the rosary.

She went home late and came back early the next day and not for one minute did she stop worrying. She had a certain dignified look when she was serious, and Mrs. Colligan was now in her element; crises brought out the best in her. She loved a catastrophe—its mad chaos, the rapid-fire action and willful dispatch it demanded made her feel so alive. All women are the leaders of a family when their husbands don't get in the way. Mrs. Colligan knew this, but now she was terrified. She paced the room and fell into despair as her courage weakened; she delivered a strong reprimand to her son. Her voice was punctuated with tears as she told him that she had had enough, "If I were to tell your father about how I found you yesterday his face would get as red as the bricks he makes. He would hold me responsible for all you've become. He has always said I was too soft on you, and now I know he was right. You are on your last leg now; there is not going to be a second chance. You need to get a steady job like the doctor instructed. He scolded me for being so damn easy on you all the time. He said that unless you found a worthwhile occupation you'd be dead in a couple of months."

This sudden hard news struck the poet cold. It was doubly troubling for Colligan to hear this directly from his benevolent mother; she never lied to him. He listened intently and fell speechless; he was recoiling from the shock of the news. It was serious. He had to stop himself from falling further into the abyss. Certain facts took hold of Colligan in an unseen and mysterious way. They began to penetrate his dull and apathetic will. He looked off into the flow of traffic coming up Ellsworth Avenue and tried to figure out what words and poems really

HELL IS OTHER PEOPLE

meant. Everything drifted randomly about him. In a moment his thoughts were following a bus; they dissolved in the plume of lingering black smoke from the exhaust. He got a blanket from a nearby chair and he returned with it to his soft-cushioned couch to doze as his mother went off to the kitchen to clean up a mess of dirty dishes.

A few minutes later Colligan's mother was sure that she heard her son get out his toolbox to begin sawing logs in front of the living room fireplace. Sick men are always doing ridiculous things and now her Charlie was headed in exactly this direction. She had always told him that sawing wood had to be done outside, but he was taking the easiest way out again. He was stubbornly determined to do it inside the apartment. Mrs. Colligan stormed back to the front room to tell her son to stop sawing logs, "He's sure to get sawdust everywhere," she said to herself angrily as she stomped down the hall to the living room. The scene was a surprise. What she thought was the sound of sawing logs was her son snoring on the couch. Her face went red with anger as she yelled at him, "Get up, get up off the couch this very minute." She was utterly exasperated with her lifeless son. "I want you up and walking around and no more poetry and dreaming about Paris. I don't ever want you to tell me about how you are going to haunt the cracked and moldy streets of Paris ever again. I won't have it. This family has worked too hard to support you. Now you have to go out and get a job." Like a dutiful son Colligan sleepily rose up from the couch in a kind of dopey daze that was as gradual and lazy as it was labored. He now had to do something as a gesture to let her know that he would try to cooperate. He loved her and yet was completely forlorn about exactly what it was going to take to make her happy with him.

Colligan placed his hand on the volume of English poetry before him set on the coffee table. He gradually found his way over to the fireplace. It was now blazing; it warmed his leg, and he watched the bark on the logs slowly peel away in the fire and then gently burn up into gray ashes. Hesitation had hold of his arm as he offered the book up to the flames; he looked down as the yellowy pages were consumed by the fire. "If my old, dried-out life could be so easily done away with and begun anew," he mused weakly to himself.

Apathy consumed him. His mother was pleased but only for the moment. The sole purpose of his action was simply to appease her. "That is the trouble with you, Charles, you have taken up the wrong things in your life, and now you must make a fresh beginning. Because if you don't, you and your poetry will just end up dying in a damp and messy apartment with mice in the cupboards." Colligan's dreary face turned as white as marble when these words stormed from his mother's fearful mouth, "Unless you look after your life as though it was as precious as your poems, you will never make it through the year. When the doctor and I were out in the vestibule talking about you, he told me that he had never seen a case as serious as yours in such a young man. You should be dead; if it wasn't for me you would be in the cemetery by now." Colligan now shook with fear; his hands were trembling as he reached out for a glass of water to swallow down his pills as his mother went on, "Now we have to get you better. I will help you find your way, and your father will one day be proud of you, I promise you that. He will be as delighted about you as a man as he was the day you were born." Colligan sighed to himself for this was a troubling thought that he turned over in his tired mind. The sound of his mother's resolve decided him. It placed him on the path of survival as he mused to himself upon a certain poem of Kipling, "If . . ."

Within a week Colligan was looking as though he might make a full recovery. His hair was a clean, shiny red; and his teeth had lost their green tint. He had taken a real pleasure in flossing them and keeping them spotless. Floss was to him now a string of poems flowing between the pearls of his whitened teeth. He told his mother this, and she scowled at him furiously as he laughed light heartedly for the first time in months. Mrs. Colligan had to take immediate action before her son capriciously decided against changing his habits, his poetry reading, the very foundation of his miserable existence.

She intervened by finding a Greek woman on Highland Avenue who owned a dry cleaning business. The woman needed a presser to help her press suits, shirts, pants and women's blouses. Colligan was recruited for the job and began work the next week. His mother explained to him that unless he performed this job well he would never receive another dollar from her. The money supply was now cut off until he made good on his promise of getting himself together. Colligan reluctantly assented; he smiled slowly but agreeably and hoped for the best. Within a week a truly happy expression found itself on his face for Colligan welcomed the abrupt change in his tired routine. He readily took to the work and he made a good impression on the stern owner of the store.

Colligan cleverly found a way to work at his pressing job and keep to his old habits. A new man was already being dug out of the earth like clay and fired into a solid brick of a poet he never knew existed. Since the apartment was not far away, he could walk to work. He began to relish this morning movement among the people and the cars. The traffic flow sent his heart beating faster and more vigorously. After a few months the brisk morning exercise improved his physique and he felt livelier. His life had really changed for the better.

Colligan worked steadily at the steamy press as though it was a form of poetry. Each shirt left his ironing board with crisp lines and pleats where every button was a period upon which he paused to think about his poems for a moment. Colligan was a tireless editor of wrinkles who went avidly to work on them at the steam presser. His immense poetic enthusiasm was now moving ever more quickly and surely about the tiny wooden shop on Highland Avenue. Just up the street was the Highland Park Reservoir; several jaunty revolutions around it at sunset sent him home happy, healthy and more self assured than he had ever been. When he walked into the shop the next day, he was clear headed from a full night of solid sleep. Colligan now worked all day long and tirelessly into the evening. Buses full of office workers went past the dry cleaner's steamy front window; they wondered about who this stout happy man was for his big Irish smile was a pleasure to behold.

On Saturdays he made change and sometimes joked with the customers. At break time he retreated to a corner to read his loose sheaves of poetry. Now and then he recited them to store patrons. At the end of the day, bibliophiles from Squirrel Hill, North Side and Highland Park brought their dry cleaning to the Greek woman's store. They congregated before the long dry cleaning counter where Colligan stood on a chair with his thin volume of poetry. The continuous swooshing steam from the presser in the humid back room created an industrial-like accompaniment for his "Poems from the Ancient City of Iron and Steel." Even the Greek woman began to listen to the poet's imagery. His soaring illusions, his heart-stopping poetic tales of lost love among the coal mines, railroads and steel mills filled her with wonder. She was genuinely intrigued by her ambitious presser, he had suddenly grown charming. Colligan's thoughts and words of poetry slowly settled in the minds of his listeners. In less than six months his poetry had won over a sturdy woman's heart. Colligan and the owner began living together. Ms. Thumos was in her forties, and she carefully looked after him. Before a year went by his weight had dropped from over 240 pounds to 195. He stood taller without his paunch, and he was more confident behind the dry cleaner's counter. People saw something different in him and his new Greek love songs. It was clear the pair was destined for happiness. Every morning she arrived at the shop worn out from a night of love, and Charlie was silently satisfied. His father found out and came into the store to congratulate him. He took his son out for a beer and they talked about women, sex and the great oyster of the world that is love. The two of them walked along Highland Avenue like two proud spirits awash in the spirit of a new-found friendship. Father and son became one dialogue, an animated series of sparkling stories about the importance of words, poetry and the brimming vitality of sex in world literature. They talked for hours about the wisdom of a wonderful wild romp in the hay on a long and wintry Sunday afternoon, in front of a blazing fire inside an old Pittsburgh mansion.

When the young Colligan got back to the dry cleaners, his face was something wonderful and alive. The cold winter air and the thrill of being with his father had recharged him; his father's love sent him swimming free in a sea of true self-affection. He was the prodigal son that had come home from a wasteland of excess, of drunken reverie and dry, lifeless poetry. He had been a sparse entity, an island; he was a living and breathing paradise lost, and now it was a paradise regained. It was in him brimming, swirling, spinning away within him. This was an Eden fresh and wholesome. Its glorious emotion was now unencumbered by fear and jealousy, meanness and bad poetry born of too little sense. This was the winey new poetry of Whitman and Henry Miller, and it was gloriously at work. It roiled up inside the poet of life and his head was now fresh. He was a man whose humble lips sang out in harmony, "Look at me, I'm in love. All women are beautiful, they shear the wolves who are as foolish as sheep."

Colligan charged behind the dry cleaner's counter and said to his dear and loving Helen, "You are the Greek goddess looking over my little love life." The Greek woman stood over him and took him in her arms. She was taller by a foot and she poured her tongue down into his mouth. It lived there for a while squirming for the grip of his delicious teeth. A long wet kiss ensued and then it consumed them. The tongue of the woman lounged on the teeth of the man and soon she was on her knees. Her teeth went down on his throbbing love. When she freed it they laughed gloriously aloud among their love-looks. Their winking took over and they nibbled at one another and the morning turned into afternoon. Then she whispered long and lovingly to him, "I am your woman and your Venus."

They hugged and laughed and chased one another amorously around the dry cleaners. Their feet roared around the wooden counter and then among the plastic-wrapped coated suits, dresses and fur coats. Their work on the wrinkles and lost buttons, torn sweaters and hemmed skirts was forgotten in a thousand kisses and cooings, pinches and hand holdings, glances and self-styled expressions of love. Then they locked the door and rubbed against one another for over an hour. Their romantic spirits drew them off alone into their own little world not far away from the dry cleaners steam compressor. City buses pulled past them on Penn Avenue and they never noticed them. Their hearts were at work. It was the work that had been delayed for too long for both of them. Love was the most serious of work, and it could never give way to the trivial, mundane and the monotonous side of life. They toiled among the hangers in the back room of love, and their kisses were a series of old sales receipts that would never be lost in the dusty corners of life. Their lives flowed together among the books of poetry that were piling up inside the steamy front window of the busy dry cleaners. It grew crowded with more people and books everyday. Whitman was there and they read him aloud deliciously as they sang the body electric. Their hearts sang out to one another in a thousand new and sparkling ways. The light from their smiles was given off and it soon was taken up and passed on, one to the other and then onto the next. Customers would visit the store and leave, joyous and enthusiastic about the wonder of their young love! They were busy at work and it was not meant for a stuffy old museum. Their hearts brimmed with the art that was the poetry of their lives.

 The ever battling and mulish bibliophiles throughout Pittsburgh slowly came to realize that one of the most forlorn and faithful members of their troupe had now been unearthed like a bit of clay, molded into new brick and cemented like a man in a place that was secure. Colligan heaped praises upon them, and he explained himself in a new volume of poetry that he dedicated to his Grecian goddess. He sang poetry to Apollo, Dionysus and Athena, and no one would ever be so full of poesy as this Pittsburgh poet would. Fresh from the press his slim book of rhyming and words listed the many trials and hidden beauties of his life.

Colligan discussed the wild laughter of librarians and the wretched loneliness of lawyers that he had suffered over the years in his little bit of Pittsburgh, on its streets, in its bars and in the swirling throb of its Shadyside cafes. The poet beamed and his love gushed for his dearest in new poetry. Its opening epigram told the whole truth about the past, present and future of his existence:

> We are thrown into the world and we then throw ourselves into our Art.

These thoughts pounded the great anvil of his heart like mighty, iron hammers. All his days and nights were rugged hammer blows on the chisel of his steel pen; his scribbling never ceased. Along with his great Grecian love, his poems spoke of the furious glory of the great steel mills along the rivers, their soft steamy beauty echoed off the brick rowhouses in McKeesport, Duquesne, Clairton, Braddock and Homestead. Gradually, silently and mysteriously the bibliophiles gave up their hard-hearted and divisive words once they understood the truths he had rendered on behalf of the brick city, its hardened citizens, the rough hewn hearts and faces of the many mill towns' downtrodden. The accusations and literary jealousies that spoiled the city's perfect and silent peace disappeared from the chaotic community of their false lives. Their hypocrisy faded like the dry print of cheap paperbacks and then died off for lack of attention.

*

* *

Inside the shabby, wood-floored dry cleaners every Saturday morning Colligan makes a pulpit of a sturdy wooden chair. As he mounts it his feet stand upon the seat and his sweating head peers out like a gentle megaphone addressing customers and bibliophiles gathered around him. The poetic faithful gather to mouth and fondle his poems like favorite words. Poets lounge about as in ancient times. A dozen or so of them are always in attendance. They raptly stare at his solemness; ever searching for the truth in his eyes. It never fails them as he announces, "Every true poet is eternal and Homeric. We must carry on in his tradition as though his Grecian wisdom were our own. We must make Homer's city right here within our hearts." Colligan's silence then fills the room and his weary poetic face looks hopelessly out among the eternity of curious faces. He is truly an oddity no one really understands. His sanity belongs to those whose dusty wonder is piled up on book shelves throughout Pittsburgh's many private and public libraries.

Now and then Colligan's gray-haired father drops by and makes a seat of a bundle of dirty clothes thrown into a corner. He looks up and his Notre Dame sweatshirt is proudly worn like a vain banner. The father marvels at the blossoming spirit of his greathearted son. The strong, young voice of his only offspring swirls about the steam and swooshing of the dry cleaning presses. Thoughts of Grandfather Colligan collect within him as he dwells upon the wisdom of his vast industrial experience down among the clay pits, the barges, the kilns and the brick stock yard. It is destined to be inherited by Charles Colligan III who will hire managers to run it for him and turn over piles of money to be deposited into his account at the Pittsburgh National Bank. The father is happy; he has always loved and enjoyed his son's love for he has never tired of their beautiful walks along the reservoir or their being together and singing the praises of Yeats, Joyce and Beckett. These poets have woven their lives together and made them who they are. They are in a sense, father and son poets, mirror images of one another who will never stop loving what they see in the other. Theirs is a fiery affection, a brick-like love that nobody will ever fully understand. It is the beer and the whiskey of their crazy world they have struggled to hold together for a while, for life never changes, as Grandfather Colligan always used to say. Colligan often says that each of us makes the world over in our own certain fashion, and that no two bricks are exactly alike. Like snowflakes or poems each is unique and beautiful.

Pittsburgh's bibliophiles all talk about the latest rumor. The poet and the Greek woman have decided to spend a month in Paris once another tough snowy Pittsburgh winter is over and done with. Virtually all of the bibliophiles across the city are now able to see that Colligan's whole life seems to be a dreamy poem of sorts. It is completely his own and nobody really understands it. The youthful lines of Colligan's poetry are mined like coal from his life and fired in the smithy of his vast soul. The poems are iron-hard and strong as steel and they are known and appreciated for the truth they contain. What they lack in polish and workmanship they make up for in worldly wisdom. The friendly and yet ever shy and somewhat uncertain Colligan is anything but professional. He is an amateur forever sweeping up the crumbs from the white, pristine tablecloth that is Literature. His is an ideal world only he can understand. Like his poetry it is a bit of an enigma shared with others once a week. He always ends his Saturday morning poetry readings by concluding with the same sentiment from his first and favorite poem, "My father built this city of brick and called it home. I will cement my words together and live them out like a poem."

As the people trudge out the door of the dry cleaners words of good cheer are exchanged. The manly comments and whiney woman chatter takes off into the frigid air and evaporates like their steamy breath. Hearty laughter takes hold of them and warms the winter morning. A fresh new day is at hand and a dozen hearts sing out the same cheery song, "Colligan! What a beautiful poem he is! What a man! Thank God for Colligan! We love you, Colligan! We love you! We love your Poems!" Their voices chime in unison as their feet hit the silence of the snowy pavement. Off in the distance of East Liberty is the Tallest Tomb rising up into the sky.

Among the band of poets, a tiny masculine voice set out to prove a point with the rumors he'd heard. Among the motley crowd he now captured the attention of all as he spoke of a secret. "A friend of mine who used to make deliveries for Schoyer's Books told me he carted over 2000 pounds of poetry, history and literature to old man Colligan's private library one afternoon a couple of years ago. The Library floor was sagging in the middle and the plaster walls were cracking in such a way that even the ceiling looked as though it might come down. The oak mantle was buckling under the weight of all the books that were piled up on it. They were in stacks that reached the ceiling, and you couldn't even see the two dusty portraits hanging over the fireplace. This guy told me that old man Colligan was a bibliomaniac who spent $5,000-10,000 a month making book purchases from all over. He told me that Colligan's son just signed the delivery receipt and said to him, "Just tell the folks over at Schoyer's my dad will send payment over in the morning, even if I have to take it over to them." Now that just shows you how a dedicated poet like Colligan really is. He wasn't even concerned that his dad was suffering from that dreadful sickness that is book collecting. He just let the guy go hoarding whatever texts he wanted for his collection. I mean it takes real love for a son to put up with a crazy father like that whose insatiable book collecting could have destroyed the very house they were living in. Now that is a committed poet and I think it's proof of Colligan's poetic nature too." The crowd was very impressed, and they now decided to share more of their thoughts with one another.

They headed to the trolley stop but practical matters took over as a man said, "Did you see his father sitting there on that bundle of dirty clothes? That was Colligan's father. He's the man who built Pittsburgh and the Pittsburgh Wool Company. He knows everyone. I'm telling you they're a clever Irish clan if ever I've seen one. They're one of the greatest Pittsburgh families ever. God! I wish I had been born into one of those great families! What luck! How is it some people have all the damn luck in this world? Oh, what I wouldn't give to be a wealthy man like Colligan. I'd give up my soul to get inside one of his poems! Now there's a great living poet for you! You can tell he really loves Poetry. He is Whitman all over again and words to him are food. He eats and drinks and sleeps Poetry. It's in his blood and his lungs; he breathes Poetry!"

A small exhuberant woman now took the lead on the sidewalk. She let the tiny band of poets there know exactly what she thought, "I tell you I've never seen such a man such as him; he's the real thing . . . His poetry is an alarm clock and it wakes you up. And to top it all off he's got his dad's money behind him. He has knowledge, the power of words and money too! These Colligans own this damn city and don't think that they don't know it, they reign over Pittsburgh like the Medici in Florence during the Renaissance."

A backward and somewhat scholarly poet among the crowd now felt as though he should say something about Colligan. He measured his words carefully and tried to appear certain about himself. Everyone gathered there listened to him speak, their searching eyes sought to encourage him, "I believe Colligan's father is the true poet because it's only these sorts of men who can praise and encourage youth. These are the men who are truly important. Everyone else attempts to thwart young men and their passionate love of living but not a man like Collgian's father. He knows that the good life is always worth living. It takes an old man like him to know this too. Even the ancient philosophers all agree on this one point; the future belongs to youth. Colligan's father has truly nurtured him in the right way." Everyone on the sidewalk silently agreed, and then all sorts of things that were not so serious began to be discussed.

A meek but excitable, red-haired woman spoke up. Her voice was trembling with great excitement, for she too was dying to be heard by the other poets. "I hear the Colligans own most of downtown Pittsburgh and almost half of Ireland." The startled faces in the crowd turned to her, and all were taken off guard by wonder and disbelief. "How could it be?" A sour, Swissvale woman finally brought a bit of common sense and a great smile to their gossip, "And with all of their money don't think these Irishmen don't know the truth about the great state of their affairs too. They own the politicians and a good part of the clergy. Even the newspapers and the local media do what they want done . . . they cater to their every whim . . . that's the way it is when you got money . . .

you get whatever you want when you want it and nobody can push you around . . ."

The young, buxom red-headed woman now faced the Swissvale woman who gave out her hard-bitten, womanly advice with a bit of a sly wink, "I saw you eyeing the poet all right. What you're interested in doing, young lady, is poetry of a different kind and it can only be found in bed by becoming Colligan's lover." One of the men swallowed hard as the woman said this. She never paused for a moment, "I saw the passion in your eyes when he was standing there in front of you just now. He held the door open for you as we left the dry cleaners and you were actually swooning before him. You should know more than to look upon your betters like that." The woman blushed and refused to deny anything. The old woman finished her up with a quick retort, "Oh, you love the poet and his poetry, and if you found your way into his bed you think you'd be just like Colligan now wouldn't you? Yes, and your precious little hands would have his world by the ass too!" And the crowd let out a great laugh. It echoed off the Tallest Tomb like a chime. It rang like poetry in the air and they went their separate ways on a snow-covered, herringbone sidewalk made completely out of great grandfather Colligan's very first batch of red bricks.

A MODERN SCRIVENER

Presentiments of strange discoveries hovered round me. The scrivener's pale form appeared to me laid out, among uncaring strangers, in its shivering winding sheet.

-Herman Melville

All men suffer the same uncertainties; these doubts are the calculus from the forgotten blast furnaces inside the city of my youth. This city only became clear to me after I finished my university lessons in the Laws of Life; they were learned in the heart of Pittsburgh. It was only then that I realized that my experience embraced doubtful truths, which could not be denied. I found them in the judges and lawyers when I went off to work in the city's august Law courts. The courtrooms themselves quickly beckoned me with my solemn and youthful hopefulness; practical matters soon took over. It was then that the cherished and dusty halls of academe softly faded away into insignificance.

Once the pressing reality of legal practice rose up before me as a form of survival, it consumed my whole existence. I became drunk with doing good; I furiously threw myself into the court cases piled up on my wobbly, wooden desk. I had inherited it and some law books from an anonymous attorney. He had spent over 46 years in the same cramped and dingy courthouse office I now occupied. When I asked about this nameless lawyer who nobody remembered anymore, one of the legal secretaries thought his name was Mr. Hollowster. There was a painful look of regret on the faces of lawyers who sought to deny his existence; the old law clerks sought to convince me that he never existed. I was saddened by a secret they were hiding from me and I became suspicious that something was not right. How could this poor man have spent so many years in so crummy an office? Its only window looked out on a brick wall, I felt cramped, and the wall made me feel insignificant. After a while this thought faded away in the regularity of my routine. The very fiber of my life was taken over by the pursuit of the Law.

The laws of the Commonwealth of Pennsylvania and its many statutes literally kept me alive. They paid the rent and put food on the table. My tongue and my teeth, my very guts were made of these statutes and the debating that took place regarding their uncertainty and precedents. The enthusiastic glint in my lackluster eye depended upon some lawbreaker seeking to get off or escape the spirit and intent of the Law. Like all lawyers I soon came to relish those delicious little legal conflicts of will for they paid my way in life.

The true hero of my first year of law practice was a Pittsburgh skinflint. He walked right out of the pages of Daumier and into my office. This small greasy man wanted to sue his poor mother-in-law for breach of promise, his wife was not living up to his lofty expectations. "Thank God for these lousy skinflints," I thought to myself over and over, "They make the legal world of human action go round and we lawyers collect the fee." This wretched man and two dozen of pathetic others like him kept food in my mouth that first year. I knew just how serious this thing called Justice really was. Men like me could not live in this world without it. I attacked these trivial cases with enormous zeal and soon, I had won a bit of a reputation for myself in provincial Pittsburgh. The legal secretaries and stenographers inside the courthouse soon labeled me a confirmed workaholic. They had me pegged. They held that I would eventually fall in love with money like most lawyers, and my search for Justice and ideals would disappear in a vapor, like the smoke from the steel mills just down the street. I set out to overturn their rumors. Their opinion became a crucial court case I took to heart every day when I went to work. I was determined to refute them and their view of me.

The first thing I did was go on the attack; this always emboldens the heart. I would make them see the real me. I asked a few of the pretty ones to go out for lunch, but I was continually turned down. This surprised me because I really didn't know why they refused me. Then I got wise to them, the situation varied but the conditions of their refusal were always the same. It was usually one reason or another and, like court cases, their excuses were unending. Their alibis began to annoy me. To subdue this nagging annoyance I worked harder and with greater determination.

One short, buttery blonde I had my eye on for months was truly a goddess whom I refused to give up. I worshipped her every morning that I arrived at the courthouse where I waited at the cold coffee counter sipping my morning coffee. This woman filled my thoughts throughout the whole course of a day. When I was freed from my work I walked down to see her sitting at her desk. Inevitably her hands were busy with a lipstick, mirror or a magazine where she sought out the semblance of her perfect image. Every evening, when I left the courthouse I watched her; I concluded my day with a ritual.

Before I headed off to the dreary clutter of my apartment I made it a point to walk by her sleek and polished desk, it did not wobble like the one I leaned upon all day long. I envied that desk and the order of the files. The envelopes and the papers positioned on it in a certain way were a tribute to her poise and sophistication. Now and then, I glimpsed these attributes in her glossy fashion magazines. Her beauty was an ideal I desperately sought for my own; I wanted her all for myself. This woman and her sexy curves sat behind this square, trim plane of wood and I often could not take my eyes off her white hands setting gently upon that dull wooden desk top. I wanted those hands, the smooth white stockings and the lipstick and its mirrored face whose look gave me a view of the heaven that she possessed in her heart. That fine beauty was my great goal in life; its name was Emma and she was as Edenic and as eternal as the Bible.

Words went around the courthouse chamber and I slowly began to suspect that she too was doting on me. Rumors and whispers reached my keen ears. Besides, there were things that went on that did not escape the scrutiny of my constant vigilance. A hasty, unseen glance my way now and then kept my budding passions fired with a warm and lovely future that was awaiting me. Only time and a little patience were necessary. After all, heaven is not achieved in a single day. A whole life could be devoted to pondering its glorious wonders. This is where I was at the moment, and fortunately things were going my way. The precious thought of this beautiful woman promised to make me very glad.

One of the old gray lawyers in the court even mentioned my good fortune to me at the bar one afternoon. My heart swelled with such pride that vanity took hold of me for good. There is nothing like it to make men do something truly stupid. The gray lawyer thought he saw Emma taking notice of me. He said she was not like most pretty girls who outfox men without imagination. Her beauty was lasting and perhaps even eternal and it was meant for one special man. I told him that I was just thinking about this same thing recently and he smiled. He then said to me that he had to confide a secret, "She was watching you with more than a little interest when you walked by her desk this very afternoon." From these facts I was now sure of one thing; I knew I really existed as someone special in her eyes. I reveled in the fact that this goddess was warmly looking upon me with an unmatched kindness and love. I saw such sweet things in her thick and pouty red lips. My confidence, thus increased by my own delicious urgings for Emma, sent my fears skulking away like a lost court case. I knew for certain that her short ivory skirt was nothing more than a promise of our imminent nights of wondrous passion.

After a few more beers I took action by calling the bartender over. A little whiskey was poured into a shot glass, and I mulled over my dreamy desire. I needed courage to do something on this dour and rainy afternoon. I was a little dispirited following a tough court case I had just succeeded in winning against all the odds. It concerned a lawyer who had sued his son whom I had very ably defended; a technicality won out in the end. The case went quite badly for the father and I needed a diversion from the immense pressure this case had brought on. The talk of the lawyers gathered about the mahogany bar centered upon the fact that I should never have taken on a case against a colleague. I ignored their advice. I was now being ostracized for my independence and devotion to the Law. To forget the miserable details of the case, I fiddled with my whiskey and my beer and decided to involve myself in something I had desired to do for a long time.

During the course of the afternoon inside the oak-paneled bar, I slowly resolved to ask my dear Emma out for dinner. A year had gone by since my first glimpse of her; I was now ready. The filthy looking lawyers all about me would be put to shame once I had someone like Emma on my arm when I arrived at the Court in the morning. I would show these rascals what was what. I slyly worked up enough courage with another quick double of whiskey; I walked briskly back to the courthouse to ask Emma to join me at a nearby restaurant frequented by the city's legal elite. A few of these scoundrels were sure to turn up there later, and I could really make them envious. They would feel even worse going home in their fancy, lonely cars on this wretched rainy night. I could see it now, Emma would strut in with me, and she'd look down on these lawyers in a way that I had observed with great relish. She treated most men as nothing more than trash; she had a real knack for putting some of these lusty devils in their proper place. I loved her when she did this for it was just another example of her pristine character; it made me admire her all the more.

I went directly to her desk in the Office of the Clerk of Courts and our eyes quickly met for a moment, I knew this had not happened by chance. Nothing so beautiful happens purely at random. A truly, beautiful woman like her is one in a million and my sucker-like soul knew it. This Emma was a swell, slender woman who had many admirers among the lawyers for a simple reason; she was simply beautiful. Her coy look had a hold of me, and she was willing me forward toward her charms. I was in the power of her beauty as it toyed with me in subtle waves of sweet imaginings. All my sensations were scintillating with the same passion that shone in her cool, curt look. What precision was there! Her neck was a perfect soft sculpture of white marble I contemplated for more than a few minutes. Then my curiosity had to have more. I gazed deeply down into her wondrous abyss where just a little taste of her warm, perfumed bosom was softly teasing my eyes. She was occupied; a gray skinflint lawyer had all of her attention for a moment. He was handing her a legal file and giving her specific directions. His dark fussy hand was in the way of my line of vision of a very beautiful situation. It would soon be mine, all mine, I felt warm inside as my assured sense of self filtered down into my happy heart. Then that big, gray hand appeared even larger as it cast a shadow on her two warm mounds. I stood there impatient, and my mind went off on its own. It was thinking fondly about her ivory skirt as it became lost in the surrender of my passionate hands and kisses. We would soon be plunging desperately into our wild joy together.

Then the drip, drip, drip from my raincoat diverted my thoughts of Emma. Her heavenly scent had found me, and thoughts took me off into a certain imagining that could not be denied. A woman without perfume is like a rainy day without an umbrella, ruined. A sweet waft of her dewiness tugged at my curious nose. It pulled me in as her lips moved softly. She was decisive, and I liked that in her for it spoke so assertively to me that I had to wonder about her no longer. Those luscious red lips now had hold of me and me alone. I bent down into her scent and asked her out to dinner. Then I listened and her face struck me as rather temperamental and even a little odd at this moment. Her icy voice, which I had never heard before, was not soft.

"You gotta be kidding! Your old clothes are too shabby and worn out for my tastes. I want a man with a ton of money and some real style." She laughed cynically at me; "I turn down silly guys like you for dates every twenty minutes. Besides, the Judge told me to keep an eye on you. He's still suspicious of your antics with his daughter." My face tightened up, frowny wrinkles sagged to my ankles and my heart stopped as she continued, "Look," she said matter of factly, "You have to understan' somethin', it's nothin' personal see. I mean you don't even drive your own car. I mean . . . I always see you out there on the corner slouching down by the bus stop. Ya' gotta know my situation. I'm just a lousy workin' girl but I hafta have a guy with some dough . . .That's what it takes if you want to be seen with me . . ." At that moment my heart turned into a lead anvil, it sank deep down into my skinny chest, I staggered back and began gasping for air. My throat wouldn't work, and I suddenly realized I was being overtaken by something beyond me. It was as quick as the nasty glance from her petulant vanity, and it was now looking down on me. I was a nothing in her eyes. I staggered amid the marbled walls and floor. The ceiling riveted my eye to itself and wouldn't let go of me. Despair was everywhere. My arms were flailing sightlessly out in front of me like a hasty blind man. My feet began to move faster and faster and then I was out of the courthouse and sweating profusely. I was soaked through, and my heart was now pounding so hard that I was deafened by the noise inside me. I was about to die, I could feel myself falling over and then the granite wall of the courthouse came forward to hold me up. I grabbed at its hard stony silence. Then there was a sense that I was not destined to die just yet, I was frozen to the wall like an ugly brown gargoyle wearing a rain-soaked trench coat.

A broken man within me now took my place on the gray, dripping sidewalk where people were moving about. My eyes barely knew what they saw on this teary street. The rainy evening scene became a mirage of watery red stop lights and car turn signals. I felt as though I was drowning in an angry dream, and I didn't know which way to swim. My lungs couldn't get any air. Something told me I had forgotten my umbrella, and I was instantly soaked through. I was standing right under Kaufmanns's brass clock. It looked down on me saying, "Time waits for no fool." My coat was wet with cold, hard rain, and water soaked through me as if my clothes were nothing more than the rotted timbers of an old wooden coal barge out on the Ohio River. A song from a steel banjo nearby got a hold of my ears; it was the Pittsburgh Banjo Club in the distance where a strumming noise was pouring out onto the sidewalk. I heard Stephen Foster singing, he was leaning against this bald headed Negro, and they were motionlessly crooning about how Old Man River was a clock who recorded a certain moment. And they said that soon it would be lost forever in the flowing river of music along the forgotten shores of Time.

The rain washed over me until a face appeared up ahead. A kindly businessman noticed my struggling; he gently pointed me toward a bus stop. God, how I love businessmen who know what's what. Their directions are a godsend that keeps everyone going in the right way. I wanted to thank him; but I forgot, and he was gone home probably or maybe to his mistress's cozy apartment. This was all I could imagine; it was now swimming frantically inside my head where my Emma was drowning inside me as I sought to forget her. The pain inside my heavy heart was dragging me down toward the pavement, I had to try to pull myself up. Then my feet moved as I looked down on my briefcase suspended from my hand like a thing unto itself. Its soggy brown leather convinced me that a pathetic state of being was seeping like rain into my life.

A long silvery cylinder appeared out of nowhere as I climbed some steps. An old arthritic woman on the bus stood up and gave me her seat. It was done out of pity for my condition, her wrinkled brow knew that I could not find myself. Years passed by me on the way home inside that bus. My devotion to Emma was so serious that I actually thought I was dressed in black and set on going to a smoke-filled funeral home or toward a sooty and blackened cemetery tomb. The 88 Frankstown bus went on and on past the lives of the poor standing silently in front of me. They newspaper under my tired and lonely arm was a wilted, wet loaf of dreary news. The pages stuck to one another like the sweaty people standing in the aisle. Halfway home to Highland Park I gradually came to my senses. They were full of heartache until my scheming thoughts ripened amid the humid mass before me as my mind came back into focus. I finally found a way out of this mess. I began to devise a clever plan of action that would soon have my dear Emma and her beautiful blondness pining to go out with me. The very next day, certain tentative actions sprang like dreams into my thoughts and then crawled into me in a slow and snail-like fashion, I would head down into the heart of Pittsburgh's department store district to look for a new suit, a tailor-made shirt and a shiny silk tie.

*
* *

At noontime on my lunch break I went to the Gimbels Department Store to get some new clothes, I had to have the best. The handsome clerk in the Men's Department fussed over me for some time, and this pleased me in a certain way. Once I was all fitted out he proudly told me how good I looked. That was proof enough for me. There is nothing better than looking good when you have to make a big impression on a woman. I was set, I had just purchased a brand new summer suit with a cool blue shirt and a soft, yellow silk tie, all of which I wore out of the store. My old clothes were left behind since I wanted to start over. New clothes can often make a real change in a person's attitude. Even the weather was cooperating; the sun was out for once in over a week. I was turning a corner downtown with thoughts of a happy song in my heart when a tall, thinly bearded man summoned me.

He had the shining face of a repenting and often sinning saint with long, stringy hair. He was loitering on a Pittsburgh street not far from the Ohio River and he seemed odd but then maybe not. Everything can be found on the street nowadays. The situation somehow reminded me of a classic story from ancient times which

I had once read in college. It concerned Alexander the Great and Diogenes. There was something about it that jogged my memory into worrying about the essence of reality as I was now experiencing it. Here and now were suddenly within me. I realized my whole life was being lived out in the stifling heat of the grimy Law Courts that were never swept clean.

The thin man stood there like a white stone statue or a deity from olden times. He was framed by the Bridge of Sighs, I didn't want to hesitate and talk to this poor guy; people might see me. Besides, Emma was waiting to get a glimpse of my new clothes. I was in a big hurry to get back and see her too. All I really wanted was just a little more time to myself before I returned to the stifling heat of the Law Courts. Hypocrisy was awaiting me there, and I dreaded it more than a little bit. The silent granite of the courtroom windowsills loomed before me. The massive Court of Law was an enormous heap of stone massed upon stone, like a municipal mountain of fortressed rock; it was tied together with unseen laws, penalties and deadlines. Inside, the lawyers, clerks, bailiffs and judges patiently trudged about under the weight of this lofty structure. The building forced them to move like snails with a great brown shell of granite upon their backs; they slid slowly from one august court to the next to protect civil society under the Law.

A thought turned over in my mind like an old Roman coin. I knew I had been deceiving myself all along, only I refused to admit this simple fact. It seized hold of me in a way I could not deny. My own silent thoughts formed a testimony that would, in and of itself, be tangible evidence that I could not refute in the end. It was as though I was nothing more than a modern scrivener, who hurriedly traveled among the shadows of life cast by the fading, fiery light of my flat computer screen. It was a mistake that often deadened the senses and manipulated the minds of puny lawyers like me into believing that they were nothing more than its lowly appendage. It now ruled over my schedule like a selfish tyrant greedy for attention. A small suspicion slowly pursued me; it lifted my eyes up to the power of reason where truth is only achieved through doubt. It swallowed me up, and nothing appeared to be what it was. For once the city was merely a series of people busy about their own personal interests.

As I paused on the granite steps of the County Law Courts, their civil solidity crumbled into insignificance beneath my feet. The perfect bubble-like daydream of the present was being exploded as I began to question myself. What had I been doing and where it might lead me? What did the future of the Law hold for me anyway? What good are all the things in life if one is not happy to be alive? All I could see was a series of skinflints weaving in and out of wooden doorways along the endless hallway that was my routine day in court. At that very moment I was cautiously reaching out for a different course of action. Someone told me that words in the end make the man. I looked at my new suit of clothes and suspected that my clothier was clearly not the answer. If I didn't change something more than my attire, I was soon going to be stuck in a rut for good.

These doubts hounded me relentlessly, and it seemed as though the personal ecology of my own computer-like consumerism was the only constant in my life. For a while I actually believed that something beyond myself was molding all of my habits. The television ruled over people like me, and I didn't even realize it. I was no different than the next guy but I was becoming a person I didn't like, and there wasn't anything I could do about it. Maybe all of us were just programmed at birth to become what we would be. I began to sense that the myths which had been fed to me from the information food chain of my youth were all wrong-headed. For a moment I actually convinced myself that freedom didn't really exist. Who could prove it? I began wondering about my true mission in life. Who was I? The golden rule stuck in my mind like a coal shovel in front of the fiery smithy of my soul. What good was I doing? I had no idea. Laws and lawyers suddenly seemed nothing more than falsehood and illusion—phony motives surrounded me on every side of the courthouse. I secretly had a terrific hatred of myself for having joined their smiling ranks; they were all smilers at heart who were selfishly out for only themselves. Every move they made was calculated for self-interest. Stock market percentages clicked off in their heads like the time on a clock. Tick, tick, tick. Deep down within me this sickening aversion to my own beliefs was now slowly growing into a warm puddle of resentment. Its terrible pull was beyond the power of my own will, and it was taking over my whole consciousness. In the midst of the world it was what it was not, and it was not what it was. I sensed that what I had to do was just to figure out exactly who I was, and where I was going. After that I would be fine. But there never seemed to be enough time. I suddenly felt deep within me that America was the land of opportunity where there was never enough time for anyone to be honest with themselves. I looked out into this America and down the concrete canyons of our cities. Everywhere that things were rushing about, there everything was wrong. And I was moving about hurriedly along the boulevards and avenues of the city of my youth. It was then and there that I said to myself, "I, too, am wrong. I'm always headed in the wrong direction."

My own existence was a complete mystery to me. There were times when I busied myself in order to forget who I was, my will power and desires ever diverting me away from who I really was. Activity was a mirage in which I was captured. My thoughtlessness was a mirror of my soul walking across the Plain of Oblivion or along the nearby River of Forgetfulness. The passionate thrills of youth were never going to capture the beautiful economy of my heart. I was so dearly longing to understand things amid the futility of my many faultless dreams. Only one thing can dispel the nagging of a spurious illusion, and that is the dawn of reason. I impatiently ran from it. My legal cases, trips to the courthouse, judge's chambers and Saturday mornings to the dry cleaners were footnotes of who I was; and at bottom, I was nothing more than mere motion.

The only happy man I ever met was inside the dry cleaners. He was an absent-minded poet who hummed to himself while he stood next to an ironing board pressing pants. He was completely self-possessed as he stood there like a wrinkly statue in his ragged corduroy pants. Contentment flowed out from him as from a rock. I went to him to see what happiness looked like; he was always beaming and glorious. I could see bits of happiness in the cracker crumbs sticking to his rumpled sweater. My life in contrast was nothing more than hurried motion, I was always running back and forth between the Law Courts and the Law Library. My constant work had made me wretched. I was drinking too much too often and studying and working too hard. I was a man of too much motion who was devoid of a rudder. I suspected I was slipping overboard and would soon be drifting downstream. The river of life was moving ahead of me faster and faster, and the world I lived in was spinning out of control all around me. My friends were getting married and having children and buying their own homes, and here I was nothing but a nervous bundle of confused and noisy desperation. Behind every failure is an unexamined life and a lack of self knowledge, this was at the heart of all my troubles and I couldn't run away from it anymore. My head pounded inside the heart of the maddening crowd. A mass of men surrounded me on all sides. I was a cork on a shifting sea of continuous chaos; confusion was my sole mode of being.

As I rode into Pittsburgh on the slow, iron bus every morning, I couldn't figure out what it was I was supposed to do to change myself. The future was greedily gobbling up my existence, and I was utterly helpless. I felt that I was holed up like an animal in a small apartment. I knew I was missing out on something. I couldn't even get a girlfriend. Women were sometimes afraid of me and I hated to admit this fact. I realized that the truth had to be faced. I decided to do something different. I started dating the daughter of one of the Judges.

One day, on a picnic with this woman she told me my eyes paralyzed her, and she ran home from Highland Park in terror. She was completely frightened by me, and she told her father I had no business in the pursuit of the Law. It took me more than two years to get over her. Her wily father still lurks about the courts looking to catch me mishandling legal matters so that he can have me disbarred. This woman taught me an important lesson—stay away from Judge's daughters. Things never got any better. Every time I found another one, some guy came along and just stole her from me. I usually give up pretty easily on women. Since they are so numerous, another one can always be found. At other times it seemed as though women only wanted to talk to me because I was a lawyer who had lots of money. They even told the secretaries at the courthouse that then chatted about me to the other lawyers. I felt I was lost in the presence of my own mind where the words of others echoed within my head and sounded hollow.

My thoughts were nothing more than sad country and western songs echoing from the radio sitting on the nightstand next to my bed. I was unsure that I would ever accomplish anything; the law courts were merely a way for lawyers to make piles of money and nothing more. The corporate lawyers proved this to me once I saw them in action. It seemed as if my new law degree was about to end up just being an enormous waste of time and that each new case would, in a sense, turn into selfish profit. I was merely stealing money from people in the name of Justice. It was as though the practice of Law had become nothing but a personal appeal, now languishing in the high court of futility. I wanted so much to have time to think, but I was always impatient and ever in a hurry; haste was the way of all men. There just wasn't enough time to think things through anymore. The maddening rush of city life prevented any self-reflection about what was truly going on.

I silently felt something within that compelled me to delay returning to the Law Courts this afternoon. The first sunny day of summer rose up to hold me back. Returning to work now seemed to be the real trial of my existence. The furious routine of my life was always the same. Monotony ruled over my habits like a tyrant who refused to give up control over the day to day events. I had to get to court to try a new case in front of some cranky judge. I feared them, and they fell into two categories of men: mercilessly mean or unknown. All of them were monsters for curious legal minutae which I struggled desperately to remember.

*
* *

As I was walking down the dreary part of a dull and shady avenue, I saw myself mirrored in the Frick Building's glossy windows. I was consumed by my harried image hurrying along Grant Street and then my impatient reflection disappeared. It was replaced by a luminous shadow rising up in front of me. It was that of a robed figure that could have been an ancient statue. It patiently beckoned me forward like a lovely vision. He was about seventy years old and he was humming to himself stoically as he patiently came along in my direction. He looked like a calm and peaceful being on the streets of confusion, and it was evident to me that he was out of his element. I felt as though he was a simple man who was now remaking the world according to a higher plan. It was clear he was content with the harmony of everything around him. He casually walked up to me in his ancient ivory robe as though he were a legal colleague from long ago. He could have been one of the great lawmakers, Solon or Socrates, Moses or Napoleon or even a solemn Washington. His feet were propelled toward a higher goal, and he was looking at me as if I was the only real person in the entire world. I couldn't figure out why he desired my attention. There was nothing remarkable about me. I was merely another one of the city's greenhorn lawyers, fresh out of college and returning to the Law Courts after gulping down a hasty lunch.

This guy began talking directly to me in a melodious and

friendly voice. His lips moved, and I heard him speak softly, "Show me an honest man and perhaps even Diogenes can live again on the streets of America." This statement immediately challenged me. I was captivated by him and his thoughtful and penetrating look. His hands demanded my sympathy, and the smell of his breath reminded me of the cooking oil from my grandmother's old cooking stove in the German section of Pittsburgh where I grew up. The beauty of my childhood and the idealism of my youth were now decades away, and yet they seemed to be back again in the form of this tired-looking man's presence. I sensed that the essence of the whole world was secretly in his grasp. There was a certain form of beauty in the way he and his long white robe were carried out into the green and shiny summer of the street. His face had a peculiar Socratic ugliness to it and, it made him appear almost lovable. He possessed a calm, casual air about him and his simple mannerisms confided something about the eternity of an idea like the Promised Land.

"The face of the world lives on inside the confines of your own heart, and it is there that we must start over again to remake ourselves," he bellowed out like a street crier from the rough-hewn days of revolutionary America. His confident voice pierced my heart of hearts. It spoke directly to my whole being, and I immediately realized I wanted to see the world through his eyes. As he spoke to me with these simple words I was overcome with an inner certainty that he proclaimed, "Your memory is a dream you must never forget; in it is the art of all remembrance. Each man's memory is only what he creates and thus, all of us are the humble gods of our own haphazard creation."

Stunned by his simple admission of fact, I was instantly awakened. My ever-pressing need to hurry toward the Law Courts felt as though it was subsiding, and yet it still nagged at me a bit. I wanted to rapidly give this man an offering and be on my way. If I hurried I could get back to work within five minutes. If I gave him a dollar, I could then be done with him for good. I knew that these panhandlers possess one thing—

able feet and they are always headed to the State Store to buy booze. They are a timeless burden on the public purse only because they are always running from themselves or the police. I wanted nothing to do with this curious man. All I really wanted to do was forget the lingering pain that was hidden deeply within my own heart. Then this man smiled at me and it was instantly clear. He somehow instinctively understood my inner anguish. He realized I wanted him to know me once and for all. His words drew me closer and closer toward him, and I could not ignore the gentle spirit of his kindness; his poetic friendliness was a magnet.

I strolled along the avenue with him for a while, and we moved onto that great limestone heart of the Law Court pavement. Soaring glass towers rose up into sparkling pinnacles of truth and wisdom. A great granite obelisk stood like a monument to Justice. I suddenly felt out of place here on the stony plain of the city. It was as though I didn't belong in these august Law Courts anymore. A whole world of falsehood seemed to mimic my own fickle heart whose fleeting glances sent me ever this way and that. In the presence of this solemn-faced man, everything looked new and different. His eyes shone with the love of wisdom and grace. In him lived the whole of a certain civilization which I longed to know about. His calm look silently made promises of salvation. I could sense in a certain way that there was a real perfection in the things he wanted to show me. It was as though I saw the wasteland of our earthly existence for the very first time. It was barren as the gray moon in all its bleakness. On this sun-parched and desperate plane of existence, all of humanity appeared to mean nothing more than a simple voice standing here before me sharing its kind and gentle words, which he himself had spoken in pursuit of Justice and Art, Literature and History. I heard these words call out to me. They fell to the depths of my iron soul, and I decided a radical change of heart was needed at that moment. I resolved to rethink myself and travel about the cities of the world with this man.

The soft and philosophical pleading of his sappy eyes bespoke a search for true justice. In them I saw a sense of self that I could only wish for in the greedy faces of my fellow lawyers. These lowly, boy-like men would be lining up in the courts like a bunch of mischievous school boys by now since it was almost time to start the afternoon session of the court's agenda. I felt the ideals of my youth appear and bubble up in memories from the past. They sought to flow from my soul and into the chalices of heaven like the wine of truth. I was standing there mesmerized by the scene of beauty before me. In looking upward I saw two pigeons land on the scales of justice atop the courthouse. They pecked away at my robotic and thoughtless existence. I felt deeply within me something say that it was futile to fight City Hall now. I wanted only to be through with them and their mindless hypocrisy and their laws over life. Their cases were a frivolous jungle of contradictions, political lies and dreamy delusions. I took out a tablet of paper and some envelopes from my leather briefcase and immediately began scribbling with a worn out pencil I found at my feet on the avenue. I was sure some good and benevolent god had placed it there for me to pick up so that I might put things right for once. I wrote out a series of letters like a true scrivener. They then went off into a nearby mailbox; I sent the same note to everyone I knew:

> I am posting this notice to my friends and family now. Let this hasty message serve as my letter of resignation from the Law Courts. I will have nothing to do with the haughty and pretentious lawyers who believe they are the real defenders of the common good. Many of them are godless and false-hearted men. The Law Courts are only a mirage of justice for the only real justice rules over our hearts every day of our lives, I have now discovered this truth, it can only exist in the creation of our own existence. God is my witness and I can now feel his presence beside me in this decision.

Although I had reservations, a moment later I was secretly glad at having just resolved to retire from the Law Courts. Even though I knew there was an important case waiting for me that was supposed to be heard that very afternoon, I had reached another verdict. Acting as a judge, I decided my own case. I would live anew in the land of freedom. The glorious moment of salvation was to be found here on earth. For once I actually began to believe I could cancel a meeting with my next skinflint. My worldview was actually nothing more than what I saw through my own actions. Freedom was real to me for once; it was in every one of my decisions. Even the simplest of choices was saturated with it. My whole being roared with a crazy love of freedom and I suddenly knew this truth could never be denied. Freedom is a thoroughly maddening experience to certain men. I had feared it and now I was definitely growing mad with happiness and laughter in understanding this newly found thing within me.

My robed friend was smiling on me like an eternal and happy father; his contentment was simple and clear. The inner beauty of this man's voice rang out in the empty chambers of my poor heart, "The truth is everywhere, and yet it never exists as an absolute as we ourselves imagine." Here was a man who understood something that was greater than himself; his words announced it simply. "Our hearts must always be full of joy so that it can be given to the downtrodden." The presence of these words struck me like lightning in the midst of my turbulent misery as it swirled deep within me; the shock of these words broke open something new. The presence of my own mind was glorious and wonderful and this robed man was making it all clear to me. He called out to passing strangers, but they did not understand. They refused to stop and listen to him, and this immediately confirmed my belief in a significant sort of way. They were the sheep he was sent to tend to as they became lost in their confusion; they did not even want to admit the purpose of this holy man's existence. Surely the full goodness of his words was the true flower of life, and they couldn't see the miracles blossoming all around them.

My heart was brimming with new and important information, and it was taken over with wondrous imaginings. I sat down beside this man; sunshine glinted in his sincere eyes like a magnificent kind of wisdom, and it graced all he said to me. I felt an immense sense of relief as I put my legal briefs down on the sidewalk and anxiously pulled off my shoes and socks. As I felt the warm street and the summer sun on my feet, I knew that I was going to give up my false life and become a true disciple. Freedom of religion was here and now, and it had an anchor in my own troubled heart. The fancy false heavens promised by Hollywood that I witnessed on the nearby theatre marquee across the way suddenly repulsed me. Didn't the newspapers always print the truth? A laugh slowly welled up inside me when I looked down at the box holding the newspapers chained to a rusty steel pole. If only the truth could be so easily found on every street corner, all would be right with the world!

I hurriedly hung up my new suit coat on a lamppost and followed this strange, ragged creature I had just befriended. He told me that we should set off to find a white sheet I could wear like a Greek toga. He promised to turn me into a new man with his words of love and kindness. I suddenly felt good inside; this new and exciting prospect was just what I needed. The stranger guided me down Fifth Avenue and into a haughty department store. A slim, smartly dressed woman handed me a flowing white satin bed sheet to inspect. What a beautiful woman she was! Her delicious hands were as silken as the sheet she exhibited for me. My hasty eyes told me something; clearly the finest women were not to be found behind the desks with their magazines inside the courthouse but in the department stores! I must have seen her a thousand times and never took the time to notice how sweet her eyes were. I profusely thanked her for her kindness, and as I looked for freedom, an exit appeared out of nowhere. The old man sensed that we had to get out of the store quickly. My clever eyes found some light near a wall, and I headed for the door. As I glanced back, the beautiful woman was looking at me with a strange look as though I had forgotten something, then her face turned into an angry canvas set on revenge. She promptly faded from view as she hurried behind her cash register.

I walked briskly with my new friend onto the glittering and sunny avenues of the steel city. The smoke-filled and cloudy Pittsburgh streets that once looked littered and dirty to me exuded an innocent glow that felt like home. We went quickly into a State Store and loaded up on some pints of whiskey. When we shot out of that store the manager had his fist raised and was cursing at us as we ran, "I'll get you two, you can't get away this time." The teacher laughed it off, and I just went along with him in that ever evolving maze of Pittsburgh's many sidewalks. We walked out into the crowds of people with wild smiles on our faces and we now felt how good life was. We were joyous for the world to be alive; every living thing in it was perfect. My newly made friend was a dedicated teacher who was leading me this way and that through the pulsating crowd, and I was sure they would soon come upon his wholesome and redeeming spirit.

When he smiled I could feel myself being drawn to the great cities of the New World where the masses of the downtrodden were in need of his message of salvation. New York, Philadelphia, Boston and Chicago appeared to beckon me by way of the highway and the turnpike; this man was a savior and a law unto himself. I knew that these great cities were the places where I intended to live on the streets of wonder and drunkenness. Together he and I would preach the word of joy and light. Poetic sermons would fill these great cities and would become the heavenly abode of the New World. I began to hold onto the promises of paradise, for like this recently found friend of mine, this was where the future was surely going to be perfect.

He boldly informed me that he would be the next Philosopher King. What a shining joy his face was when he told me this! He then showed me something silvery. He told me he had the

Ring of Gyges' ancestor and once he slipped it on his finger, the wearer of this ring would then be made invisible. Truth would be given absolute access to the invisible wearer who could travel undetected throughout the city. I was wholeheartedly taken up and I vowed to him that I would be his faithful follower for all time. He would be my hero everlasting, the eternal King of the Road and the maker of a new heaven and earth. The New World was our oyster, and soon its great pearl would belong to us. The soft pearly whiteness of this truth burned within. Our sudden laughter was a great uproar bearing our hearts aloft as we looked at the pigeons slowly circling overhead in the bright sky above the Law Courts. Freedom was here; the perfect moment is always now, today, this moment burning away in time. A wild volcano of joyous freedom of religion and free speech was now shooting mad glee into our hearts as we laughed like innocent children. The whole of a hard sunny afternoon wore on effortlessly in the midst of our mindless mirth.

    Slowly as the immense, unmerciful sun beat down on us he told me that we were going to build a magnificent arch of pure light. The robed teacher said that we were destined to start the *School of Athens*. It would be painted by an Italian artist he knew, named Raphael. My heart leaped with a silent joy. I immediately realized this guy was omniscient. He could foretell the future by simply remembering bits and pieces of the past at random that most people like myself barely knew about. I was utterly amazed to be in his presence. I felt I was in the heart of something supernatural and more beautiful than anything known to mankind. His voice was that of freedom and it was greater than anything I had ever known.

    He promised that he was going to make me one of his chosen few; I was trembling with honor. The hot sun rained down on us in sweaty circles of pulsating heat so we ran over and stood under a department store's canvas awning to get into its shade. That damned hot sun just beat down on us like a white-hot spotlight; the sunny pavement even burned our bare feet.

Then my friend took a drink of something from a flask and suddenly turned toward my ear. He whispered another secret to me cautiously, "You will be welcomed into this School of Athens and in it you will always be able to find friendship along the boulevards of life. Once it is founded, we will invent gods so that men will worship more than just the sensual pleasures with which they enslave themselves. We will teach the workers of the world that they have nothing to lose but their chains. We will show all men and women how to be true friends of man right here in the midst of the city. We will take on the world and conquer it not with swords but with words of love."

That afternoon we casually strolled out toward the university where a great gothic monument stood as a Cathedral of Learning. The robed man explained me, "Andrew Mellon cleared the way for this magnificent cathedral to be given to the New World and it rules over Pittsburgh like a great beacon of knowledge." His voice paused, recollected itself and then confidently announced, "This is a new and true cathedral completely unlike any of those old and crumbly, empty ones scattered throughout Europe. This mighty Pittsburgh cathedral was the work of men whose hopes were for their children set upon the conquest of learning and knowledge." My meek eyes took in the soaring stone, and they could barely believe the great wonder in the sky. The cathedral rose up over the city. It was barely possible to comprehend its immensity within the span of a single glance. Its walls shot up dramatically in temple-like fashion, they beckoned the eye and the soul heavenward toward the pursuit of knowledge, understanding and judgment. A fiery passion for reason and certainty had launched this university into the unknown. Here was science and engineering carved delicately like lace into imperishable stone. Dead wall reveries took the teacher's eyes up into the heavens; I felt my self giving way to its lofty ether. We were deranged by its soaring truth; this was the philosophy of learning magnificently carved out for men and women of the New World.

His words softly reached my ears in praise, "There is nothing in the Americas quite like this massive skyscraper. There is nothing so good and so true as its lofty love of ideals. They soar heavenward like the birds. Its great shoulders are drawn from the strength of American workingmen from the coal mines and steel mills, the railroads and Pennsylvania limestone quarries. It stands as a lasting monument to their industry and their struggles. It is an abiding tribute to their dreams for their children who are a part of the vast glory of humanity passing beneath its secular portals." My eyes were taken up; they soared into the sunny sky where my vision was soon blinded by the university's luminous presence. I could barely hold the image of this great cathedral within me; I couldn't comprehend the immensity of its soaring limestone for it was far beyond me. Within the chambers of this cathedral were the whole of my own iron will and my heart's great desire. I had finally found my home here in the land of freedom.

My teacher now walked on confidently with great zeal. He detailed to me how the hills of Pittsburgh were set on a bluff where an acropolis would soon be poised like another polished ideal overlooking the city. It would be the city of our dreams where the Philosopher King would soon rule. The rusty barge inlets set into the rivers for the iron and steel mills would be turned into the ancient port of Piraeus. Tugboat whistles would echo like Sirens from the books of Homer and they would soon capture unsuspecting men adrift on the wine-dark sea of life. Each man would be an odyssey, each a solitary Ulysses on the roads and avenues and boulevards of Pittsburgh. The *School of Athens* would be painted again in a dreamy flood of consciousness.

The old teacher's wizened head was as gray and as stubborn as a Belgian block on the side street where we were now standing. In it was an illusory and wordy blending of the past and the present. He was dreaming me into a perfect future that would soon see the true light of day. His ideal world was his own that no one had ever experienced before. He had this vision of both of us walking arm and arm down the steps of Mellon

Institute like Plato and Aristotle. Its sober limestone columns would rise up and loom over us in Doric simplicity. Our Grecian wisdom would become reminicent of ancient monuments leaping into the abyss where Apollo would jealously guard over us in childlike wonder and amusement. We would be philosophers discussing the great themes of truth, beauty and goodness from the ancient world. The sun of a new day would rise up and fall upon our own magnificent Parthenon just down the street from where we were now standing. His pearly voice was certain, "The Agora will be built nearby of pure marble and nude maidens and nymphs will be found there smiling upon us in wonder and glee. They will dream of us as though we were gods." I took his words into me and turned them into a new and dreamy vision. He intimated that philosophy and religion were to be linked arm in arm and would soon be walking like Athenians all across America. Little towns would be graced with their architecture and pediments; columns and Roman porticoes would soon follow behind them.

Like a foolish king rushing into the hall of mirrors at Versailles, I strode about the city exhausted by my own reverie. No stranger could hold me back as I leaped out onto Fifth Avenue and pointed up to the vast assemblage of stone before us and excitedly exclaimed, "The Masonic Temple will become Plato's Academy." His eyes lit up with an inspired sort of hope. Wild optimism overtook him as I admired his happy face brimming with a curious charm, "Listen now, you've got it, my boy." We laughed aloud at our soppy wisdom. It splashed from a bottle into our mouths on the boulevards of life. It seemed the oyster-like world fell open before us like a great and simple Cartesian text. My teacher hugged himself with certainty. He was sure the University of Pittsburgh would hand over the Frick Art Museum so it could be used as Aristotle's Lyceum. His solemn voice now took hold of me, "Do not be inspired. Be convinced that the truth is always possible." With these words I was wedded to the freedom of the future. Nothing else mattered to me anymore. This living madness was life and its perfect moment was here and now. It was burning within my useless and passionate heart.

I was quickly overtaken with new plans. I felt this wonderful feeling of freedom gush up from deep inside me. I was shaking with a joy that had to be shared with all the politicians and lady shopkeepers, clever students and lonely housewives. Little boys, miserly lawyers and pedantic hoboes would be thrilled when they took this ideal into themselves and remade the streets of democracy into a new world for all time. I felt all the problems were over; they melted away like the buttery blonde truth that was now setting me free. I was on the road to philosophy and right around the corner from salvation. I was getting a little smug. That only happens when you are selfishly convinced that the future is going to be good. I was sure this was my lucky day, and my teacher now whispered confidently into my ear with great excitement, "If we could get hold of a printing press, then we would be set for good. Then we could print up our own bibles. I am certain we could print our own money and buy a radio station or even a television antenna. Once we go worldwide, our wireless voices will conquer every human need, and we will fill them up with our hopes for salvation. The kingdom of heaven will glow as true and as bright as the light of knowledge within us." I trembled before the full and mighty voice of this man; powerful leaders always send a thrill through me. The whole of my gentle spirit felt as fragile as some litter blowing down Forbes Avenue in the sunny, summery wind of time.

We walked further on up Fifth Avenue and our eyes swam in an ancient dream of taking over the earth. Time seemed to pass away into nothing as we paused on the corner of History. There was a crowd of resolute newspaper boxes stationed there next to a wooden telegraph pole, and they were intent upon getting the word out to the masses.

The teacher's voice now boomed drunkenly on as it announced his new view of the world, "Once the Americans are through with their monumental building, their steel skyscrapers will rise up to rule over New York, Chicago, Philadelphia and Pittsburgh; and they will eclipse the old world that is Europe. Enormous feats of engineering will soar up over the boroughs of New York where the masses have flocked upon the shores of America in dreary desperation. Who can truly say how great this shining city of New York is? No man. Who can say how much it has given to America? No man. To humanity? Again, no man can fully capture in words what greatness this city has held within its endless borders. Perhaps there is a little clue to be found in its skyline, beneath which the masses labor anonymously. From the colossal corporate egos of the industrial age the life of the great city grew and prospered. Their swagger is gone; but the skyscrapers they built are still busy cities unto themselves. These monuments are the forgotten tomb of the executive's selfish, shadowy self. Oh what glorious opinions they possessed of themselves! Like the masses they too are all forgotten. Like the masses they too sweated and suffered so that their titanic egos could temporarily bask in the pride that their industry succeeded for the merest of moments. New York with its steel skyline is the nation's finest hour created by a century of building. It reveals a little bit of the imagination that is afoot in America. Only in New York is our truest greatness observed. Only there can the vast canyons of man's eternal vanity be glimpsed."

The old man now set about a plan. I was to be part of it, and I was unsuspecting of its complexity. He took swig after swig from the bottle, and then his words leaped into my ears, "You and I will go to New York to tend to our flock. We will work like scriveners to print the eternal word about America. We will be poets who hand out our true poems of beauty and light to the people on littered street corners. Millions of them will walk by and give us a buck, and before long we'll have a church of our own and we'll be swimming in money!"

My heart was flowering into the visions of this sparkling man's winey rendition of the past and the future. His voice rang out along the boulevards like a great gong. "Nowhere else but in New York can our freedom of religion be viewed whole and complete.

In that great city can be found the finest men of our civilization. They are awaiting us. When we are on the avenues and boulevards of that great shining metropolis, we will see ourselves truly for once. There, you and I will soon discover something new and glorious in the sky; it is Chrysler's shiny Pittsburgh steel. It stands like a mighty miter upon the wide, wild avenues of all Manhattan. Now then. Stop for a moment to figure things out." His arm now stretched out before me and pointed toward some nearby tombs. "Look off into the cemetery over there, and you will see the monuments to the fine people who manufactured this steel for these great and wondrous New Yorkers. These dead men once turned the elements of the earth into stainless steel sheets, steel beams and girders, iron rivets and nails, wash basins and ironing boards, automobiles and Ferris wheels, wire rope and skyscrapers."

The teacher now took a long swallow from a bottle he brought to his lips, and his madness flowed out, word after word. The man's voice now bellowed out in a parade of proud preachings. He loved the city of his youth more than anything in the world. I saw this in his riveting eyes; he looked up at the Cathedral of Learning and was completely enthralled by its crazy gothic beauty as it shone in the honeyed sunlight. Even his vanity seemed to be buttressed by its flying limestone supports. I was in the throbbing heart of this magnificent industrial capital and I couldn't break free of the place.

The robed teacher launched into a wild torrent of imperious words, "And Pittsburgh and Philadelphia, Chicago and New York City have already exceeded the Caesars of Rome by preserving their stony ruins in a new way no one ever expected. The freedom of Europe was stolen from the vile German menace that not even God or the evil genius of Descartes could have imagined. The Empire of Capitalism and Democracy now rules over the world with shiny new religions. The poor and the downtrodden will soon be willing and faithful masses seeking out its opiates. Americans worship new gods that are, only now, being seen truly for what they are: Power and Money. Especially the Almighty Dollar. You and I, young fella, will sing its praises and the faithful and true believers will flow toward us en masse. But we've got to get to work, today. Today is the beginning of the future. You must live for today. You must take up the bucket, and you will have to panhandle and beg if this great dream of ours will come true. Our lives depend upon it!" My willing head assented and my heart roared for the discipleship. I pledged that I would follow him wherever he went. I would be his willing acolyte. This pleased him and, I was committed to become someone truly holy.

The robed man now strode fearlessly out into the street, pointing up at the massive stone of the Cathedral of Learning. His voice rang out with a new and powerful light, "It was here to Pittsburgh that the people flocked from all over Europe. They escaped the cracked and lifeless fields of their homelands. It was here to this American city and its three rivers' many shores, to its coal mines and its many mill towns that they found a refuge. These dilapidated mining and mill towns freed them for once from the chains of their stubborn and ignorant ancestors. They escaped their dull hovels of rotten agrarian misery passed down to them endlessly, from father to son wearing the same rotten shoes out into the fields of their own wretchedness for centuries. In desperation they sought to give up the poverty of Europe for the New World, America . . . Who can say how truly great Pittsburgh is? No man. Who can record what wondrous things went on here for the sake of humanity? No man. Who can say what the world would be like today if this industrial capital did not exist? No man." The wiry old man stood on a street corner to make an announcement to the students of life who paused between classes at a stoplight.

"The work of the great and anonymous masses from this city helped to produce the armaments that freed Europe from the wicked grip of tyranny. The bombs, shipyard steel, aluminum airplanes and metal landing crafts of D-Day gave new freedom to the Old World. This liberty was forged in the furnaces of Pittsburgh; its men and women created it from raw materials taken from the earth. These are the people we will always be indebted to. They were a part of the past that helped to create the conditions for the possibility of the future." The students may have been sleepy; they walked on as the tired voice of history trailed off from the pearly heights of a certain marbly pedestal. His great sweaty head seemed to be looking for a place to set its thoughts. Another swig was stolen from the bottle, and he renewed his crazy litany, "Only now, from the industrial capital of the twentieth century can you see Neptune's silvery steel and glass, aluminum and oil rising up and spouting right out of the dreary earth. These materials were mined and milled on the backs of Pittsburgh workingmen. These shiny and prosperous things were created here and then went forever flowing toward the rivers and oceans across the Earth."

The bottle was now making regular trips from hip to lip. He pulled it out from beneath the robe and from it a great, gurgling swallow was taken in gulp after gulp. This fortified his voice, and then the list went on and on in wild panegyric praise, "In the beginning All was America and not even a god in a heavenly slumber could ever create such a fine thing. It was as close to an ideal as ever existed. Thomas Cole had even taken the time to paint it in *The Architect's Dream*." This all-consuming, robed teacher told me this hastily as though he had to get it all out before it was too late. He now beckoned me to come closer. He had calmed down a good bit only because his teaching took him to the brink and had worn him away. His face was that of exhaustion; he got his breath back slowly. He wanted to recollect himself for a moment. Time passed, and then he looked at me. His eyes were serious now, and he demanded I listen. His voice spoke slowly and sweetly now to me in the tired fashion that sounded like wisdom to my anxious ears.

"I want to ask you this my friend. What is the use of living if you cannot love your fellow man?" A greathearted gentleness dripped from his slobbery words full of the utmost gravity. His sharp and critical eye caught mine, an answer was expected of me. As always I hesitated, he was wiping his slippery mouth on the saliva-soiled sleeve of his ragged robe. A pause surrounded us as I stood there before him and pondered this question for a long time.

The whole afternoon of my existence had been eaten up by this question; it humbled me as it does all men intent upon the Good. My heart slowly grew as hard and as heavy as an anvil and all anvils take a lot of pounding. Like Damascus steel my own was set sure and certain upon its myriad intentions. I carefully came to one conclusion, and it was formed of itself slowly as the whisper that silently roared in my heart. This existence of ours is a damn serious business if ever there was one, but it is solely our actions and our words that count. Our only conscience is our memory forged into words; they pass judgement upon us each and every day. It is only when we stop the march of time with Art that we begin to see what's what. It is a silent necessity, a threat to those who live in the mammony womb of the world where lovely blonde women in courthouse offices dream of brand names. That is the only stinking shit of heaven they will ever know! Art to their shiny eyes is face powder and magazines, dough.

I looked down the long drab and sintering streets of the shabby city. They were singed by the dark sun of ignorance and now worn weary with hopelessness and unemployment. The shiny steel dreams of my youth were but crumbly rust; my own poverty was preserved for eternity in the black and white alley of family photographs. The gray wretchedness of my former life seeped into me like doubts from an oily unknown source. The cracked and moldy pediments and peaked roofs of Pere Lachaise pried open the dark and dingy vault of all my many fears. I tried to deny it, but the damned search for truth was taking hold of me for once and it wasn't going to be anything more than my own dust before long. Time was fastened upon the present, and it was running out on me like a thief in the night.

I glanced over at the bleached statuary figure standing as proud as a deity before me; his graven image of himself was affixed to an invisible object that eluded me. There was something amiss in the bleak robes we were wearing like Pharisees; their vanity was now flapping gaily in the sunny summer breeze. The hollow cheeked high priest strutting proudly before me now looked odd and mean; his ringed hands and gnawing teeth were clenched tightly upon an unseen purpose. Mammon was entwined about his bony fingers where his breath tasted of wrath and hatred. He had fed himself with the misanthropic wine of truth, and it had turned to the Nietzschean vinegar of fear. With this bottle that he offered me was a rotten chance for me to quench my thirst. I swallowed his raw, hard whiskey; it was warm from setting next to his skin all day. Then he meanly grabbed it from my innocent hands, and he took a great swig. Then he selfishly forced it back under his robed belt.

I looked around but no one could help me now; my own wit was all I had. This city of ours did not look right at all. My eyes fell down at my feet. They were clean and shiny, and yet his own body suddenly seemed foul and wrong-headed. It struck me very odd that this priestly man's toes were so dirty and worn out by the hard and wretched road of life. Like a self-satisfied bishop or a cardinal, this preacher's gray beard was mangy with mammon taken from the masses that swarmed upon this city's streets. I felt a glorious and powerful man like him ought to be omnipotent enough to take better care of himself here on earth. He had me carrying this bucket of coins, and his eye never left its shiny surface. The thing weighed me down terribly and was starting to make my arm sore.

For the first time I saw that his teeth looked as if they had been stubbornly carved from a dull ivory tusk or precious bits of knotty mahogany. His saliva was brown, and when he spat upon the pavement it left a sickening stain that could not be forgotten. It was the echo of his words and all of their false promises. My hungry nose began sniffing about and I got the impression that he hadn't had a bath in weeks. I was rapidly growing sour in the stomach. A taste of bile was in my mouth, and it was soon moving like a worm upon my tongue. That smell of cooking oil I had noticed earlier was not his breath at all—it was emanating from his oily skin. Flies were buzzing about him as though he promised to be their next meal.

We walked on through the Southside of Pittsburgh where the

great steel mills were spewing out their industrial smoke. Steel, steam and coke fumes drifted out of Hazelwood. A coal black darkness reigned in the soot-caked calculus of the city that would never go away. I knew that I had to do something, so I asked the robed man his name. He turned to me cautiously and waited a while before he answered me, his actions were full of hesitation as he delayed. He smiled in an unusual way, and he took a hit from his handy hip flask that he continually kept hidden under his robe. He considered my words for a time, and he paused before speaking. Then his fanatical eyes rolled about in his head like that of a madman. Zealotry blazed hotly within his words as he spoke directly to me, "I am the savior; the living god of all creation. I am Dionysus and the drink of imagination that will set you free."

Something made my throat suddenly close up; it preventing me from screaming for help. My mouth dried up before these perilous eyes that were now intent upon my soul. His hard heart, gleaming brown teeth and eyes ate through me like greedy pieces of buttery sweetness; it felt as though they were powered by an electric current. I didn't know what to do before their damned, iron-hard judgement and I had to look away from this maddening terror. It had hold of my arm but it wouldn't let go of me. I sought to escape from this decrepitude; its sun-like smile then burst into wild-eyed laughter.

Like all men I craved light, and he had offered me up a false lamp of oil in the darkness. I was eminently mistaken about this ancient prophet who now stood almost naked and bowlegged before me. His tattered sheet was slipping haphazardly from his bony shoulders. His powerful voice rang out loudly as an advertisement. It was as though he meant for the whole world to obey his laws and worship his crazed ego. He pulled out from under his tattered, oily robe a list of commandments that had been scribbled on the writing materials I myself had abandoned earlier in the day. My personal letterhead was at the top of each sheet. His tasks were listed in order of importance. He went down the sidewalk with them extolling their virtues and the need to achieve a certain end, the promised land was ours if we only applied ourselves. Then his lackluster spirit had an idea; if begging for money doesn't work, use force. He got hold of a man's shirt collar and was shaking him to listen to God's holy word right now, right this very minute. The poor man's terrified eyes pleaded for me to help him. I reached out and separated these two battling souls that were locked together for a moment by madness. I pulled the men apart and the scared guy moved quickly away. He soon ran off down Liberty Avenue. The danger of this insanity quickly echoed within my hollow heart, and it suddenly overtook me. I myself was now terrified, shaking and I felt nauseous. This greedy god-like man was clearly a real threat, and I was his shy and reluctant apostle. The white-robed man was set on finding more men like me. He pointed at the Ohio River and said to me, "Let's look for some real men down by the Galilee over there."

I was immediately uncertain and paralyzed by my own fear. My heart sickened and began to beat wildly, and it cleverly got my attention. Its noise roared loudly in my ears. Desperation now set out for me from every direction. I was being bombarded with information, and there were no real answers. Everyone chose their own way. I suspected that if I have sinned, it was only the sin of omission. I was one of the innocents who had no self-knowledge. Up until this moment, ignorance was for me merely an abstract concept. A man. He stood before me, and I was completely lost in the chaotic thrill of hasty sensations. Then from out of nowhere the humble voice of sanity and knowledge somehow leaped into my ears like a silvery shield to protect me. "Run, fly away, escape before it's too late. You are being led by a wild-eyed skinflint who is out to take over the whole world with his mad-hearted and faithless zeal."

Now a great fear pounced upon my thoughts. It swarmed within as sweat poured over me like the great Niagara. I felt as though a Wailing Wall of stone had fallen on me, and I could barely pick myself up off the ground. This thought about the ancient snake crawling out from the Edenic deception of Adam's garden suddenly made me dizzy with apprehension. I became terrified at once by what I had done. My precious god had now become a desperate self-styled preacher who panhandled for the Almighty Dollar. I myself was rabidly badgering people for it on the street, and they had the gall to look at me sourly. I was a minister of the Lord and they looked down upon me. Then I caught myself for a moment. They were right the whole time! I had no idea how truly right they were since I always distrusted their unusual stares.

The visage of the teacher had taught me to face each person man to man, put my hand out and beg money from them until they gave up some change. My pleading palm then turned into a demand for their help. This was all mean and wrong-headed work. What was I doing out here on the Boulevard of the Allies wearing only a bed sheet and begging money from these poor citizens? This stern and cranky teacher used his stick of guilt on me again and again. He told me to get to work and he yelled at me mercilessly, "Tell them to donate the their lives to the love of money. It is the root of all evil, but only it can save them from poverty. We need all their cash and anything else they have. We must get it all out of them as soon as we can. We need their money for my kingdom of heaven here on this earth. Tell people that money is everything, and life is nothing. Sure enough some of them will slowly begin believing it. Those are the ones we want to get a hold of! We have to find the gullible ones. We have to convince them that this is the American way, and we are its religious leaders. Start telling them that I am going to build a new Rome. And upon this rock, right here on the sandy shores of America, I will rule over the freedom of religion, and it will live on forever and ever."

Something suddenly fell upon me, and it was doubt, the patient arbiter of all truth. It abandoned me for a moment but it had returned to deliver me from this mad falsehood. The lovely, liquid vision I had been imbibing flowed through my veins to form a certain thing. I could sense its power in a new way. My imagination forced its forgetfulness upon me for a moment and its presence formed the absence of my memory. This thought now awoke me from my dogmatic slumbers. My dream city of youthful ideals was swiftly turning to rust within me. For solace I helplessly threw myself into the memory world; it lived within me along a stone wall in a brick alley always in the shadow of the Church. It was here that God beckoned me toward the truth as I ran from citizen to citizen begging for alms. My feet were wild with fervor and the love of motion. I couldn't escape what was set to happen to me next. My head was being clawed by a frightening image that led me this way and then that. There rose up within me a single thought—there is only one thing in life more fickle than women, and it is a man intent on finding heaven here on earth.

I had to find a way out of this winey world of faithless madness, and the finale was suddenly thrust upon me. It had a chrome grill and it was moving in slow motion toward me in a shiny blur. It resembled a car, and then there was a vision from which I could not flee. Smoke and mirrors and a red light whirled around me as I looked up at the Pennsylvania and Lake Erie Railroad station. Coal cars and a locomotive passed by, and, a creaky old patrol car bumped along amidst some city potholes. Its wary headlights sneaked up alongside us in the wretched alley of poverty where we were hiding from the flimsy railroad police.

At first it looked like Valhalla and then I could see we were on the Southside of Pittsburgh not far from the incline inching up the hill like a slow wooden worm. We crouched down; our knees were up against our chins as we settled in behind some warped, wooden pallets of the Terminal Buildings jutting out of the earth near the river. Hiding was becoming impossible and all of our attempts at being invisible just wouldn't work. The Ring of Gyges wasn't getting us out of this mess, and I was now desperate. I hid my face and wanted to be out of here. I prayed for God to strike me dead, but nothing happened. The terrible false stranger was right here at my elbow.

A second later two ornery Pittsburgh policemen jumped out of their car with billy clubs ready to go to work on our sweaty heads. One of them announced that they were looking for a man wearing a stolen winding sheet. I gasped desperately for air as they anxiously poked around at some cardboard boxes with great rapidity; we were about to be found out. We jumped from our snug hiding place and suddenly retreated. They started yelling at us to surrender, I wanted to give up but the old man refused. He had a plan, we swiftly got moving from behind our little cave of wooden pallets and took off toward the Ohio River. More police spotted us and were determined to help their friends who were now in mad pursuit. They were all chasing us down along the river of my forsaken dreams. I had been sold into the slavery of false beliefs, and my voice rang out like an innocent church bell. "Jesus Christ," I shouted out to my companion as I ran after him, "What the hell have I gotten myself into now?"

The answer wasn't far off. I watched it as the other sheet quickly ran past me in a crazy zigzag down the embankment and then toward the river. Its feet were slipping in the mud along a hillside. I caught up with it, and we got behind some foliage and doubled back along the camouflage offered to us by some bushes. I have to tell you this old guy must have been a real sprinter in his day because I could barely keep up with him. He was a wily son of a gun. We thought we had the cops outfoxed when we headed up a back alley. We had to retrieve our bucket of coins stashed behind some boards. Our dirty sheets were now snug up against a brick wall, and we were both chuckling to ourselves. Then the old man got a worried look on his face and he told me, "When you think you're lucky, start praying because that's when all hell usually breaks loose and ends up in your lap. I know, it's happened to me a thousands of times."

I didn't want to believe him, but it was then that I found out that the Southside of Pittsburgh wasn't as big as I thought it was. The cops suddenly appeared out of nowhere and there was a small army of them, they got us cornered inside one of the Terminal Building. One of the policewomen said she knew the old man would never abandon his bucket of money. She was genuinely amused when she said, "We caught you with your own bait." The cops were all smiling about it, and even the old man had a good chuckle because he knew it was true. They took us downtown to the jail and, we had to give up the sheets we were wearing since they said they needed them for evidence. We were given some clean clothes and I swear I have never had clothes that felt so good. That sheet had gotten a little mangy after a single day of running around along the riverbanks.

It turned out the pints of whiskey they found on the old man, which he had been drinking all day, had been stolen from a State Store. The wily manager of the store showed up at our hearing the next day and he said he had to press charges against us. His voice was full of condemnation. His frustration and hard-hearted accusations swayed the judge to hold us for court, "This was only about the thousandth time this has happened and it's always the same. He strolls into the store when we're busy around noon. He reaches over the counter, grabs a pint, and in less than a second he's out the door. And now he's got an accomplice who he is training to help him. The two of them were in my store only yesterday, and they got away with six pints of whiskey."

I could barely believe my ears. It was suddenly clear to me that this old guy really had me fooled the whole time we were together. He had told me that he had a deal with the State Store, and that what we were taking really belonged to heaven. It was supposed to be ours for the taking, and I never gave it much thought. The damned old guy always seemed to know what he was doing. When they took us back to the cell after the hearing, I sat there glumly for a long while. I didn't really know what had happened to me then. I had a chance to understand it because I had a little leisure for once. No time passes as slowly as that inside a prison cell. We then sat for over three months in jail, the snail-like, granite Court was moving slowly. Justice never comes too quickly for the wicked, and that was evident for it had taken them that long to finally assign us a public attorney.

I will never forget the look on this young lawyer's face when he came into our dingy jail cell. This must have been his first case because he peered at the two of us suspiciously. We were not so much clients in his eyes as we were a couple of lousy skinflints. I took offense at this at first but after a while I warmed up to him. He definitely was a pretty decent fellow. His frayed shirt cuffs were really ragged around the edges and the gravy stain on his tie had thrown me off track. This skinny and balding lawyer actually wanted to help us, so I told him the truth about what had happened. He appeared sympathetic about my case when I told him, "I really believe that if I could only stop hurrying about from one thing to another, my whole life would fall together of its own accord." The old man nodded in sad agreement with me on this point. He was sober for once in his life; he was pretty damn hard on himself now that he was in jail. Being cooped up in the damp cell had seriously changed his outlook on life and it was anything but optimistic. He told me that every day he spent in jail permitted reality to seep into him a little. It was now telling him he had to start all over. Again.

Then the hopeful lawyer said, "Well, I am pretty sure I can get you guys off. We'll figure out an alibi and a defense strategy, and you'll be back on the street again in no time." The old man gave him a sour look of disbelief when he heard these words; he motioned for the lawyer to stop talking by putting up his hand. There was a peculiar expression on his face that took the lawyer by surprise, "Look, we're all guilty of something, for me it's a lack of self-knowledge and for my young friend here . . . Well, he got to believing in the wrong prophet, the wrong screwy, street genius. This sort of thing happens everyday, and it's not a crime punishable in a court of law. You can't send a man to jail for following the wrong goddamned role model." The lawyer took this all in and was patiently willing to admit some of it might be worth using in court. Then his listening sharpened as the old man said, "Now, then, let's be honest about this lock up. None of us can get off. There is no way to deny certain charges, and nobody can truly justify their existence."

The cell resounded with a silence that fell as pure and as absolute as poetry inside me. For once I had found peace in a few well-turned words. A clear sense of resignation ruled over the lawyer's solemn face as he contemplated what the old man had said. There was no doubting that some of the things were off base but some of it wasn't. The old guy made sense, and he really liked me in a certain way. I could see that now for he was really intent upon looking after my welfare. He treated me as if I might be his own Prodigal son who had taken up with the wrong crowd for a while.

During the last few months in this prison cell, he had been torturing himself dreadfully about our being in jail. I told him it was therapeutic and that it happened so that I could become a better person. He grew irate and just smirked at my comments in disbelief, he then looked at me with a hard gaze. His eyes were very serious when he spoke, "You're innocent, and you don't understand what's going on here yet. Jail is a damn serious business. I'm not even sure of half the crimes I've committed, but once they start digging into my past, they'll lodge dozens of additional charges against me. And they'll hold you as my accessory. I'm telling you these prosecutors are out to crucify us."

We needed help and he was set on finding it somewhere. He began thumbing through a book for assistance. I knew that this is never a good sign. When a man needs a book to support his case, things are always a lot worse than you might suspect. This is one of the first lessons I learned in Law school and I was now getting a bit nervous. He tacked up on the cell wall a quote from this book he lugged around with him. It was *The Tropic of Cancer*, which he had smuggled past the jailer. The words were from this bible of his that he read every morning when he woke up. I was forced to read this quote a thousand times. It was stuck up on the wall with pieces of dirty Scotch tape that were curling around the edges. He said I had to read it so that I would understand what was what:

> I am living at the Villa Borghese. There is not a crumb of dirt anywhere, nor a chair misplaced. We are all alone here and we are dead.
>
> -Henry Miller

The quote finally wormed its way into my stubborn head, and it served a purpose. The poor, old man was made happy by this. He was absolutely gleeful when I asked to borrow his Bible. He rubbed his hands with joy that morning. In the afternoon he was as somber as a parish priest after hearing a hundred confessions. He was filled with anguish and fretting but it wasn't so bad; he wasn't grinding his teeth anymore. He might be a little whiney and mulish, but he was wrapped very lightly in dread, it was the dark doom of thought about being accountable for his fellow man. This didn't worry me much since the old man thought he was to blame for all kinds of things that went wrong. His heart was like a piece of soft clay or a bit of soap that takes the shape of its container. I had to continually tell him to stop worrying because we were going to be all right, no matter what the court decided. He moped about the cell endlessly critical of himself. He was sick and tired of running from the cops. The people he badgered on the avenues for money pained his memory. The hard, vicious hammer of the world that was pounding away inside the anvil of his aching heart seemed like it might give out. It had molded his whole life into something I didn't even know about.

Then he spoke somberly to me in a confessional tone. "I've been trying to escape from reality ever since I was born, and now they've put me away and made it so I can't run anywhere for once. And this has finally got me thinking about myself." I told him not to be so damn stubborn and so hard on himself. "You're going to give yourself an ulcer and that won't do you any good. Once the surgeons get ahold of you whatever money you got, you might as well kiss it good-bye." This may have brought him around a little bit because the miserly side of him knew I was now making sense. Nobody knows doctors better than a lawyer. If anything, I did get him to go a little easier on himself after a while, but it was only the fear of surgery that kept him on guard. I knew he would never want to part with all the coins he and I had collected out on the avenues. We had a whole bucket full, and the guards often asked us to make change for them.

At certain times the prison cell was full of unknown surprises.

One morning I got up, and it was during one of the periods when the old man had not slept for several weeks. He paced the cell endlessly and made notes to himself. One day underneath the curling quote I found the following lines scribbled on a dirty scrap of ragged brown paper. One of the guard's lunch bags had been turned into a biography, this was a remnant of his latest hope. The old man had tacked it up to remind himself who he was, his ideas were no longer dreamy but real. The writing on this scrap of a brown paper bag was in pencil. It was neurotically written in small letters by a cramped and humble hand.

> *Uhr* is the German word for clock. And it has not escaped my attention that I am a clockmaker of sorts. My clock will now tick away inside the clock-watcher's internal time consciousness for a while and then pass away. Time does that. It is a very swiftly moving thing that no one can fully grasp. Perhaps the clock-watcher will one day understand that each of us is a single grain of sand journeying down the glassy funnel of an hourglass. If I remember this now and then, I will eventually become a true clock maker. This clock is, in the end, the face of Time that I am tinkering with impatiently. It is truly the only moment I'll ever know or understand.

Once he had tacked this wrinkled note up on the grimy cell wall as a reminder to himself, he was less impatient and a little wiser although not much. He began to relax a little and even sleep better. He was not so troubled and anxious as before. Another thing that happened gradually was that he wasn't anywhere near as miserable as when we were first locked up inside the cell. Back then, he'd look in the mirror in the morning and tell himself, "I am a condemned prisoner locked within a cave of my own false reflections . . . I am a damned demented fool who runs from one passionate falsehood to the next. Hasty impulses and motion are my false gods, and I cannot flee from them. But at least now I have been forced to see them for once as they truly are. Reality has finally caught up with me here inside this jail cell; this place is proof of all mankind's confusion and heartache. I might wish it was not so but the truth cannot be denied me. It's telling me that something is dreadfully amiss and false; and it's not the world that's crazy, it's me."

After these episodes of harsh and critical soul searching, his iron teeth would be grinding away. Then his face would get a desperate look upon it that wouldn't go away for hours. He might not talk all day, and his silence would sometimes go on for weeks. If I asked him something during these quiet moments, he'd write a little note to me on a dirty piece of scrap paper, and its printing was scrawled and dreadfully serious when I read it, "Silence is the keystone of the thoughtful."

One day he told me that he was truly trying to forgive himself for his mistakes, but it was virtually impossible. "Lying has become such a source of life that I doubt if I can really change it now. It's too late in the game for me . . . perhaps I will find the truth before you are done with me. Lies are the real rubbish in life, and I've swallowed them down with every drunken day of self-deception. I'm a hypocrite and I cannot run from the delusions that are my life. Life is nothing more than what you make it, and I have made a living hell of it. So it goes."

*

* *

The public attorney appeared again one day around noon, and he fidgeted with some paper work which he sought to hand over to the old man. It was a Confession and a Power of Attorney, and he wanted them signed. The rheumy eyes of the old guy looked at the papers with a sneer. He signed them and then handed them over, guilt was etched on his frail face. As the attorney was heading out the door in a perfunctory manner that his job was now done, the old man's voice caught the guy off guard since it was clear that we would go to trial alone without legal counsel. The plan was simple, we would have to defend most our actions based solely upon our own intentions. The old man wanted to tell the lawyer what was what, and his sad voice sounded pathetic and dreadful. It was even a little comical as he spoke, "Look, we know you public defenders mean well but we've made a God-damn hell of our lives. Can you understand that?" The old man's thinning gray hair glistened on his sweaty head that was full of frustrated admissions he could no longer conceal; he slowly nodded my way. His hard face was a stony portrait of dark regret as he concluded that the lawyer ought not return to offer us any more help, "I and this young guy here are two damn skinflints, and we're just going to stay in this jail for a while so we can get a new start. Maybe we'll have to be in here forever before we find ourselves."

My mouth dropped open in angry disbelief. I didn't believe what I had just heard, and I immediately wanted to contradict him. I had to tell this old bastard he had it all wrong. He was supposed to be my friend. And here he was double crossing me and lying to me again. My thoughts were spinning out of control. I tensed up, and I couldn't even move because his words stunned the hell out of me. The tension in the room mounted, and I felt it was going to crush me. It was making me angrier; it was set to drive me mad. I was in turmoil, and I wanted to scream at him; but my heart wasn't in it for some reason. Apathy had taken over and I soon felt that it wouldn't do me any good anyway. Things inside me slowly eased up and fell into place. My silence finally killed the terrible revulsion, and I just gave in to the peace and quiet of the cell. The simple sanity and goodness of things settled into me in a way I had never known. Knowledge flowed into me, it came from every direction out of nowhere in the form of nothingness. I leaned back on my prison cot, and I felt calm as I sat still and waited patiently for the worst to happen. I decided not to fight the old man this time.

He could see I was struggling with his view of things and he told the lawyer, "Let's just say instead that we might be in this cell a long time, maybe it will take us a while to figure out who we are and what we did wrong. We have to work on knowing ourselves. That is at least the only thing I have learned inside this rotten concrete cave full of frightful illusions. Now then, let's just say this young man will be leaving here before too long for you will see that Justice is served. My formal confession should be enough to get him free. I wish it were not so, but I am certain it's for the best. I pity the man who has everything he desires for if he does not have one true friend, he has nothing at all. Well, I will be nothing once my young friend here is released for good." There was a pause, and the old man had become a little more respectful of my concerns as he continued, "I can't speak for this young fella, but I have to be more honest with myself. Right now I don't need a lawyer or an alibi so much as I need to think about how I am going to quit doing foolish things that I have been doing all my life."

As the steel door of the jail shut with a metallic thud, the lawyer walked off toward the Bridge of Sighs, and I could hear the cleats on his shiny black shoes echoing down along the hallway of my old and forgotten dreams. They haunted my memories of poor Emma, what a lonely and selfish creature she was! To think that I once worshipped her as though she was a goddess from heaven that I had been longing for with all my desire! Her heart was as black as the Judges' robes and as fleeting as the false friendships of the Lawyers. If I had come upon this truth, then it was worth going to jail. I felt like I was nothing more than the old man's scrivener, his curious shadow. If I was anything it was a cheap facsimile of him, a poor copy of the true and the good and the beautiful being that is an honest man.

Later on that afternoon the old man's attitude became pensive and before long, he wanted to believe things were soon going to be looking up. But his face was still scarred by uncertainty and doubt. There was a minute bit of enduring hope in him that could not be diminished. It was born of an eternal desire he felt when he was dreaming about his people. Now and then he'd say, "I will attempt to treat others not as a means but as an end, as I wish to be treated." I didn't know all that he meant by this, and he remained silent for a while. It seemed he knew what was destined for me.

When the jailer came to tell me I could go, I was free to leave the jail cell. The charges against me had been dropped and heaped on the old man since he was a chronic offender. They said he had a history of destroying the order of the status quo, and he would now have to repay Society by spending his life behind bars. He was not going free, and he knew it. He had suspected it since we had arrived but this didn't seem to faze him. The notice of my immediate release brought a wild gladness to the old man's face as the stern, officious guard opened the jail's door for me. I almost didn't want to leave this cell since it had become a kind of home where I had found friendship for once.

The old man turned to me and shook my hand with a great grip, and he seemed pleased to be rid of my incarceration. For the first time I saw the name on his prison uniform, it was Mr. Hollowster, the man who had occupied my wobbly wooden desk for 46 years in the County Courthouse. I had finally met the man. This was the guy nobody remembered for he had gone mad, and their heartbreak was a reason for their forgetfulness. Everyone had lost a friend they could not bear to recall, the memory of his hardship was simply too painful for the lawyers and the secretaries to recollect. And here he was, a Savior on the streets of Pittsburgh. He now said something to me with a delicious smile that was full of clear-headed certainty. His solid and unwavering voice conveyed to me that his bright heart was bursting with joy because he was ready to begin his old life anew, I saw what was in his eyes. Hell was not an abstract thing to him; he was an expert at it! And his smelly, rotten teeth beamed confidently at me in the face of death. His humble visage reached out to me in the steel doorway as my dazzled eyes took in his glorious voice, "Everyman makes his own advice and some of it ain't too good. That is just the way it should be, and it will never change. All I know anymore is this. Starting over is the easiest thing to do in America; I've done it a thousand times. And I have failed a thousand times, and each time my most sincere dreams had to die a certain death on the iron-hard anvil of hard times. Every failure has been a great hammer blow upon my heart, and look at me," He stood up straight, and his face was a portrait of staunch, human kindness, "I am three score and ten, and I am still alive!" His eyes had a magnificent gleam in them for a moment, and then he paused. The old man now became more serious; an expansive look filtered into his eyes as he concluded by turning to face me directly. He clearly wanted me to understand what was what, and he spoke honestly to me for the very first time.

"Young man, you must listen to your own heart and the thoughts within your own head as you walk across the hard and stubborn streets of America where mammon-love is a rotten way of life. You must not make the love of money your one, true god, for in it is only emptiness and the nothingness of hopeless despair. You must do many things, and their truth, beauty and goodness must never be forgotten. Hold dear the memories of your parents for Mother and Father are the finest and most precious of words that live inside the language that is Civilization. You must refuse to succumb to the ignorance of others like myself who seek to secretly destroy you with false dreams of a hollow heaven."

I saw the old man was tired of the old forms of life and that he wanted only the one true form of Justice that I myself had been longing for from the beginning. His gray, sweaty head was now a noble thing set upon the isthmus-like pedestal of his thick, marbly neck. His bony arm rose up and was outstretched and it pointed down the hall of this cave-like prison. As he bid me to look upon a strange vision of his words beyond the Bridge of Sighs, there was something out in the future which I had been too impatient to consider. Before me his whole attitude was pious and full of Socratic resolve, his hearty voice bellowed within the chambers of my happy heart. My yearning was now leaping with the new joy of anticipation; all the promises worth keeping were now within me.

With a great sense of purpose he looked into my hopeful eyes. I saw within him the friendliness that is common among the broken-hearted and the downtrodden. Here before me stood a man of passionate strength and epic certainty. He urged me not to remain disillusioned in one place for too long. His last words were full of confidence. It resounded with great force deep within me. The fury of him propelled me along as my patient eyes set upon his dreamy nothingness for the last time, "Go. Go and open yourself up to the great book that is the world. Go. Go and become something of the hope of heaven here on the Earth for your fellow man who is, in essence, your other self and the ear for all your words. Go. Go now for he needs you; he is waiting for you with his uncertain heart on that dreary street corner that is your place in the world. Go. Go and find your self in every part of that great and glorious whole that is the New World, that is America. Go."

*
* *

ABOUT THE AUTHOR

Michael Uhrin was born in 1953 in the heart of Pittsburgh, Pennsylvania when the city was an industrial capital. Mr. Uhrin and his wife now live on the outskirts of Pittsburgh not far from the few remaining steel mills that once made the city and its citizens prominent during the Industrial Era.